HEAVY DIRTY SOUL

A. A. WARNE

HEAVY DIRTY SOUL
First edition.
© A.A. Warne 2019

ISBN-13: 978 0 6485253 4 9 (Paperback)
ISBN-13: 978 0 6485253 3 2 (eBook)

Cover © Elena Dudina
Developmental editor: Amy Elmore
Editor: Jennifer L. Collins Gorman
Format by A.A. Warne

This is a work of fiction. Any similarity between the characters and situations within its pages and places or persons, living or dead, is unintentional and co-incidental.

A catalogue record for this book is available from the National Library of Australia

To anyone who has ever tried
and to my family who have stood by me while I tried.

~

...and to Tyler Joseph, Josh Dun and the muse that inspires them.
Thank you for the music.

*To anyone who has ever tried
and to my family who have stood by me while I tried.*

~

*...and to Tyler Joseph, Josh Dun and the muse that inspires them.
Thank you for the music.*

Heavy Dirty Soul

PROLOGUE

1440

*I*rene moaned as her stomach tightened. Clutching at her side, she slowly sat up in bed. She took in deep, large breaths to soothe the pain, but this time was different. This time, she felt the baby was ready.

Beside her, Walter sighed, then sat up and swung his legs off the bed. He left the room silently, just like he had every other morning. He hadn't spoken a word to her in weeks because he'd had enough of the lost sleep, poor dinners, and unwashed clothes.

Yet, Irene was thankful for the space.

She counted the seconds until the rickety wooden door slammed, then pulled back the covers and planted her swollen feet on the cold dirt floor. Breathing in and out slowly, she wrapped her hands underneath her stomach and hoisted herself up to stand. Moans quickly turned into yelps and she found herself counting her breaths.

Bent over with her palms firmly pressed against the wall, she felt her swollen stomach tighten, and then relax and tighten again. A breath in and then a breath out.

Then she paused because the front door had opened again.

"Mrs. Buckley?" The woman's voice echoed throughout the tiny cottage.

Irene sighed and held back a curse to the gods. "I'm in here, June!" Irene yelled out as she pushed herself upright, then labored one heavy foot in front of the other until she stood in the doorway.

Somehow, all the wrinkles in the old crone's face pulled back and she let out a gasp. "It's time!" June said as she clapped her hands together before she disappeared out the door.

Irene started to breathe again. For some reason, she always seemed to hold her breath around that woman. Shuffling across the room, Irene stood at their tin bucket and drank from the wooden lave. Welcoming the cool water down her throat and into her restless stomach, she somehow forgot the winter remained in the air.

Without even knocking, June burst back through the door with the midwife in tow.

Irene dropped the lave back into the bucket and clutched at her stomach once more. "June, please. You startled me."

"Never mind that," she said to Irene before turning to the short midwife. "Here she is, love," June sang out, closing the door after the midwife's entrance.

"June?" Irene's voice broke and she panted her words between breaths. "How did you know it's time?"

Flashing her long dark lashes back at Irene and raising a single eyebrow, June appeared unimpressed. "You know that I consult the stars," she said in a serious tone. "I've been telling you all along that this child would arrive on the last day of winter," she pointed out, speaking in a matter of fact tone.

Holding the bench for support, Irene spread her legs to even out her weight, convinced it would help her breathe better. Desperately, she wanted to send June out, back to her own house to mind her own business, but at the present time and with the way the pain was taking its toll, Irene couldn't muster up that type of energy.

The midwife remained silent as she took a seat at the room's sturdy table and went through her large bag. Seeing her pull out knives, rags, bowls, and scissors, Irene unable to face the reality, turned away to gaze out the window. June's stone cottage was all that Irene could see.

She breathed again, in and out, trying to let her mind wander off and think of something else. But all that came to mind was how she'd gotten into this mess in the first place.

It had been only days after her birthday when her insistent father had requested she come into the sunroom.

"What is it, Father?"

"Sit," he said from the opposite seat at their small round table.

Irene squeezed her hands tight, wondering what had placed her father in such a mood. She sensed something strange, like a block over his heart.

"We need to discuss the terms of your betrothal."

Irene laughed. "Oh." Her palms went clammy. "You're serious?"

"I would never joke about such matters." The bags under his eyes more prominent now.

Her eyes went wide. "But, father," she protested, standing and leaning on the table. "I… I can't!"

"Why not? You are of marrying age. A suitable man has come forward, and I have approved."

Irene slammed her hand on the table. "How dare you!" But she stopped herself from going any further. There had only been one time before then that Irene had raised her voice to her father, and that had been just after her mother's death. She couldn't remember what it had been about, but he had slapped her across the face and sent her to her room for a week. When she'd finally emerged, she hadn't spoken for a month, but after that she'd never raised her voice to him again.

"Do not speak to me like that," he warned her now.

She looked for the door and felt like running. But instead she stood her ground. "How could you?" she asked, speaking through her teeth this time. "I never wanted this. I can't believe you would do such a thing behind my back, Father." Tears filled her eyes, but she forced herself to keep going. "You know I wanted to be like Mother, and learn her craft. How am I going to do that now with a horrible husband telling me what to do?" The tears ran, soaking her cheeks.

Her father sat in silence. It was like he was just a shell, no longer the man he'd once been.

"So, if you've made your decision and already told them yes, what are the terms to discuss?" Her voice croaked, sounding out her pain.

He dropped his chin to his chest. "I don't know," he said in a small voice.

"You always do what everyone else tells you to do" She raised her voice again. "Don't I get a say in my own life?"

He looked up then. "I've always let you speak your mind, Irene. But you've never known your place."

She turned away and stormed off, knowing that if she stood with him any longer, she would reach across the table and wrap her hands around his neck.

"Stop, Irene!"

Irene's feet automatically planted themselves into the floor, but she didn't turn around to face him.

"It'll do our family great honor, if you accept."

Irene flinched. "You've already made the decision," she said, clenching her jaw. And then she left the room as quick as she could—before she said something she'd regret. As she left him alone, she thumped her feet throughout the house.

"Irene!" He yelled.

She raised her fist into the air, drawing the pressure from within her and holding it inside her hand. Then, with a flick of her wrist, she released her fingers wide, causing an explosion of energy from her hand. The flowers around the house burst into flames.

"Irene!" her father screamed.

Within the fortnight, on the Sabbath day, Irene's father picked fresh flowers from the garden to hide the smell of the week's work. He handed them to Irene as they entered the small church. With her father by her side, she refused to hold his arm as they walked down the aisle. Everyone stood and smiled as she walked to the end of her life and watched her father shake Walter's hand.

I'm like the deal made in hell.

Her father wiped at his own tears, then took a seat.

Irene couldn't muster up tears of her own. Fury burnt them before they formed.

"We gather here today, before God, to wed this man and this woman together."

The priest went on, but Irene tuned him out. She lowered her head, and yet her gaze held, eyes boring into the priest's head.

If only... she stopped that thought dead in its tracks. It wasn't the priest's fault that she was here.

It's their fault!

"Now, turn and face each other to say your vows," the priest said.

Irene refused. She spoke her vows through clenched teeth, but didn't take her eyes off the priest once.

He squirmed under her stare.

"The rings," the priest said. "Hold out your hand," he whispered as Walter turned his back for a brief moment.

Irene lifted her right hand, not wanting the correct hand to be used.

"Other one," Walter said.

With a sigh, Irene swapped hands. He placed the ring gently on her finger and spoke after the priest just as he was told.

"Irene, the ring?"

Irene could have exploded right then and there, taking the whole church with her.

Walter nudged her in the arm.

Don't you dare...

"Here you go, dear," a woman's voice spoke from beside her.

Irene looked to her and noticed she was just as old as Walter, if not older. *Where's my cousin?* Over her shoulder, among the watching faces behind her, Irene saw her cousin sitting in the second row behind her father. *Not even she does what she wants!*

Irene grabbed the ring from the old woman's palm and jammed it onto her groom's finger.

He flinched. Irene held in her laughter.

"Under the watchful eye of our almighty God," the priest bellowed out, "I now pronounce you husband and wife!"

Walter turned and faced Irene. She shrank under his stare.

"Mr. and Mrs. Buckley," the priest added.

In that moment, everyone behind them got to their feet clapping. Walter Buckley leaned in and kissed Irene on the cheek. Irene inched as far away she could without her father noticing, and the woman beside her began to weep and blubber.

Irene turned to her. "Who are you?"

"June, dear," she said, lifting an already soaked handkerchief to her eyes.

Mr. Buckley grabbed Irene by the hand and all but dragged her straight for the door.

Halfway down the aisle, in amongst the sea of cheering faces, Irene looked back to the older woman. She could sense her pain, her yearning, and somehow in their exchanged glances, Irene knew she had taken the woman's place.

But why? she thought for days, and then weeks, even months after. That was, until she fell pregnant.

Irene had mentioned it to her husband several times over the months.

"I married you," he said. "Not her! So, I'll hear no more to it." After a moment of awkward silence between them, he'd add. "Don't bring it up again."

But quite often she did. *Why marry me?* She stomped around, annoyed, often running to her father's home and begging him to let her return. But he held her there until Walter came and got her.

Never speaking, Irene was stuck in a loveless marriage at the age of fifteen to Walter, who'd already had salt and pepper hair and wrinkles around the eyes. Captured by her spoken vows that informed her what part she had to play, that was, to provide children and watch the woman next door love the man she was forced to marry.

Even though he could never provide a decent reason for June's constant lingering presence, he always denied Irene's accusations. Perhaps it was that June had been well past child-bearing age, otherwise, Irene might have married someone else.

Since the wedding, Irene had spent her days performing house duties like all the other wives did, and yet she pushed her imagination. Constant thoughts of all the different possibilities to be used to speed up his aging occupied her; it was a matter of forming a plan into action

All too often, Irene dreamt of the day she would live in widowhood.

"Ah!" she cried out beside the tin bucket sink, contractions snapping her from her thoughts.

June rushed to her side and began rubbing her back. As annoying as the old hag could be, June knew how to soothe her.

"Can't we do something for the pain?" June snapped to the midwife.

"Sure, sure," the short, curly-haired woman answered as she shifted items that clicked around her bag. Before Irene knew it, the midwife had shoved a vile-tasting liquid into her mouth.

Irene gasped at her burning throat.

The midwife chuckled, then took the concoction away and drank some for herself. "You're going to have to get used to little tricks like that, if you want to get through this alive!" She returned the bottle to the bag, then turned on her heels, setting her sights on Irene's husband's comfortable chair.

"What is she doing?" Irene whispered to June a minute later, staring at the sight of the half-slumped and apparently sleeping woman.

"She's getting rest. Doesn't look like this little one will be here for a while!" June said as she continued to rub her back.

"But it's the middle of the day," Irene said. "Didn't she sleep last night?"

"Most likely not. Tis babe-arriving season after all." June's hands ran up and down Irene's back ever so gently. It soothed the tension in her stomach and the rest of her body as Irene shifted her weight from one foot to the other.

"It will do you some good if you can get some sleep, too," June said.

It was as if June's words weighed Irene down. She had felt so tired for far too long, but even though rest was tempting, she couldn't bring herself to move. Standing at the kitchen bench and swaying her weight, her body set into a relaxed motion. Her breaths in and out created a rhythm that matched her heartbeat. All these tiny actions rolled together like a liquid-warm cuddle, making the tightness around her stomach so much more bearable.

Eyelids heavy, she lifted them slowly to look out the window, and noticed that nighttime had already fallen.

"How did that happen?" she asked, pointing into the darkness, but she didn't stop swaying.

"It's the pain, love." June giggled, tired herself. "And the gin."

"But I only had a sip."

"Then you must have fallen asleep, because you've drank more than me and the midwife put together."

A small burp left Irene's lips. She reached for the wooden lave again, pressing the icy cold water to her lips. Was she drunk? She couldn't tell because the pain was so much stronger than before.

"We've got more gin when you're ready. It'll help you cope, and before you know it, morning will rise."

The door opened.

Irene twisted to look.

Walter stood in the doorway and looked straight at June.

How dare he cause me this much pain and not even glance in my direction?

"The babe still hasn't arrived," June said, always speaking first when the two of them were present, as if Irene wasn't there.

He averted his eyes, looking to the ground.

Since Irene had mentioned his feelings for June the first time, he always made an effort to avoid looking at the other woman whenever he was in the presence of Irene. Yet, Irene saw the truth in his face. He had feelings for the woman, no matter how much he denied it. And that made Irene's pain even worse because he'd still gone ahead and bid for her hand in marriage.

"Go to *my* house, love," June said. "There's clean sheets on the bed and salted meat in the icebox."

With a grunt, he was gone.

Again, Irene was thankful for the space.

Irene had long drifted off to sleep, yet still she remained standing at the sink, swaying from one foot to the other. A soft warmth touched her face and she opened her eyes, noticing the sun peeking through the window.

June leant in closer and whispered. "The first day of spring, love."

Irene stopped swaying and stared at the brightness. "But you said the babe would arrive on the last day of winter!" she snapped.

June laughed. "Yes, yes, I did," she said, and held up the lave to Irene's lips. "But this babe must have a mind of its own."

Irene sighed and finished the water before closing her eyes again to continue her mindless sway.

"It is also the equinox," June added.

On the other side of the room, the midwife moaned. "I'm glad the babe didn't come through the night," she said, standing from the armchair and stretching out her limbs.

Irene's eyes were on the chair. *Why does she get to sit in that chair?* Even when she was in this much pain, she'd never have been forgiven for sitting down there, not by Walter.

"Did you see that full moon last night?" The midwife cracked her neck and crossed the room, stopping just before the tin bucket.

Watching the midwife drink, Irene shook her head.

"It was the largest full moon I'd ever seen. Had crisp edges that glowed the ground like sunlight." She took a sip of water and dropped the lave into the bucket, splashing up water. "I didn't like that at all," she said. "Especially since the babe was coming."

As the midwife continued her mumbling, Irene looked around the room. June was no longer rubbing her back; instead, she had taken her husband's armchair and quickly fallen asleep.

The midwife left her side and kneeled down by the potbelly stove, throwing the last few pieces of wood onto the fire. She returned to the window then and extended her neck, searching the morning sky.

"Blasted!" she cursed so loudly that June sat straight up, wide-eyed.

"What is the matter?" June asked as she got to her feet.

The midwife mumbled again, pacing the room back and forth, and then began rummaging through her large bag.

Ignoring them both, Irene turned back to the window and looked for herself. Right in the middle of the sky sat a perfectly full moon, glistening in the sunlight.

Closing her eyes and taking in a large, deep breath, Irene felt its energy. An image formed in her mind. It reminded her of what love felt like. Not the fake love that she was to pretend for her husband, but rather a real and natural love like that which she'd had for her own mother, that her mother had given to her, and the love she now felt for the little kicks and rolls in her stomach.

It was as if the moon was sending her love. Pure, untainted love.

Irene breathed it in, basking in its richness.

She opened her eyes again a moment later, annoyed at the chaos behind her.

"What is the matter?" June snapped at the midwife while she leaned across the large oak table.

"That moon!" the midwife yelled. "It shouldn't show itself now. It should have disappeared into the night. This is not good news." She paced the room. "This is not good news at all!"

Ignoring them once again, Irene turned back to the window and yearned for June to rub her back. The pain in her stomach had intensified, and she realized just how long she'd been standing on her feet. Crunching her elbows into the wooden kitchen bench, she hoped that it would release the pressure in her heels.

The women behind her began arguing.

"Energy!" the midwife said. "Too much energy."

Like a swirl inside Irene's head, the midwife's voice echoed the word 'energy' around and around. Irene leaned back over the tin bucket, ready to be sick.

Energy! But that's a good thing? Irene internally argued back at the midwife. *Why is she saying these nonsense things while I'm in labor?*

Irene had blurred out the quarrel behind her. She didn't have the strength to stand up for her unborn child and demand that the woman explain these weird superstitions. Turning herself around, to face them front-on, Irene felt her third eye flicker open. A flash of something familiar crossed her mind. She thought back to her cousin, Annabella, who'd given birth just two years prior. Weeks after Annabella's own delivery, she had pulled Irene aside and whispered that there were men in spirit form guarding her room. She was worried that they were there, ready to take her in death. But nothing out of the ordinary had happened, and she'd delivered a healthy boy.

The memory disappeared from Irene's mind, clearing her sight. In the room, Irene suddenly saw four men, just as described by her cousin.

"I need to lay down," Irene said, but her voice was drowned out by the ongoing argument.

"The marriage was before God!" June yelled.

"That doesn't have anything to do with this."

"Of course, it does! The child is born to wedlock, you superstitious fool!" June said, pointing a finger right in the midwife's face.

Irene reached out and grabbed June by the arm.

With the midwife continuing to squabble, June stopped, turned, and faced Irene.

"What is the matter, dear?"

"I don't feel good at all," Irene said, her words barely able to leave her mouth. "Can I lay down?"

"Of course, dear." June pushed the midwife's bag off the table and helped Irene up to recline back on it.

Irene hesitated. "Wouldn't the bed be better?"

"No, dear." June shook her head. "The blood is easier to clean here."

The midwife was out the door, pacing nearby. Then she returned, drank the last of the gin, and stood beside Irene, positioning herself on the opposite side of June.

"My stomach is so tense," Irene said, the comment coming out more like a moan.

"It's time," June said, and then both June and the midwife rushed around the room, getting things ready. Sheets, water, knives, and all the things that Irene had never expected to be needed seemingly appeared out of nowhere.

"We need to wait," the midwife said under her breath.

June shook her head. "If the babe is ready, then now is the time."

Irene rolled her head to the side and saw the same spirit man that Annabella once saw, standing there. He was as tall as the roof and he clutched a long sword in his hands; it reached to the ground. He stared across the top of Irene to the other side. She rolled her head to see what he was staring at and saw another spirit, similar to the first, staring back.

Why are you here? Irene asked them in her mind, but neither of them answered. Instead, they turned around and walked through the walls. Her eyes could no longer see them, but her mind's eye saw them stop and keep guard. Then her eye flooded with a bright light. It was warm and inviting and the purest of all things. As it calmed in brightness, it drew back to the outskirts of the house, enclosing it somehow, and on that border remained just as bright.

They're creating a barrier! Irene gasped. It was powerful, and she felt it go right through her. *They're protecting us! Annabella was wrong! They're here to protect me!*

Irene rested her head back on the table, letting it support her. With her new support outside, she felt safe, even more loved, and excited for her babe to arrive. *I just need to rest my eyes for just a second...*

"Wake up!" the midwife yelled. "This is no time to sleep." The short woman slapped her legs to get her attention.

Irene looked over her round belly and noticed that her legs were up, knees apart, and, somehow, her dress lay crumpled on the floor.

Irene turned to June. "Why am I naked?"

"Easier that way."

"But how?"

"Never mind that now, dear." June showed her the knife and winked. "It's time for the babe to arrive."

June lifted Irene's head and slipped a pillow beneath it, helping Irene to stay upright. Then she reached for her hand and squeezed it tight.

"I'm not ready," Irene whimpered as her stomach tensed fiercely.

"Yes, you are," June said, pushing Irene's hair out of her face.

Arching her back, every single muscle in her stomach pushed downwards. A slight moment of relief came as the muscles relaxed before they tightened and pushed again. With her spare hand, Irene clutched the table with one hand and, in her other, she crushed June's knuckles.

She opened her eyes, and on her left side, just behind the midwife, a bright light appeared. Irene gasped. *What is that? Am I hallucinating?* The light stepped forward, making it easier for her to make out the shape of a person.

A sharp pain and a fierce burn between her legs caused Irene to exhale a scream.

"She's crowning!" the midwife announced.

The light on the left moved closer.

"No!" Irene cried, but the light didn't listen.

"One more push, Irene."

The light being leaned over the midwife and hovered above Irene's legs. Irene felt its energy, a fierce contrast to the pressure in her body. She looked down and held her breath. In its arms was a small round orb.

Irene gasped.

It was a light baby.

"Push, Irene!" the midwife snapped.

As if her body was the one listening, Irene's stomach pressured downwards. Then there came a weird movement inside, and the babe slipped through her legs.

The light baby lifted out of the arms of the being, and into Irene's babe.

"A girl!" June exclaimed.

The babe's cries filled the air.

The light being leaned in and kissed the babe on the forehead.

She stopped crying and looked at the midwife.

The midwife gasped, immediately holding out her arms and flopping the babe onto Irene's stomach.

Irene wrapped her arms safely around the child, pulling her closer to her chest. As she drew in the beautiful small face, the baby girl's third eye closed.

What was that? Irene thought, but then she was all too distracted by the swelling of her heart and the excitement of her soul.

"A girl indeed," the midwife said, answering June.

Irene glared at the midwife, not liking the lace of acid to her voice.

As June helped with the umbilical cord and then with the afterbirth, she kept telling the midwife to hush.

"What is the matter?" Irene asked, speaking over them.

"Nothing, dear. Everything looks good." She gestured to Irene's lower region. "What have you named the babe?"

Irene smiled down at her sleeping child. "My precious Ivy."

Cradling the child against her chest, she slowly and painfully raised up off the table and wrapped a blanket around her naked body.

The two women fussed around the room as they removed the blood and any remaining traces of the event.

Crossing the room, Irene had her sights on her husband's armchair. *I gave him a child, so I'm sitting in it!* As she sank into its comfort, Irene pressed Ivy firmly to her chest so that she could begin suckling.

When the babe finished, it cuddled into her neck and they both drifted off to sleep.

Irene opened her eyes to the sound of the women's consistent arguing. "What's going on?" she demanded.

They stopped and stared down at her. "Never mind, dear," June said, and the midwife hmphed. "Get some more sleep."

The two hustled outside to continue their argument.

Irene watched after them, needing to know what the quarrel was about. She pushed her tired, heavy body up and out of the armchair. Keeping Ivy in her arms, and the blanket around her, she stood beside the ajar door. Staying very still, she listened intently to their harsh tones.

The midwife spoke with the same acid voice as before. "We can't let this go on!"

"Don't be stupid, it's just a babe," June said. "People read things wrong. Look at me, for instance—I read the day wrong, it's that easy."

"But it exposed itself!" the midwife snapped. "It showed me its evil eye!"

June gasped.

Irene slapped a hand over her own mouth.

"In all my years," the midwife continued, "I've never seen such a thing. And on its way out of the womb! My only guess..." She paused. "The plague it *would* set on this world!"

It! Irene cradled her babe even tighter to her chest and stared in horror. *How dare that old harridan call my precious little Ivy it! I will never, ever let anyone call her that again. She will always be the most beautiful Ivy the world has ever known.*

"Look," June went on, pleading with the midwife, "I'll watch them both carefully, especially the child. I'm already here every day, and if anything were to happen, even the slightest of things, *then* we could deal with it. But right now! It's murderous! To think of such an evil act—"

"—Oh, I'm thinking that keeping this *thing* alive is an evil act in itself," the woman cut her off. "It must be dealt with urgently. I'm fetching her husband, and the town's priest. Make sure you keep her here for when I get back, because that *thing* will be destroyed today!"

Irene's entire body shook. *Destroyed!* She couldn't think, couldn't believe her ears. *That's not going to happen.* Eyes darting around the room for something to defend herself and the babe with, she saw the pan tucked neatly under the bench.

Dropping the blanket, she rushed across the room and reached for the pan. Slipping back into the armchair quietly, she wrapped herself once more, and pretended to be asleep.

June remained outside for several more moments before coming in.

Irene's heart pounded against her chest.

What is June going to do? Is she going to tell me what the midwife is planning? Will she save me and the babe and protect us from that madness?

June closed the door and stood still for a moment.

Irene struggled to remain calm.

If she's going to do anything, now is the time.

Irene heard her footsteps. Waiting for June to wake her, she all but jumped when she heard the tin bucket in the sink move.

Oh my. She's not going to protect us! Irene's mouth went dry.

She opened one eyelid slightly and saw that June was wiping the kitchen bench once more.

How could she? They plan on murdering my baby! Does June hate me that much? Irene shook violently.

June returned to the sink with her back to Irene. Quietly as possible, Irene got to her feet. With the pan firmly in one hand, and her babe in the other, she let the blanket drop to the ground. She crept barefoot across the dirt floor. June turned around, mouth wide open.

"Oh dear, you scared me." She looked Irene up and down, noticing the pan firmly gripped by her side. "Give me the babe, dear, and it'll be all over."

A deep anger raised up and exploded from Irene. Rushing at June, she arched her arm back before she flung the pan down with force, so that it collided with June's skull.

June toppled backwards into the sink before her knees wobbled and she crumbled sideways to sprawl across the floor. A pool of blood spurted from the open wound and sprayed across the dirt.

Standing in place, unable to take her eyes away from the unconscious woman, Irene dropped the pan beside her. She had long fantasized about hurting June, but never thought about making it a reality. Rather than the excitement she'd imagined, a numbness washed over her. Irene inched away from her heinous crime. Inhaling largely, filling her chest deep with courage, she looked down to her sleeping babe, knowing she'd do just about anything to protect her. Still bare naked, Irene crossed the room and picked up her dress. It fell straight through her hands and crumbled to the floor. Slashed up the side, the midwife had cut it off her.

Quickly looking around, Irene grabbed the blanket and wrapped herself up. With her babe nestled tightly against her, she turned her back on June and fled through the open door.

Outside, she stopped, not knowing which direction to head.

Father will send me back and he won't protect my child. He always does as everyone tells him to.

She thought about her cousins. *Would they help?*

Tears rose in her eyes.

She had made her decision. Turning away from the town, Irene faced an the direction of the unknown.

Knowing not a single soul would protect her, Irene had to do that all on her own. Not letting her fears slow her down, she ran across the fields and into the nearby forest as quickly as possible—where she disappeared, never to be seen again.

ENGLAND

1457

"*How* ow much further?" Ivy yelled from the back of the rickety wagon. The deafening squawks of the chickens caged at her feet almost drowned out her voice, competing with the draft horse's clunking hooves as it plodded down the road.

"Pipe down, Ivy!" her mother reprimanded her over her shoulder.

Ivy sighed and shifted her sore body. It was as if the wagon hit every stone, pebble, and rock along the road, and by doing so rocketed uncomfortable vibrations up through the wooden bench seat and into the base of her spine.

"I want to stop and get out," she half-pleaded, half-demanded.

Irene's shoulders went upwards, curling around her own tension. After a long, drawn out moment of silence, she twisted and handed the reins to John, Ivy's stepfather.

Maneuvering herself into the back of the wagon, Irene sat opposite of Ivy. She didn't say a word.

Ivy sat very still, trying to anticipate what might occur.

Instead of speaking, Irene leaned over, opened a chicken

cage, and grabbed one by the neck. She pulled it out and closed the cage quickly so that the others wouldn't escape. Snapping its neck, she laid it across her lap and began plucking its feathers. One by one at first, followed by whole fistfuls.

Ivy couldn't determine what mood she was in. Glancing up at her every so often, Ivy kept her head down and continued plucking. Once the wooden box beside her was full of feathers, Ivy closed the lid, slipped it under the bench, and retrieved another.

Quickly finishing the bird, Irene placed the prepared chicken in an above compartment so that Gold, their shaggy mutt, couldn't reach it. Then she sat back down, fetched another chicken, and repeated the process.

Not wanting to break the silence, but tempted anyway, Ivy spoke as nicely as she could. "How much further?"

Irene sighed. "Can we please have more whining? You got that?" She wasn't harsh this time but simply sounded exhausted. She yanked each feather violently until none were left before flopping the bird down on the bench seat beside her.

Gold always sat with his back to the birds, but now he turned around and barked.

"Shush up, you," Irene snapped. Even though Gold remained on guard, constantly watching and forever protecting, no one trusted him when it came to the chickens.

Irene picked up another and continued.

"Once we arrive," Ivy started off nervously, diverting her eyes to the ground, "what will we sell?" Knowing her mother's exact worries about finances, food, and whether or not they were making the right choices, Ivy couldn't help but look up and read her mother's face.

"What we've always sold. Pillows." She sighed. "And prepared chickens."

"And..." Ivy opened her mouth, yet her mother held up a hand.

"Don't," she said. "I've been in this wagon for far too long. It's time to stop."

"I know!" Ivy stood, stretching her body and moving too quickly with excitement, scaring the chickens.

"Pipe down, Ivy." Irene clicked her fingers and pointed downwards.

Rolling her eyes, Ivy sat back down and returned to her boring work.

They had spent Ivy's entire life on the road, going from one town to the next without spending a single night more than they had to in any one place. Wherever they were, they bought live chickens, cotton, or wool and, along their journey, they'd pluck the chickens, make pillows, and sell them at the next town, living off a tidy profit. Any eggs the chickens laid were theirs for the keeping. It wasn't the best of trades, especially for wanderers like them—however, it had kept them hidden for almost twenty years and they never went a day without food.

But that was all about to change.

"Tell me about it," Ivy insisted.

"You've been told so many times, Ivy. Nothing has changed since the last time I told you or even since the very first time I told you."

"Just tell me it all again anyway." Ivy wiggled her bum towards the edge of the bench seat, nodding for her mother to speak.

Irene sighed long and deep. "Okay." She took in a large breath and held it, then let out a long sigh. "Your father—" and here she gestured to the smelly drunk male up front who held the reins, "has a cousin, Geoffrey, or George or for God's whatever his name is." She sighed. "He built a beautiful little cottage on the far end of his property just for us. Complete with an outhouse and a vegetable garden and—"

"Don't forget," Ivy cut her off, "the stone chimney!"

"It has a fireplace attached to that chimney; you do know that, right?"

"Umm...." Ivy looked baffled. She didn't think she had ever been inside another person's home. She had always seen chimneys above rooftops, and along the sides of buildings, which had only left her to imagine what they were used for.

Irene glared at her.

Ivy shifted under her gaze. Living a life in the back of a moving wagon with no connection to younglings her own age was hard to stomach. Especially when riding into town and seeing them laugh and smile at whatever festivities were going on.

"Farming," Irene spat out.

"What?" Ivy twisted her head, confused.

"We'll grow potatoes, and pumpkins, and anything else we could steal from neighboring farms."

Ivy smiled, and it matched her mother's.

"Then," Irene continued, "once we have an abundance, we'll sell it to the neighbors we stole it from."

They both chuckled.

"Quiet down back there," the drunk, chubby half-wit burped out, not even bothering to speak over his shoulder. John sat with protruding bags under his bloodshot eyes, hair missing from his bulbous dome, and with a stained tunic that had buttons struggling under the pressure of his ever-growing stomach.

Ivy rolled her eyes while Irene humphed. Placing the bird on Ivy's side, Irene left her to finish the pillows on her own.

Ivy slumped back into the hard wooden bench seat and sighed. As she remained slouched, she studied the feathers chaotically decorating her worn-out, patched brown dress, and then felt a pinch right in the middle of her palms.

Her magic was restless.

Sitting up tall, she checked to see if her mother was

distracted. Then she returned her sights to the loose feathers and concentrated.

Energies made themselves known around her. She never had seen them, but she had often felt them. She had no idea what they looked like, but something in her mind told her who they are and why they were there. One was a spirit standing nearby, always eager to watch her. Another, a goddess watching over the animals. Two more arrived with a purpose of their own.

Ivy drew on their strengths, pulling on their power. It enhanced the pinch in her palms and created a glow.

The feathers lightly lifted off her dress, and all the ones that had fallen to the floor now rose up and gathered together. As they hovered in the air, right in front of her face, she make them dance above her hands.

Trying desperately to hold back her excited laugh, a small giggle escaped her lips. She moved one hand in a circular movement, shaping the feathers into a tornado. They clustered together and swirled through the air, speeding up with each twist and turn. The remaining chickens violently flapped their wings against the cage. The faster the feathered tornado spun, the harder Ivy struggled to contain it. Gold turned his back on the outside road and barked ferociously at Ivy. Spinning dangerously out of control, the feathered tornado ripped around the back of the wagon, causing an almighty mess in its wind storm.

The horse up front reared up and shuddered the wagon to a halt.

"Ivy!" Irene screamed.

Ivy dropped her arms to her sides. The feathers scattered all over the wagon. Turning, Ivy faced her scolding mother. Beside her, her stepfather wore a pale white expression. Blank with terror, he sat glaring at Ivy with his mouth wide open.

"Not again!" Irene howled. "You stupid child!"

"I am *not* a child," Ivy barked back.

"You *are* a child, and continue to *be* a child because you're careless and reckless and stupid!" She didn't bother getting up from her seat, and rather grinded her teeth together and pointed at the feathers and then to the pillowcase. Irene turned back to her husband and handed him the reins again.

He faced the dirt road and his bushy grey eyebrows clustered together. He recognized something was out of the ordinary, but Irene's particular mind-training had him questioning other possibilities that were far from the truth.

The horse broke into a steady trot while Gold turned his back on Ivy and the wagon, and went back to being on guard.

Motionless, John watched the road ahead.

Irene hovered over her husband and placed her fingertips gently on his temples. In a small circular motion, the very tips of her fingers warmed as they released energy directly into the depths of his skull. In a low murmur, she spoke the words of her ancestors, and cast the spell she'd always used on him. One that would force him to forget. To only know a world that didn't contain magic. To remain blatantly ignorant.

Ivy rolled her eyes. "If you keep doing that, there won't be anything left of his brain to remove."

Irene returned a savage stare.

Instantly, Ivy looked away.

Sitting beside her quiet husband, Irene handed him another glass of the cheaply brewed ale that she had picked up in the last town.

He pressed the wooden chalice to his dried lips and drank it absentmindedly.

"It's your fault," her mother scolded. "Always using your magic so blatantly! You know I can't keep you hidden forever!"

"Good!" Ivy snapped. "I'm not going to hide forever." Ivy crossed her arms and stared at her mother—knowing she wouldn't look back, but on the off chance she did, and then Irene could suffer one of those horrid stares. While Ivy positioned her face and glared, she watched her mother breathe deep. She looked down at her old hands, turning them one way and then another.

Ivy had seen her do that before. Realize how old she was getting, how tired she was from continuing to argue when Ivy could easily argue all night. But it was her fault, Ivy convinced herself. She'd chosen to tell Ivy a veiled version of the truth, leaving Ivy to live as a lonely child. Things could have been much different, if her mother would only be forthcoming with the details, but the details fell where they did, and here they were, spending their entire lives still on the run.

Ivy stood and went to her mother's side. Gently, she shook her shoulder.

Irene looked up and smiled.

Ivy pointed up ahead. In the very far distance, still on the horizon, a small and yet narrow church tower came into view.

Leaning over her stepfather's slumped body, Ivy jiggled the reins so that the draft horse sped up its pace.

As they got closer, Ivy couldn't contain her excitement, and she swayed from one foot to the other.

"Sit down, Ivy," Irene nagged.

But Ivy shook her head, embracing the new-found energy and slipping into a dance, unable to keep still.

"I've never seen you so excited to go into a town."

"That's because we've never stayed in a town for more than one night!" Ivy said, nearly falling into song. "This town, we can call home."

"Maybe," Irene corrected her.

Ivy froze. With one finger, she poked her mother firmly in the back. "No! Not maybe," Ivy spoke with her mother's own tone. She demanded attention. "I'm *never* getting back into this wagon *ever* again!"

Irene paused, trying to find the right words. "Well, if it

doesn't work out, then your father and I will get into this very wagon while you ride horseback."

Ivy shook her head, ignoring her words, and then let the excitement take over again, quickly returning to her excited dance. "We will see about that," she mused.

Within an hour, the draft horse had reached town.

"Ivy!" her mother snapped. "I need you to act like a lady."

Ivy had heard the lecture many times before. Tuning out the warnings and the threats, Ivy took in the sights. Pebbled cottages enveloped in the thick smell of soot. Dark green shrubs covered in half-melted snow. The chilly breeze that carried the chimney smoke away from town caused Ivy to shiver.

The wagon pulled up in the middle of a mud-slick street, stopping at a trough in front of a shop. Ivy shook her hips side to side to celebrate.

Quickly turning, Irene latched onto Ivy's wrist. "Calm down right now," she said through clenched teeth.

"I'm not going to do anything," Ivy retorted back as she reclaimed her arm.

Irene puffed out her chest. It was something she'd always done when she held back an argument. Knowing not to provoke her, Ivy averted her eyes, dropping them to her sore wrist, where her mother's fingernails had left indents in her skin.

Ivy smiled, turned, and climbed over the cages.

"Ivy!" her mother called, using her warning tone. But Ivy didn't respond. Rather, she lurched forward, jumping from the back of the wagon, and flew through the air until her heavy leather heels crunched down on the dirt road.

Her dress had caught the wind, collecting up around her head. Frantically, she pushed it down and gathered herself.

Oh my! If anyone had seen... She snapped her head each way, hoping that no prying eyes had seen.

Instead of seeing faces, though, Ivy was instantly distracted by the surrounding town. On each side of the road were little stores with fronts big enough for a small door and a narrow bay window. Yet, as a whole street, it all gave the impression of a collection of clustered boxes, lined up one beside the other.

From where she stood, Ivy could only see blurry figures inside the boxes, as the hand-pressed glass was too thick, bubbled, and it distorted the view. She thought about pressing her face to the glass, but decided against it. *First impressions last a lifetime*, she thought in the nagging tone of her mother, and she could just imagine how horrible she'd look from the other side.

Shivering at the thought, Ivy twisted and turned, taking in the sights. It wasn't until she connected with the nearby faces that she realized her error.

There were several people along the street, some together, while most walked alone. One paused to stare with dissatisfaction while others kept moving, giggling to one another. Ivy had made her entrance. Exposed undergarments and all.

"Stay with the horse, Ivy."

"Yes, Mother." She walked to the front of the wagon and stood holding onto the reins, realizing that she had left Gold unattended to guard the wagon. Before she moved, she caught sight of her mother linking arms with her drunken, half-witted husband to cross the road and move into a little shop with signage labelling the locale of the mayor.

Standing beside the horse's head, Ivy gawked after them, imagining the mayor only wanting to speak to John, and yet he wouldn't be able to get a word in. Irene was the one that did the talking, and after a solid seventeen years of being stuck beside her, being manipulated and drained whenever she saw fit, Ivy doubted John would be able to muster up any words even if he wanted to.

Ivy's senses tingled. She felt a presence behind her. She twisted her body to inspect the source of the feeling, but as she turned, her heel clipped the edge of a small hole and rolled her ankle to the ground.

Her arms flung out to the side as her body tilted before she toppled over and the ground came up to meet her. But, halfway down, something unexpected happened. A pair of bulky arms wrapped around her, squeezing her tight and cushioning her landing.

She gasped when her head impacted a bony chest instead of ground.

"Miss?" a voice shook her to attention.

Ivy sat up, dazed, confused and looking towards the voice expectantly. Two almond eyes looked back at her.

"Miss," he said again, "are you alright?"

Leaning away from the unfamiliar face, Ivy gathered her dress and tried to stand.

"Here, let me help you." His musical tone danced around her. In one fluid movement, he was on his feet, standing tall and looking down at her while he held out his hand.

She looked at it carefully, inspecting him closely. Her mouth went instantly dry.

Reluctantly, she slipped her hand into his, hoping her mother was still in the mayor's office. As he pulled her to her feet, her knees wobbled and she bellowed out. "Ouch!"

"Oh my!" He grabbed her by the shoulders to steady her sway. "I've hurt you," he commented.

"No, no," she said politely, softly pushing him away and searching the ground for the culprit. "If there's a small hole in the road, it's bound to find my feet." She laughed. "These matters seem to find me often, so please don't burden yourself with blame or guilt."

He stood smiling and his eyes softened.

Don't think about the pain. Act strong, Ivy. She breathed in and then out again. *Oh, ouch!*

She latched onto the horse's harness for support and to

relieve the pressure from her throbbing ankle.

"May I have your name, Miss?" For a tall man, stubble at his chin, and a day's work under his fingernails, he spoke gently.

The heat radiated underneath Ivy's cheeks, which turned a darker shade of red. "Um..." Ivy looked him up and down. He couldn't be any older than she was and he wore nice clean clothing had been made to fit his shape. Someone had taken the time to make him presentable and decent. Ivy instantly hated the dress she wore. Made of a collection of old rags, torn blankets, and left-over pillow stripping, the dress had turned an ugly color of brown. "Ivy," she whispered, keeping her voice low to avoid suggesting the pain she was in.

"It is nice to meet you, Miss Ivy." He'd said her name with such sweetness. It reminded Ivy of that one time she'd tried a sugar drop and rolled it around her tongue. "Are you in town for long? Or passing by?"

"My mother is inside meeting with the mayor. We've just been given a cottage on the outskirts of town." She wasn't quite sure what her mother would think of her telling a strange young men of their intentions, but Ivy couldn't care less. She wanted him to know.

He rolled back on his heels, and smiled, then lunged forward to grab hold of Ivy as she toppled to the ground once more.

"Dang!" she moaned. "That *stupid* horse moved so I let go."

He extended his hand and helped her to her feet.

"Let's get you seated." He looked to the front of the wagon.

"Can you help me to the back."

Smiling, he came in real close, wrapped his arm around her waist and lifted her up, so that her sore ankle no longer touched the ground.

Hobbling on one foot, he assisted her all the way to the back of the wagon and helped her to the ladder.

"You haven't told me your name, Mr...?"

"Thomas."

She pulled herself up and swung her legs around to sit beside Gold, who was nuzzling Thomas's hands.

Ivy's mouth dropped open.

"What's the matter?" Thomas laughed.

"That dog." She shook her head, amazed at the dirty long-hair guard. "He doesn't allow anyone to touch him."

Thomas dropped his hands to his side. "Are you sure? He likes me." Gold wagged his tail, wanting more pats.

"It's a first," Ivy said as she looked to the people walking by. It was like they came out of nowhere but had some place to go. She noticed several blank faces pretending not to stared as they passed, and when she looked directly at them, they quickly turned away, going on with their business.

"There's a lot of people in this town," Ivy said.

"Sure, you could say that. Not too many that don't talk to my mother," he said, winking. "And all of them are probably on their way there this very instant, to tell her how I carried a young maiden to the back of a wagon."

"Well, when you put it like that, I'm sure they're running."

He laughed and shook his head. "Wouldn't surprise me in the slightest." He sighed, and Ivy twisted her head for an explanation. He sighed again. "Well, you see..." In his hesitation, his face turned a darker shade of red. Ivy could see his embarrassment, but instead of helping him, she remained silent, desperately wanting to know what he'd say. "The maidens in town have been courting me," he said. "You see, it is very embarrassing for my mother, who thinks that it is not proper behavior for a young lady." He averted his eyes, and even his cheeks beneath his stubble reddened.

Her eyes wandered away from him and into the nearby buildings, where people sat behind windows watching, or stood on the balconies pretending to do something and then quickly glanced over their shoulder, towards Ivy and Thomas.

It appears I've made my entrance. She sighed.

She searched for the maidens that he spoke of and quickly found three of them. Their dresses were perfect, clean with crisp lines. Pure colors that not even Ivy's mother could master.

None of them were tall and Ivy could easily enough be a whole head above them, but there were something about their milky skin, their shiny hair and the light that seemed to follow them.

But as they came into view and locked their sights onto Thomas, their jealousy radiated from them like poison in the air.

"Well, *I* wasn't courting!" she insisted.

He smiled. "No, you were not, Miss Ivy."

Now, Ivy's pulse raced..

"Ah, hum." A young woman, one of the maidens that she had seen across the other side of town, stood beside Thomas clearing her throat.

Ivy looked down at her. Although she was not tall, only making it to Thomas's shoulders, her tight blond curls sat neatly around her face. If it hadn't been for the sour look and the angry glare, Ivy would have thought she was beautiful.

Thomas snapped his gaze away from Ivy and turned to the young woman. With her arms crossed and with her eyebrows scrunched together, she looked up to Thomas furiously.

Is this a lover's tiff? Ivy's heart sank.

Feeling like she should give them some space, Ivy fumbled for what to do; she had nowhere to go. Stuck with a throbbing ankle, she shifted in her seat uncomfortably.

"Miss Rose," he said ever so politely and tilted his hat, quickly returning it to his head.

Ivy couldn't help but notice the difference in his manner. His greeting had been much more relaxed with Ivy than with this beautiful young woman.

Did he treat me better because I hurt myself?

The girl mumbled under her breath so that only he could hear, and Thomas's face twisted at her words.

"Please, Miss Rose, you are mistaken." He straightened his back. "It was the proper thing to do."

She hmphed, then turned and stormed off in the opposite direction.

Ivy squeezed her lips together, forcing herself not to laugh.

He bowed his head, not bothering to watch her walk away. Once she went out of sight, he lifted his head and looked up to Ivy. Something sparked in his eyes.

Ivy sensed a shift in him.

He leaned in a little closer. Eyes wide and bright, and his face held a glow.

She could feel deep within her the impact she was having on him. All her senses tingled, her chest swelled, heartbeat quickened and she felt like she was loosing her breath.

He smiled again, and his eyes shined even brighter. It was like he was looking into the sun and Ivy was brightening up his entire existence.

She took a deep breath in, feeling the magic dance around them.

There was more to Thomas than she'd realized. She not only felt it, but she sensed it in the universe.

In the corner of her eye, Ivy noticed her mother had exited the mayor's office.

"I must go," Thomas said softly.

Ivy nodded. The timing was perfect. "Will you come and see me at the cottage?"

"If my mother allows it." He tilted his hat and smiled so brightly that it made his eyes glow.

"I won't tell if you won't." She smiled.

Thomas took a few steps backwards before turning around. In that last moment, as he looked away, once his eyes were no longer on her, it was like she no longer shined so bright.

The ride out of town took longer than Ivy would have liked.

"If you ask me one more question about the things I don't know, I'm going to banish you from the house and can live in the wagon."

Ivy rolled her eyes. "I thought you said would live *in* town!"

"The land is part of the town. Be grateful, Ivy," Irene snapped.

John coughed. "How did you injure your ankle?"

"That is a very good question," Irene said, twisting herself around to glare.

Ivy took a deep breath in and held it. "It was the horse's fault," she blurted out releasing the air from her lungs. "I was holding the harness and he stomped on my ankle."

Irene's face went flat. "He would have broken the bones."

"Er... I moved my foot out of the way in time."

"If you're not going to tell the truth, then don't speak at all." She turned back to face the road.

That afternoon, Irene and John moved all of their belongings from the wagon and laid them across their new cottage's floor. There really wasn't much—just enough clothing for each of them, enough food to last a week, and most important of all, the pillows and related items to help them make money in the near future.

Ivy left them to figure out what to do with it all and hobbled to the back door. Sitting down on the back step to rest her swollen, aching ankle, she pulled a little box from her pocket. Inside were small, earthly pieces.

Irene appeared behind her. "How are you feeling?"

"Fine."

"Lies. Always lies with you."

Ivy smiled wide as Irene sat beside her.

"Don't say it—" Irene said.

"Got it from you."

Irene shook her head. "Wicked child."

"Stop calling me a child."

Ivy looked out across the field and noticed a forest bordering the left side. As the sun began to lower, it cast an eerie shadow over the dark greenery and the temperature dropped.

"You know what needs to be done," Irene said quietly.

"Of course, Mother. I've healed myself many times."

Irene nodded. "I know. I just wish I could be there to help you."

Ivy reached out and wrapped her hand around her mother's. "Are you ready?"

"What? Now?" Ivy shook her head. "But it's still daylight."

"By the time you get down there, it'll be well dark."

Twisting around to watch John huddle over the items inside, Ivy took a breath to calm her nerves. She nodded.

After Irene helped Ivy to her feet, she slung a small bag over her shoulder and shoved the box back into her pocket.

"You've got everything, right?"

"Yes, Mother." Ivy leaned into Irene's support, keeping the pressure off her sore ankle. They went down the back steps and onto the soft grass, Ivy hobbling as they moved through the back garden and into the darkening forest. As soon as they reached the tree line, Ivy felt different.

The tall trees had spikes down the trunks, which were a luscious brown, with thick greenery overhead. The smell of pine and fresh air invaded her nose and she breathed it down deep into her lungs, letting the purity elevate her senses. As they passed several trees, Ivy stopped and looked back.

"It's not far enough," Irene said.

"But look," Ivy turned around and pointed back to the house. "I can't even sense John from here."

Irene froze. "Me, neither."

"There's something about this forest."

"You feel it, too, huh?"

Ivy nodded and let her mother lead the way. They stepped over twigs and small branches, leaves and large tree roots. The ground was covered in a thick moss and, where it was bare, soft and luscious dirt full of minerals. Ivy knew she'd return soon—she was in need of fresh materials.

Each time she placed her foot onto the ground, Ivy flinched. The pain throbbed around the base of her foot and shot all the way up into her hip.

"How much further?" she whined. "All this walking is making it worse."

"As far as we need to." Irene sighed. "You know the dangers if anyone sees. We just can't risk—"

Ivy cut her off. "I know, you've said it a million times."

"Stop exaggerating," Irene scolded. "I need to say it because you can't die a million times."

Ivy fell silent. Her mother was right. Annoying and consistent, but always right. They continued their walk in silence, and the sky darkened. The moon, fully round with sharp, crisp edges, trickled bright light though the canopy to provide just enough illumination for them to see their surroundings.

An old fallen tree trunk, hollowed out in the middle, was sturdy enough to sit upon. Ivy let go of her mother and placed the bag beside her as she sat to catch her breath.

In the looming darkness, Irene kissed Ivy on the forehead and then left in silence. Ivy watched until she was out of sight, heading back to the cottage in preparation for distracting her stepfather—hoping, praying even, that he'd already passed out.

In the dark, Ivy pulled from her bag a large pendulum. She stood, wobbling a couple of times before reaching up high above her to clip the chain onto the closest tree branch. She sat back down and watched as a bright moonbeam hit the red gem and made her surroundings glisten.

When she stood again, she reached for another nearby branch, and Ivy there placed dried pieces of mushroom, cobbled wood, and fresh lavender. Carefully, so that she didn't put too much pressure on her foot, she sat back down. Ever so gently, she unbuttoned the side of her leather boot. The release of pressure felt good, like somehow the circulation could start again.

She placed her foot onto some soft, moist grass and dirt threaded between her toes.

Quickly taking off her other boot, she realized that her sore ankle was now swelling even faster. Purple and black swirls replaced the color of her pale skin. Trying to ignore the pain, she stood up and fiddled with the clips of her dress, letting it fall to the ground. The cool night air danced across her bare skin.

Kicking her ruffled dress to the side, she positioned herself right beneath the pendulum. Palms wide beside her, she felt the energy around her exposed body. Strong, it came in fast. Closing her eyes, she inhaled deep breaths of the exotically fragrant air and her skin began to tingle. Sensing the power around her, Ivy drew it in.

Standing tall, straightening her back, she stretched her limbs long.

She had done this at least a handful of times before, but the power was like nothing she'd ever experienced. She opened her eyes and saw several spirits clustered over to the right.

She paused trying to take them all in. They stood too close together, like their light had merged as one, yet their heads were clearly separate. Four, maybe five stood but a few meters away, staring back at her.

In her mind, she was receiving messages but it was like they weren't for her. Not able to hear it clearly, she could make out that the voices were communicating with one another.

"Who are you?" she asked out loud.

In an instant, all of their information and conversation was inserted into her mind. The energy was heavy, and she nearly stumbled backwards.

"Understand?" an internal voice asked.

"Wait!" she said; she needed a moment to unpack it all. There was too much, all too quickly. It hurt her head to take it all in at once.

Struggling to breathe, she felt overwhelmed. "Who is she?" one asked. "Why is she so important?" The questions came one after the other, bringing up things that Ivy had never considered.

They went on, as a group and individually. Ivy struggled to keep up. "She belongs to no one."

"No tribe has claimed her."

"Nor a clan or a coven."

"Unusual for a witch of her strength."

"Her heart is pure."

"But her mind is tainted."

"Tainted thoughts are natural of humans."

"Thoughts wash away like the blood on their hands."

"Deeds that are done never wash away, they stain the soul."

"But her deeds are before her, not in the past."

"We can only make judgement for the things she has done, not which lies ahead."

"Exactly. Given the chance, she'll change the world."

"That's what I'm worried about."

Ivy's breath caught in the back of her throat. *Change the world? But how?* She didn't have a moment to wrestle with the thought. The voices were still coming at her, forcing her to unpack them in her mind.

"Her power is something," one continued.

"Why? What is she?"

"Good question."

Then they went silent. Ivy felt something come between them and her. It was a different energy altogether. She sensed it in her mind's eye, but her other eyes were blind to the glow across the floor. The planet's energy itself had made itself known.

"What's going on?" Ivy asked.

"There's nothing to fear, child." When they spoke, their words were all inserted into her mind without a single sound reaching her ears. "Gaia is with us."

"The planet?"

"Yes. We are her pledged spirits, and she would like you to join us while you still walk the earth."

"And before you reach spirit," another one added.

Ivy didn't know what that meant. She took a moment to think, but she couldn't hear her own thoughts. The voices of the spirits started a conversation once more.

"What is she?"

"She has to be a Daemon."

"What's that?"

"A god."

"No, not a god, it's a power and a fate."

"That's the same as a god."

"She's not a Daemon," a different voice sounded out, but Ivy couldn't determine which one was talking since they were nothing but pure white. Shimmering against the faded light, they only thing Ivy could make out clear enough was their outlines. "She's the other type."

"There's more than one?"

"Of course, there is. Do you remember who kissed her at her birth?"

"I wasn't watching."

"The energy was powerful."

"Yes, the old energies of the earth."

"She's a Diamon."

"What's that?"

"A Diamon?" Ivy asked out loud.

"You are the provider of destinies, child. Join us, and together we can heal the earth."

Ivy paused again, wanting to push them out of her head to

think her own thoughts. These spirits were strong, demanding, and pressuring Ivy to submit.

What do they really want? Are they trying to turn me into some sort of sacrificial lamb and bow down?

Ivy eyes darted around. Something beneath her feet was making itself known. She felt it and its power and it tingled her entire body. It was stronger than she could ever have imagined. But it wanted something from her, and she would never bow to a sacrificial pledge, even if it was to gain more power.

She took a deep breath, pulling in more strength, drawing it in from around her.

Filling her body with the power it let her take, she raised up, suspended in the air, just above the ground. Her toes pointed downwards, lightly touched the grass.

The power pulsated in strength again. It demanded that she submit.

"Never," she whispered, and instead she pulsated back her own strength, demonstrating that she was worthy of more than being its subject. If she was going to tie herself to a power, then she wanted nothing less than to be an equal partner.

A lamb would have been long slaughtered. But the power source made itself known. Gaia was intrigued by Ivy, and studying her carefully. The earth's spirits took Gaia's pause as an opportunity to raise themselves from the forest floor, and they reached out, touching her feet to see for themselves the mystery of Ivy.

Hungry for her uniqueness, they latched on and wrapped themselves tightly around her feet. Slowly but with great strength, they inched further up her ankles and creeped up her legs.

She sensed everything. All of Gaia's power as well as her feelings, thoughts and her intentions. Gaia desired Ivy's loyalty and full devotion, but Ivy fought back. She did not bow like the sacrificial lamb, nor did she buckle to a power much greater than her own.

Entertained by her strength, Gaia considered her further.

Ivy sensed Gaia's hesitation. The energies that had creeped up her legs, calling for Ivy to commit to Gaia, latching onto her so that she called align her loyalty, now fell back. They slowly let go, slipping down her legs, towards her feet. But Ivy didn't allow them to go too far, as she held onto them, pulling them back in, but this time in her own way.

Ivy's body swelled. A powerful surge filled her quickly, coming from both the energies at her feet and Gaia herself, demanding her intentions.

"I do not bow," she said, both out loud and in her mind's eye.

Gaia listened.

"I harness these commitment energies." She pulled on them harder. "I desire a *promise*."

She pushed out her thoughts. She felt them hear her mind, accept the ideas. Unable to form the words, she showed them pictures instead.

The whole planet came into view and the people lived in peace, never in fear and loved Gaia as she loves them.

It was a promise that no other had offered before, not in Gaia's entire existence. She felt Gaia's need, her internal yearning for the spiritual advancement of humans so Ivy gave her that possibility.

The idea had been one thought of before, yet not a single person, witch or otherwise, had the means of execution... until now, with Ivy.

Gaia remained silent, absent even, and yet the surrounding spirits, energies, and entities zinged with excitement.

As Ivy waited, she returned to the ground, her feet planting softly in the dirt. She flinched at the pain throbbing in her ankle, but pushed the thought aside. Still sensing Gaia right there, Gaia reached up and placed pure energy in the bottom of her foot. The pain was instantly gone.

Smiling, she closed her eyes and began her dance. Swaying her hips, she flicked out her feet and twirled her hands. The energy rolled across her soft skin, tingling all of her senses. Each tiny hair along her arms and down her back buzzed with every molecule.

As darkness veiled her, the night spirits gathered ever so closely. Some lingered while others merged themselves within Ivy. Swishing her arms out, flowing, twisting, swinging her hips, she lost herself. An energy swelled within her, creating a beat and a rhythmic tone that her body naturally accepted. Twirling her hands high above her head, she felt herself rise. The energies seeped into her body, down deep into her very being.

Heat, energy, and love filled her every inch and raised her up even further.

Her limbs turned and contorted, rolling in every direction. Her torso rippled as it swayed side to side. She breathed in the fresh air, deep into her lungs, allowing the purity to swarm her mind. Drawing in the earth's magic, inch by inch, her body strengthened—the surge of new power awakening her own magic anew, repairing every fiber in her body, enlivening her mind, brightening her already vibrant spirit. She, in turn, accepted this very place as home.

The nature gods delighted at her particular type of commitment, accepting her wholly. Gaia, too, accepted Ivy's promise and opened the doors for her to tap into the power she needed. The spirits that came to her first, now surrounded her, intertwining themselves until she became one with the gods. Mending her broken ankle, they relaxed the puffiness, and then, within moments the bruising softened. Soon enough, the swirls of purple and black washed away until it returned to its normal color.

The spirits returned to the earth but Ivy still felt the buzz around her.

Dropping to her feet, Ivy stood tall and strong. She took a step back and smiled at herself, wanting to feel this moment for the rest of her life.

After dressing herself, she unclipped the pendulum, and collected all of the pieces back safely into her bag. Then, without pain, she walked straight back to the cottage with her newly gained strength pulsating around her ankle and throughout her body.

Each morning, Ivy went out into the garden and picked a beautiful flower. Pulling each petal off, she'd hold it up to her lips, whisper Thomas's name, and blow it into the wind. "Thomas," she said again and again, until each petal was gone. Returning the stem back to the earth, she brushed some loose dirt over it and stood up. Since it was Sunday and with her mother away at church, she decided to walk through the neighboring forest, searching the shrubs for berries. She stopped and found ones that were particularly different to all the other types. Bright red on a green thistle bush, these ones had no smell. She couldn't figure out what they were.

Picking one, she squeezed it between her fingers, causing juices to spill out.

"They're safe to eat."

Ivy threw the berry up into the air, twisted her body around, and clutched her chest.

"Thomas!" she said, trying to catch her breath.

"I did it again," he said, frowning.

"It's okay," she said, looking around to see if he had come with anyone else.

"Your ankle!" He looked down, eyes wide, and then back to her eyes and smiled. "You're healed."

"Oh…" She leaned out and clutched the nearest tree, lifting her foot slightly off the ground. "Not fully," she said.

"It's amazing. Your mother told mine that you couldn't walk for weeks."

"My mother?" Ivy hadn't been aware that her mother had said anything to anyone.

"They're currently at church."

"I know that." She looked around, trying to see if anyone else was about. "Why aren't you?"

He shrugged. "I was there for most of it."

Ivy laughed, though it sounded more like a giggle.

"Let's just say, you bewitched me."

Ivy froze. *Does he know?*

He laughed at her expression, then looked down at the berries. "They're cranberries, and very safe to eat." He reached out and took one, popping it straight into his mouth.

"I've never seen them before," she said, softly placing it onto her tongue. As she bit down, the juices squirted, tasting bitter and sour at the same time. She had heard of cranberries, but never seen one before, let alone tasted it.

They went to the next tree and Ivy walked slowly, pretending it was sore. "Does your mother know you are here?"

He stopped and looked around, his cheeks reddening. "I should go."

"Already? But you just got here."

"If I stay any longer, it'll be harder to leave."

The swell in her stomach returned. She wanted to reach out to him, wrap her arms around him, and never let go. But she knew that if someone had followed him, or been watching, they'd get into a lot of trouble. Instead, she settled for the next best thing. She lifted her hand and reached out for his.

They touched fingers and their skin ignited between them.

"What was that?" he asked, pulling away his hand.

I haven't a clue! She looked to her own hand. It was as if a spark of sunshine had jumped out from each of their hands and met in the middle. Feeling like a prickle heat, it energized the skin and tingled all the way up her arm.

"Ivy!"

She looked back towards the house. "My mother!" she exclaimed.

"It's time for me to leave," he said nervously.

"No!" Ivy stepped closer, reaching out for him. She curled her fingers inside the seam of his vest, locking her thumb on the button.

"I must," he whispered, smiling at her.

She breathed him in. The proximity was alluring.

"Ivy!" Irene yelled again, but this time from much closer.

Ivy yelled over her shoulder. "I'm here, Mother!" Then she turned back to Thomas. "Will I see you again?"

"Of course."

Reluctantly, she let go of his vest and he inched away. He zig-zagged through the trees, keeping out of sight of her mother.

Ivy gathered as many berries as she and headed back to the house, skipping all the way.

"Why are you so cheerful?" Irene asked as Ivy appeared.

Ivy held out her hand, showing a palm-full of red berries. "Want a cranberry?"

"How do you know they're not poisonous?"

Ivy popped one into her mouth. "I'm not dead yet."

Counting the sunrises until her mother allowed her to go back into town, Ivy calculated it to be exactly a month since she'd last seen Thomas. He was the last thing she thought about at night, and the very first she thought of in the morning. But it worried her to think he mightn't have thought about her. She gazed out the window looking for another flower, but there weren't any left.

"Stand straight," her mother commanded. "Ladies don't slouch."

Ivy stood taller, waiting for her mother to lace the last of the buttons up her back.

"There," Irene aid, placing her hands on her hips. "If only you acted as nice as you looked."

Ivy laughed, then twirled around the room letting the hem breeze out to the sides. "You're the wicked one, Mother. After all, what have I ever done?"

Irene extended her neck back and let out a single laugh.

Reaching for the door, Ivy danced her way outside, and jumped off the steps, landing on the gravel.

"The basket!" Irene yelled after her. Dancing her way back, Ivy reached across the steps, took the basket of carrots and ripe tomatoes, and slid it up her arm.

With the town firmly in her sights, she skipped towards the road.

"Swap them for different foods!" her mother yelled after her. "And make sure you bring home more than you took!"

Ivy smiled, but continued to cross the front paddock to the edge of their land.

"Ivy!" her mother called. "I don't want any repeats!"

Repeats! Ivy snickered and waved a hand into the air to shoo her mother off. Irene always exaggerated the smallest things into the biggest of problems, which they weren't. Only her step-father saw things, and *he* couldn't remember a single one. Ivy wasn't stupid enough to do her magic in front of anyone, especially when she didn't want to spend the next ten years stuck in the back of that wagon again. Ivy didn't look back at the cottage where her mother was glaring from, rather turning to the road and, as her muscles warmed, falling into a long stride. The sun moved across the sky since she left home and her heart skipped a beat when she saw the town appear. Then her heart hammered against her chest when she saw Thomas.

Far ahead, Thomas stood by an elderly man. As if he sensed her staring, he turned his head and smiled. Quickly leaving the old man behind, he fell into a jog and headed straight towards her.

It gave her a second to gather herself. *Breathe, Ivy,* she repeated in her head. *Keep breathing.*

"You're here!" he said as he got closer. "I'm so glad you're all better now." His breaths were labored as he stopped just a step away. Taking his hat off and holding it in front of him, he smiled widely.

She soaked him in like a warm breeze, and then smiled back and shifted her weight from one foot to the other. Her insides could have exploded. Deep in her stomach, her emotions twisted and swirled; she desperately wanted to reach out and touch him. His eyes were eager. Her breath caught, and she realized she hadn't said anything.

"Yes, thank you," she blurted out. "Have you been waiting for me?"

He's cheeks reddened. "My mother was told you might be coming in."

She held up the basket with the vegetables over flowing. "I hope I didn't get you into any trouble."

His eyes dropped to the ground. "Oh, it's nothing," he said, running his hand through his hair and then returning his hat to his head. "I needed to see you that day."

"What happened?"

"My mother said I can speak to you in town. But coming to your house while your parents weren't home..." he stopped and looked around, pulling at his collar. He turned back and smiled. His cheeks a darker shade of red. "That's why I only made the one visit. I'm sorry for that. Mother said she already has enough to deal with, you know, with all that's going on in town."

Ivy twisted her head to the side. She didn't quite understand. *Is he trying to warn me about something?*

"I don't know," she said. "Tell me." With Ivy and her parents living on the outskirts of town, she didn't know what could be going on. She bit down on her lip. *My mother wanted me to avoid town so no one knew I used magic to heal my ankle. Was that the right thing to do?*

Being out of the loop from the town's dramas was a dangerous thing—especially for Ivy and her mother.

"Whatever do you mean?" Ivy insisted.

Thomas turned and continued to walk, Ivy pursuing him, slightly behind.

"Please tell me," she begged.

"Rumors!" He eventually answered. "There's always some rumor going around but after you arrived..." he trailed off again.

She reached out and stopped him. "Please Thomas. Tell me."

He nodded and they fell back into a slow walk.

"People are annoyed that Mr. Geoffroy has allowed you to move into his house while he is away."

"We didn't." she shook her head. "He built us a house right at the far end of his property."

"Did he really?"

Ivy was taken aback, clearly seeing why rumors took hold so easily. "He is my uncle and always wanted us to come and live with him. Why would people be annoyed at that. It doesn't make sense."

He shrugged.

Ivy's heart sunk. *It's because of me!* Her mouth went dry. *They're making up rumors because I've arrived.* She had heard of these types of stories before, back in the rural towns that they'd once travelled through, just like this one. Strange people coming and going like they always did never received any attention, only gaining notice for the goods they brought and the services they offered for the limited time that they hung around. But the ones that stayed permanently were the ones who caused the problems. Not the married couples with the really young children—never them, because those were the ones that embodied innocence. Rather, it was always the families with the young, so-called *dangerous* maidens. Those were the ones that were out looking for husbands. The ones that were sick of living under the strict rules of their parents and somehow possessed evil capabilities surrounding their desires towards a single male and their attempts for freedom. Yet, it was never the single man that caused the fear; rather, it was always the maidens who were capable of evils against the common town folk. That's what everyone said.

Ivy wanted to laugh, but she had half-suspected trouble would come her way. Why wouldn't she when the most handsome man that Ivy had ever seen, had caught her in front of every eyeball that was attached to a mouth? And to add salt to a widening wound, she'd arrived in a town as a maiden and planned on staying there permanently. It was a cooking pot of trouble that was hardly unexpected.

Ivy's clutched the handle to the basket, turning her knuckles white. She took a deep breath in, trying to hide her anger and jealousy. The maidens that had lived in town their whole life, courting young men themselves, were never subjected to such atrocities as rumored evil doings, yet Ivy had quickly been pointed out because she was a stranger.

"You've gone quiet." Thomas' voice, just loud enough for her to hear.

"Sorry." Her eyes followed their invisible path on the dirt to where they were headed. "I must tend to my duties, Mr. Thomas," Ivy said in a clear voice that nearby town folk would overhear.

"Good day, Miss." He tilted his hat, just like he'd done that day with the young girl, and with no extra effort.

Ivy's pressed her lips tight as she turned away and went to swap her vegetables.

Four days had past since Ivy saw Thomas, and as sunrise broke on Sunday morning, Ivy sank comfortably underneath the oak tree at the far end of the garden. Threading her needle and piercing the cloth in her arms, she felt she had never been so excited to make a pillowcase, because this time she wasn't going to sell it, but rather keep it for herself.

Bustling out the cottage's back door, her mother gathered her dress and ran all the way towards Ivy. Half-curled over to catch her breath, she held onto Ivy for support. "Come to the house," she managed to say before turning to run back.

Quickly, Ivy gathered her things and ran after her mother. Inside, she noticed, through the distorted front window, that a horse carriage was leaving the property, and wondered why she hadn't been pulled inside to greet the guests.

"Who was that?" she asked, studying her stepfather, who was already in his Sunday best.

"Do sit down, child." Irene pulled out the chair and pushed down on her shoulders. "Sit, sit!"

Ivy's knees buckled beneath her.

Her stepfather cleared his throat and spoke all too slowly. "That was... er... um..."

"Mrs. Guilles!" Irene snapped.

"Oh yes, so it was." His tone was flat, boring, which only dragged out his words for so much longer. "That was, er... Mrs. Guilles."

Irene frowned while Ivy uncrossed her legs then re-crossed them again.

"...And Master Guilles."

"Who?" Ivy looked between her stepfather and mother.

Irene finally took a seat. "Master Thomas Guilles," she said.

"Thomas!"

Her mother eyeballed her. "One day into town, and already you've been courted." She looked to the heavens.

"Actually..." Ivy quickly analyzed the situation. She'd neglected to tell her mother about the day they'd arrived or even the sneaky visit in the forest. She held her tongue and wondered at all the possible outcomes if she decided to speak her mind now.

"Actually, what?" Irene snapped, slamming her hand down on the table.

"He helped me with Gold on the first day we arrived."

"Gold?" John blurted out. "No one touches that dog."

Ivy laughed. It must have been the first time her stepfather had been right. The dog had gained its name for being worth its weight in gold. Not only did he guard them while they slept, but since having him, they'd never had a single item stolen from them. The only downside was that he had a temperament which meant he was always on guard. Ivy had a theory that Gold didn't think of himself as the pet, but rather kept his humans as pets.

"Thomas did!" she said. "And Gold snuggled into him like they were best of friends."

The three sat in silence, her parents not believing it possible.

"I'll have your tongue," Irene broke the silence, "...if I hear you call Master Guilles by his first name again. It's not proper for such a lady at your age."

Ivy ignored her mother and turned back to her stepfather.

"*Why* were they here?"

"He has asked permission to take you to the spring festival dance." He reached for his ale and pressed the beaker to his lips, hidden beneath his beard.

"Of course, we said yes," her mother chipped in.

Ivy jumped to her feet. "Mother!" she scolded her.

"What?" Confusion washed over her mother's face. "You would have said yes anyway."

"That's not the point." She threw her hands into the air. "I don't want to be the center of everyone's rumors!"

"We shouldn't worry about that *now*, dear." She winked.

Ivy didn't like the sound of that.

"Thomas informed us of all the rumors going around. His mother is practically grief-stricken by the drama. They are *very* nice people, Ivy. Shame about the father..." Her mother trailed off, apparently lost in thought.

"I said yes," John blurted out, slamming his beaker down onto the table.

Ivy jumped. "You said yes to what exactly?" There was nothing but silence. She looked to her mother. "Mother?"

Eyes dancing around the room, Irene was never one to look guilty. "Thomas...." She cleared her throat.

"Mother!"

"He asked for your hand," John spoke up. "And I said yes!"

"What? Are you mad?" Ivy started pacing the room. "We don't know them. You've only met them once! And you're ready to throw me away and..."

Irene cut her off. "No one is throwing you away. I know it seems irrational now, but think about it like this. Once you're married, there will be no more rumors. And you know just how out of hand rumors can get."

Her mother was right again. Ivy thought back to a remote town on the other side of the country, where twin sisters had been accused of creating a plague that had killed many livestock. They'd been captured and held down by their own townsmen, and forced to drink poisons while their parents had watched, only able to dab tears from their eyes. Coughing and choking while they'd tried to fight against their punishers, they'd both choked to death on their own vomit well before the poison had taken hold.

Ivy shuddered at the memory.

"We have a chance to calm the rumors now before they go

too far," Irene continued her nagging plea. "You've made quite an impression on Master Guilles, and he'll protect you and keep you safe." She lifted her eyebrows high, and Ivy felt the heaviness of her words. "If Master Guilles came and asked you himself, would you have said no?"

"I see what you're doing." Ivy pointed an accusing finger at her. "You're playing the safest option."

"And what's so bad about that?" her mother asked, looking towards her husband.

Ivy fumed. She stared at the drunk-turd and then back at her mother. Thomas was nothing like the safest option who her mother had chosen to endure. She bit down on her tongue and left the room in silence.

Ivy struggled to remain silent as they rode in the carriage all the way to church for Sunday service. She sank her teeth deep into her bottom lip to stop her from blurting out something she'd most likely regret.

"You can't ignore me forever," her mother said.

Ivy squeezed her eyes shut, turned her head, and opened them again. Looking out the small window, she watched the greenery pass by.

"Ivy, please can we speak about this?"

Keeping her eyes out the window, Ivy shook her head.

The wagon stopped, and suddenly John was by the door, reaching out to take her hand.

I should slap it away, she mused. *But what if I fall?*

Reluctantly, she slipped her hand into his, but as she did so, she pulsated a little bit of magic into her palm, then squeezed his hand as tight as she could.

John moaned as he tried to take his hand back.

She planted her feet firmly on the ground and let go.

Her stepfather looked down at her, surprised by her

strength, but didn't have time to say anything as he performed the orders Irene barked at him.

Noticing that the church was right beside them, Ivy turned her back on the glares and judgmental faces turned her way. Within moments, her mother exited the wagon and linked arms with her daughter.

John went back to the front of the carriage, boarded the cart, and moved it out of the way. He set the horse by the tree and detached the wagon from its back so it could rest.

Ivy remained fixated on her stepfather for the first time in her life. She figured that it was a better view than turning around to face the menacing smiles. Having seen right through their pleasant masks, Ivy quickly thought of a plan to get out of attendance and make her way home.

"Do I have—"

"Don't start!" her mother snapped. "You've missed church four times already. *Now* your ankle is better, there's no excuse." Irene tugged on Ivy's arm, causing her to turn around to face the crowd.

People turned their heads away, pretending to be in the midst of interesting conversations, but Ivy sensed their curiosity.

"Smile," her mother demanded.

Pulling at the corners of her lips, Ivy formed a half-interested smile, but her eyes fell flat.

A round, short man with a thick neck and oval glasses perched at the end of his stubby nose walked out of the crowd and straight to them.

"Mrs. Smyth," he said, pronouncing the words like they were a seduction and an announcement at the same time. His arms went wide as he approached, like somehow Irene was his favorite person in the entire world. Irene had clearly worked her usual skills. Dropping his arms to his sides, he raised a hand out for them to take.

"It is a wonderful pleasure to see you again," he said.

"Oh, you say that every Sunday, Gordon."

Ivy raised her eyebrows at her mother's unusually high tone and playful laughter, not to mention the use of this man's first name.

"And this must be the beautiful Ivy," he said.

He let go of her mother's hand and reached out to Ivy. She looked at his hand, hesitated, and then took it, but instead of shaking it like he had done with Irene's, he drew it closer to him, forcing Ivy to take a step forward. Then he pressed her hand to his lips and kissed her knuckles.

If there hadn't been so many people watching, she would have zapped him until his lips bled. But, knowing her place, she thought better of it. The second he stopped squeezing so tightly, she pulled back her hand, quickly wiping the remains down the side of her Sunday dress.

The mayor watched her every movement, but Ivy held true to her silence.

"Quiet little girl, isn't she?" he asked her mother.

She took a step back and watched as he linked arms with Irene and they turned their backs.

"There's just so many people you have to meet," he continued to talk to Irene as Ivy followed listening in. John trailed after them, going from one couple to another, remaining silent, always by her side. It was like her parents had become the most prominent people in town.

Ivy moved out of the crowd and lingered on the outskirts. It took all her energy not to run off into the fields. But she knew she would see Thomas, so she'd suffer the idea of more rumors coming her way if only for a glance to see him again.

From several feet away, Ivy heard giggles. Not bothering to see what the commotion was all about, Ivy sensed the fuss was heading her way.

"I hear that Mr. Gregory is returning first thing Tuesday morning."

"Hmmm…." Another one, just as petite and innocent-looking, stood beside her and agreed.

"And I heard," the first one said, "that when he returns home and finds these squatters living there, they are going to get kicked out."

Ivy turned and faced them straight-on. "First of all, Mr. Greggory is my father's cousin. Second, we don't live in Mr. Greggory's house, but rather the house Mr. Gregory built for us. And third, it has nothing to do with you, and therefore your opinions are irrelevant."

The four girls standing beside one another looked to Ivy with their mouth's hung wide open. By the time one managed to muster up the voice to speak back, the church bells rang, calling for service to start.

Ivy hung back, waiting for everyone to enter.

"Hurry up, Ivy." Her mother was by her side, linking arms and dragging her inside.

For every day that didn't require a church service, Ivy avoided town and remained at home, just like proper young maidens were supposed to do. Not wanting to attract any more rumors, or add fuel to the ones that were currently spinning, she thought the best thing to do was stay out of sight, and hopefully that would mean out of mind. But doubts weighed her down, and as the sun rose and set each day, she didn't see or hear from Thomas. She wondered whether or not he had changed his mind about the dance.

"What's wrong?" her mother asked.

Ivy looked to her mother, who was bent over the garden beds pulling weeds.

"What makes you think something is wrong?" Ivy snapped.

"Do I look like a fool to you?" she asked, and then half

laughed. "Actually, don't answer that." They both laughed then. "Awe, there's my girl."

Ivy sat back on her heels. "I'm nervous about tonight." She looked down, bashful. "I'm not sure if I want to go anymore."

"It's exciting to go and do new things. And I hope everything works out. But if at any time you feel out of place or uncomfortable, just remember, it's better than being stuck in the back of that old derelict wagon!"

"True," she said, and sighed. "Oh, very true."

"You'll have a wonderful time." Her mother rubbed her arm. "And Thomas is a great catch. All the woman in the town are expecting his knock on their door. You'll be the town's envy."

"That's just great." Ivy slumped.

"Don't worry about those girls. They have nothing on you."

Ivy wasn't an optimist like her mother.

"Now, go," she pressed. "Go and dress. I'll prepare the flowers."

A few minutes later, Ivy returned in her new dress, one that her mother had been sewing for days. The fabrics weren't as nice as they could have been, but after she spent a few days dyeing it, no one would be able to tell.

"See," her mother said, "you'll be the most beautiful girl there." She smiled and handed Ivy the bunch of flowers.

Smelling their sweet fragrances, Ivy handed her mother one blossoming flower at a time as Irene began to sew them onto her dress. Once she was done, they sat beside one another on the porch steps and weaved dried sticks into an oval shape to make her head piece.

"Do you think this is too much?" Ivy asked.

Irene shook her head. "Once he sees you, he won't have a single doubt."

Ivy giggled. It was also the perfect opportunity to show up those beastly girls that had once courted him.

As if her mother had read her mind, she blurted out. "Sirens!

That's what they are! Dirty little sirens. I hope they rot in their jealousy!"

Ivy paused to look at her bitter mother. She couldn't work out why such thoughts had entered her mind, even though Ivy had practically won a ballot for his hand in marriage.

Over in the side paddock, the horse reared up onto its hind legs.

Irene and Ivy paused what they were doing and watched.

The trees rustled violently against the wind and the birds changed course on their flight paths.

"Trouble!" Irene stood.

Ivy agreed; she could hear the warnings in the wind.

Irene dropped the headpiece she'd been working on on the ground. Her head snapped in each direction. "Where is that half idiot stepfather of yours?" she asked through gritted teeth.

Ivy wanted to soothe her nerves, but all her muscles tightened and she was ready to run. The tiny little hairs on each of her arms stood straight up.

Beside her, a spirit stepped forward, making itself known. White silhouette, tall and shimmering, it closed the distance between them and placed a hand softly onto her shoulder. It need not speak the trouble, because she knew exactly what that meant.

Trouble is coming.

Looking up at her mother, she gave her a worried look.

"What's that noise?" Ivy whispered. From the far distance, the wind carried chanting and shouting. It prickled the silence.

The horse back-kicked the fence and then began galloping around the field, bucking and thrashing its legs about in the air.

Irene rushed inside, and Ivy chased after her mother.

"Hide the valuables!" Irene yelled.

Ivy ran straight to her room, knowing valuables was a codeword which meant only one thing, especially considering that they didn't own anything of real value. Underneath the floor,

Ivy had dug a dirt pit just in case of moments like these arising. She threw everything she needed into the dark hole. Dried herbs, fragments of animal bones, her pendulum, and any earthly materials lying about, and then she clicked the wooden planks back into place and pulled the knitted rug across the floor. She got to her feet just as three men entered her room.

Lunging for her, they grabbed her by the arms.

"Stop!" she screamed. "Let go of me."

But they didn't listen. Instead, they dragged her through the house, out the back door, and onto the porch.

Ivy gasped. It seemed like the entire town was looking up at her.

Quickly scanning each face, Ivy looked for her mother, but stopped on one particular face.

Rose. That little short maiden, calling her siren song that interrupted me and Thomas the first day I met him. How dare she!

Standing in the front, she raised a hand. "That's her!"

People, young and old, stood behind Rose and began yelling. Some screamed and others roared profanities, but as a whole, their outburst of vengeful desires against Ivy was known.

She sighed. It didn't take much to corrupt a small mind. *Looks like we moved to a town that has only small minds.*

Ivy flinched away from their hate, but the men beside her tightened their grip.

She tried to pull her hands to her face and hide, but the men resisted, holding out her arms wide and locking her elbows in place.

"Stop!" A voice called, but was to faint against the crowd to cause real notice.

Ivy heard it, though, clear as day. Her mother, shorter than most, screamed her way into view.

She came up from beside the house, her largest carving knife in hand.

"Let go of my daughter now!" she demanded.

The crowd went quiet, looking to Irene and then back to Ivy.

Rose, with her perfect blond curls, crossed her arms and smirked.

"What is this madness?" Irene yelled.

A man stepped forward, holding Rose by the shoulder. Ivy had seen him before, but didn't know it was her true father.

"Your daughter has been busy while she's been unwell, Mrs. Smyth. Have you not been watching her?"

Irene scoffed at his remark. "How dare you come here, with all of these people, and point your wicked finger at my daughter?"

While the exchange took place, Ivy scanned the crowd of faces looking for Thomas.

He's not here. She could have cried, but forced the tears to stay back. *Where are you, Thomas?* She sent the thought out into the universe in hopes he would come.

"Hold your tongue, woman!" the man said. "I am the judge in this town and I will make sure justice is served on this, the King's land."

Ivy shuddered. She looked to the sky, noticing birds flocking in. The energy in the air hummed.

"Justice? For what crimes?" Irene pushed.

"Crimes of wickedness," he said.

"Under the King's law, there is no such thing," Irene spat back.

"I assure you, woman, that, under the God's law, the only law that truly matters, her—" he pointed a finger directly at Ivy, yet remained fixated on Irene, "—crimes will be punished here on Earth, and at the gates before God in the afterlife."

The crowd clapped their hands, and a few cheers came from the back. They supported whatever they needed to so that they would see Ivy punished.

"That doesn't make sense," Irene snapped. "A judge does *not* send a young girl to heaven to be judged before God. This is outrageous. Let my daughter go this instant."

"A woman will *not* tell me my place nor my duty, especially while she is harboring a criminal."

Ivy sensed the fury building in her mother.

"There will be no such punishment here on my land," her mother said through her teeth. "And there will be none of your justice served to my daughter." Her voice ran shivers down Ivy's spine.

The tall judge stepped around Rose, glaring at Irene. "Step aside, woman." Then he nodded to the men who held Ivy.

"Mother?" Ivy yelled as the two men who had hold of her dragged her down the back steps towards the crowd. Turning her head, she watched her mother run for her, slicing the large carving knife at anyone who dared stop her.

Bloodcurdling screams filled the air. The men beside Ivy stopped, trying to protect themselves. The crowd stepped in between Irene and the men, ripping the knife from her hands before she could slash anyone else. Lunging for her daughter, Irene fell short as several sets of hands wrapped around her body and held her back.

Kicking out her feet, she collided with one of the men's legs. He stumbled slightly before regaining his stance, and then continued to drag Ivy through the crowd.

Ivy fought back, digging her heels into the ground, shielding her face from the screaming and spitting people around her, lashing out her hands, feet, and her entire body to try and stop them from taking her away from the only home she'd ever had.

As they broke through the back of the crowd, Ivy looked up and saw the head priest standing right beside the town's judge. They didn't bother making eye contact before they turned their backs and walked towards the nearby forest.

The men holding Ivy continued to drag her along, and followed behind the leaders of the pack. She did everything she could to fight back, but they squeezed her arms tighter and often slapped her to stop her fighting.

I don't care how much pain you cause me, I'm going to fight you every step.

Ivy felt a blow to her lower back. She stumbled forward and quickly glanced over her shoulder. Someone had kicked her, and was arching their leg to do it again. She struggled to fight against it, forcing herself to lunge ahead, closer to the priest and judge.

"You can't do this to me!" she said, and turned her head to spit out blood from an oozing cut on her lip.

The priest stopped, turned, and walked back towards Ivy. "Quiet now," he said. His voice sounded soft and strangely comforting. "You'll have your chance to speak soon." He turned his back on her then, returned to the judge's side, and walked on. The men beside her tugged at her arms, causing her armpits to ache; her chest felt bruised, her energy completely depleted.

Her fighting back was no use, as she didn't have the strength, nor the ability. No young girl could possibly fight these huge men off and then outrun them, and that didn't even take into consideration the angry mob at her heels.

Arching back her head, she looked to the sky. Thousands of birds had flown in and sat on the branches high above them, looking down at the people.

Closing her eyes, Ivy felt their vibrating presence. She knew they'd risk their own lives to swoop down and save her, but she was tired of running—tired of not being able to be herself, tired of being the runaway victim. So, she sent out a vibration, telling them to wait. *Wait until the time is right,* she pleaded. *Or when I call you.* She hoped that Gaia was listening.

This time, she was going to stand her ground. She was ready to fight.

They passed the cranberry bushes where Thomas had found her on his secret visit, and then the fallen tree where Ivy and

Gaia had made their promises. But the judge and priest kept walking, deeper into the forest.

Dense and beautiful, the forest opened up to a section that seemed to have been cleared out. Circular, and empty of trees, the space appeared like a pocket had opened up right in the middle of the forest.

Ivy wondered how such a perfectly round clearing had occurred. She looked to the sky again and noticed that the trees were too tall to let the sun reach the ground.

Death. She felt it in the air. Thick, heavy, and undeniable— Ivy instantly knew that this land had been used before.

In the shaded area, barely any grass had grown, save for a few puffs here and there. Right in the middle was a thin, tall tree trunk. It was missing the top half, like it had been hit by lightning and disintegrated, leaving nothing but a hollow trunk.

The crowd spread out around the edges of the clearing and the judge stood beside the priest.

All eyes were on her as the two strong men heaved Ivy towards the trunk and bound her with rope.

Thick, long, and tight, the rope went around her several times. She could barely breathe when they forced the last knot tight. Then the two men disappeared out of sight and into the woods.

The crowd silenced itself and the priest took a step forward, and then he started flicking through an old, worn book.

From the far end of the crowd, a rock was hurled over the heads and down into the book, knocking it straight to the ground. "Your answers to this madness won't be in there!" Irene screamed at him as she pushed her way through the crowd, trying to reach her daughter.

The priest picked up his book and dusted it off, and then, without a single word, gestured for Irene to be held, still and quiet.

Irene dropped to her knees, forced down by too many hands, so that she could barely remain upright.

Ivy looked into her mother's eyes and saw the pain. She now understood why they had stayed on the road for as long as they had. Never lingering in a town for too long; never making plans to stay permanent… no matter how glorious or safe a town had seemed, it had always been just a face for what really occurred in its underbelly.

"Miss Ivy Smyth," the priest spoke loud, clearly and without any emotion to his voice whatsoever. "You have been accused of witchery, and of wickedness, as well as the heinous crimes of witchcraft. Under the eyes of God, you must pay for your sins and leave this earth to face your true trial in front of God, who will determine whether you gain access into Heaven."

The crowd's cheers now invaded Ivy like cuts across the skin.

"You're killing me so that I may face trail?" Ivy snapped.

"Madness!" Irene screamed.

Ivy looked at each person in the crowd. In their faces, she saw what they were truly feeling.

Fear.

Taken aback, she paused; she'd expected hate, or even anger, but those emotions weren't there. Even Rose, standing predominately in the front row of the crowd, clutched her hands to her chest, her eyebrows twisted upon her face like a thick indent across her forehead. The worry radiated from her like soot over a smoldering fire. Seeing the truth now, Ivy understood exactly what they were—puppets playing along in a show, doing nothing more than their designated parts so that they too didn't find themselves standing beside Ivy, held down by rope.

The priest spoke his words, but they didn't have any weight. They were puffs of air exiting his mouth, disappearing into the atmosphere and forever forgotten, like they hadn't even existed.

Ivy breathed. What the priest, nor the judge, or any of the people knew, was the presence beneath their feet.

Gaia was stirring.

Irene stopped her crying and her fight against the people holding her back, and she stared at Ivy.

Looking across to her mother, Ivy tried to decipher what she was trying to say. But Gaia pulled her attention away and pulsated through the ground and up to her bare feet, energizing her to full strength. In that moment, Gaia sent a message. Instantly, in her mind, Ivy knew Gaia was waiting for whatever Ivy wished her to do.

She wants to save me. Ivy felt the love swell inside of her.

"Miss Smyth!" the judge yelled, and Ivy snapped her head in his direction, noticing they'd been waiting for something.

The priest cleared his throat. "As I was saying, the truth, if you choose to speak it, will set you free."

Ivy looked back to her mother. It seemed like all the lines around her eyes had somehow deepened.

"If I speak the truth, you'll set me free?"

"Do you have anything you wish to say?" the priest went on. "Speak nothing but the truth in front of these people, with God as your witness."

Looking around, Ivy noticed several missing faces. The mayor was one. That shocked Ivy, because he would know where all his townsmen where. Her stepfather was another. He was one that always seemed to surprise her in her time of need. And Thomas. *Her* Thomas. The one person she wished to be here right now, saving her from these ignorant monsters.

"Ivy!" the judge spat out her name, just as vicious as before.

"I…" Ivy thought of what to say, but everything she could say would be twisted and turned or tormented into the truth that they wanted to hear. "I don't know why you would tie me to this tree. I've done nothing wrong, and—"

"How can you say that?" a voice broke her off—small, young,

and female. *Rose*. No matter how sweet her voice sounded to everyone else, Ivy saw the bitterness, spoilt and sheer evil to her facade.

Ivy remained silent and stared down at the girl.

"You come here into our town, and turn poor Master Gullies against us, and now he is going to ask for your hand in marriage?" Rose, with her little group right behind her, crossed her arms and looked Ivy up and down.

One of her friends stepped forward and wrapped her arm around Rose for support. "It's obvious that you put him under some kind of spell," the friend said. "He was going to ask Rose, and then you showed up."

Ivy closed her eyes, but so desperately wanted to close her ears. The vibration around her hummed and she wondered just how she was going to talk herself out of this one.

"Can't you see," another girl chimed in, "the damage you've caused?"

Ivy opened her eyes. She saw the evil in their eyes, all of them wanting Ivy to buckle beneath their demands. But Ivy was no follower. She pursed her lips firmly together and waited for them to stop.

But as they went on, continuing their charade, a rustle at Ivy's feet made her look down.

The two men who had dragged her from the house had now returned. Bent down at her feet, they placed sticks and small pieces of wood neatly around her legs.

"What are you doing?" She looked up at the judge, who just nodded for them to continue.

"It is obvious to us—" the priest said, gesturing to himself and the judge, "—that the final judgment must be placed before God."

"What? No! I haven't been allowed to speak," Ivy protested. She had been spoken over, losing her opportunity to argue against these ignorant claims, getting no time to talk herself out of this madness. Several more men surrounded Ivy and placed even larger pieces of wood around her, stacking it around her feet, and then they tried to hold her still as she fought against the ropes.

"This is nothing you don't deserve!" Rose yelled in her sweet voice, and the crowd erupted in support.

The priest opened his book and began reading passages, and the judge stood by witnessing it all.

Irene ran to Ivy and fought the men who held her still.

Ivy struggled against the ropes.

The men around her stood back.

First, there was heat. That was the easy part.

Ivy felt the warmth below quickly rise up around her and beads of sweat emerged across her forehead, dripping down around her face.

"Stop this madness!" she demanded. "Do you not hear me? I said, stop this right now! Or I'll... I'll..." Ivy licked her dry lips and thought of all the ways she could break free, and ruin all the people in front of her and run, not stopping until she died of old age.

But she had done that her whole life. She couldn't run again, not in that pitiful wagon through the freezing winters and without ever having a real home.

She closed her eyes and opened them again. Knowing she'd never run again, she knew exactly what she was going to do.

"No!" a man's voice erupted in front of the crowd. Hands wrapped around him, holding him back.

Ivy saw Thomas. He had found her.

But he froze, stunned to see her up there—or was he ashamed of her? Ivy couldn't tell.

The sticks at her feet were well alight now, pillowing smoke up into her face. She held her breath, trying not to breathe it in, but the smoke poured into her nostrils and left a burnt, earthy flavor in her mouth.

"What is this?" He stepped forward, trying to unhook the arms that held him back. "I demand you let her go right now!"

"On what authority?" the judge asked.

"As her—" he hesitated. "As her promised one."

"That does not give you any authority, Mister Gullies. You are not her husband, and therefore cannot claim her under the law."

"But I can! I'll take her away from here, far away, and never return. You have to free her!"

"I *am* freeing her, Mister Gullies, from this land so that she will not burden you or any of the town's folk again. She will be free to be judged before the true God."

"Don't you see, Thomas?" Rose stepped forward and took Thomas's hand. "Now you'll be free to marry who you wish."

Thomas pulled back his hand and offered her a dirty look.

Ivy was thankful that he'd never trust that little siren again. But her own sight was blurring, and the smoke had thickened. The small fire quickly flared up when men returned with more wood and poured out a liquid that enlivened the flames.

She heard both Thomas and her mother's scream. In amongst it, Ivy heard another scream, and she only realized it was her own when she stopped.

Somehow, her skin stopped sweating and the top layer dried, cracked open, and peeled itself back. The fumes blackened the edges and she felt the underneath layer begin to dry out, too.

Her swollen dry tongue licked her cracked bottom lip, only for it to feel like sandpaper.

Gaia raised up and touched her feet softly. She could no longer feel the pain from her knees down, as the heat had destroyed her nerves, cutting off any feeling.

Ivy screamed again.

Gaia reached up further, enveloping her with vibration, letting her know that she could save her from the pain, from the fire.

But Ivy pushed back, determined to do this her way.

Her beautiful dress which her mother had worked so hard on acted like a wick spreading the flames further and faster. Her thicker layer of skin became so dry it cracked before splitting open, and the tiny particles of fat underneath oozed, adding further fuel to the fire.

She'd become a living candlestick.

Screaming, she pushed through the torture and the agony, and accepted Gaia's help with relief. Not for the pain, but for the ability to breathe oxygen again. She inhaled and pulled the relief deep into her lungs.

"Thomas!" she called between coughs. "Thomas?"

"Ivy!" he yelled back, sounding surprised. Perhaps he'd thought she was already dead.

"Thomas, leave now and quickly."

"No! I can't," he started to argue, but she cut him off.

Ivy sent out a small yet powerful vibration telling him to leave this place at once. But he rejected it, fighting against everything he knew; even if it was going to kill him, he still fought.

"Then cover your ears!" she told him.

Irene heard Ivy's words, and stopped fighting the people who were holding her back. She fell to the ground and covered her own ears tightly.

Thomas—confused by her words—didn't listen. Rather, he fought harder. Desperate to get closer to her. To save her.

"Hear me!" Ivy's voice bellowed out with her last strength. "Hear me now!"

The crowd silenced and looked at Ivy like a sheen had crossed over their eyes.

She did everything possible not to include Thomas in this, but his presence was painful. She could feel his love.

"Your Lord will not save you," she called out, and laughed. "Your God will not look upon you from now on." Her words came slow and firm. Several people in the back of the crowd had turned and run back to town. But it didn't matter how far they ran, or even how fast. Ivy pulsated her power outwards and wrapped it around them like a thick blanket with no edge. "I strip you from your armor! I bare your heart. And I expose your soul. Your foolish attempts to spell my soul with your mundane ignorance falls back upon you.

"I condense your mind, suppress your thoughts, and depress all that you are to the very root of your ignorance."

Ivy laughed. The sound cracked across the circular space.

"Souls," she continued, "...are not subjected to death. Your perishable bodies will suffer the deeds of the indestructible soul.

"I bind your souls to my pain, the twisted heat that you forced upon me. I bind you to my everlasting power—" A dark flash came from within her, darkening the ground instantly. Dark clouds rolled across the sky, the air thickened, the earth rumbled, and the sky vibrated under the pressure. "—I anchor each and every soul that stands before me to a thousand lives lived and a thousand lives hereafter."

Tears formed in the eyes of each person in front of her, drowning in their exposed natures. Senseless to nothing but grief; their living flesh soaked in the tainted poison of hate. A hate that they unleashed at Ivy, and in turn, she desired to speed up their inevitable deaths, so that now they were nothing but standing corpses that had doomed their own existence.

Ivy breathed it all in: the smoke, the fire, the fear, the darkness, Gaia's power, the light, and all the workings of nightmares.

She pulsated it out, far as she could. It went past the few faces remaining in the crowd, managing to reach the town. Further on, it went, and somehow she knew it reached the ocean, but it didn't stop there. On and on, it continued until Ivy had coated the entire planet. Wrapped it like a ball and squeezed down.

Giving it all that she had, her remainder of power was extinguished, and she let go.

Leaving the curse in play for time to seed it growth.

The fire beneath her roared up and consumed her whole. But she wasn't going to be the only one that died today. She pushed it out, enveloping everyone in the area, letting the screams of those who bared witness taint the air until all of them died with her.

WALES

1574

*H*eat.

Blistering, intense smoke billowing in plumes and drying tears.

Tommie tossed in his bed.

Ash fell on his head. A painful wail surrounded him, then bore its way right to his very core.

He breathed it in—the soot, the darkness, and all the pain.

Her eyes, wild and crazed, didn't leave his sight as the crackling yellow and red blaze enveloped her.

She disappeared.

"Ivy!" Tommie screamed as he sat up and extended his arms forward. He panted to catch his breath.

His *mam* burst into the room, face twisted by torment, just touched by the soft light of the fireplace behind her.

"Awaken, child!" She reached for him and pressed him into her arms. "My poor child, awaken from your nightmare."

Tommie pressed his ear into her chest to listen to the rhythm of her heart. The constant beat reminded him of the present, the new life he was in. But the nightmares didn't allow him to forget the life that he'd once lived.

After a long moment of silence, the night air cooled his skin and his body relaxed.

"Sleep now," his mam said as she laid his body back into bed and replaced the blankets. Kissing him on the forehead, she *shooshed* him until he drifted back off to sleep.

"We should talk about this."

In the other room, Tommie heard his mam's stern voice.

"There's nothing to discuss."

"Owain, please, listen to me."

He cut her off. "*Na!* You listen to me," he said, raising his voice. "You baby that *bach*. He's not a *merch*, so let him out in the woods, with the animals; it'll do him some good for once."

"You can't mean that," she said, tears in her eyes.

Tommie sat beside the door, looking around the corner.

"You're right," his *tad* said. "I don't mean it." He slumped in his chair with his face in his hands. He looked deflated, tired, and emotional. *What is wrong with the woods?* Tommie thought. *Aren't there bears and wild animals? I'm still too small to be there all by myself.*

"My mam is coming to help," his tad broke the silence.

"She's leaving the farm?"

He nodded. "I received word this morning," he sighed, voice faltering. "My brother will have to cope without her. We need her here."

Tommie's mam reached across the table and took her husband's hand.

"She'll know what to do," his tad said, looking up at her. Tommie could see the love between them, and it brought a dull ache to his heart, knowing he caused their suffering.

"I hope you're right," she whispered.

. . .

"Tommie! Tommie." *Nain* Maude placed her wrinkly, warn out hands over both of her eyes, then lifted them instantaneously. "Boo!" she said.

Tommie eyebrows furrowed.

"What's wrong with him?"

"Nothing, Mam!" Tommie's mam shook her head as she placed hot drinks onto the table. "He just doesn't play games like the other kids."

Nain returned her hands to her eyes.

Tommie reached for her palms, forcing them away so she could see.

"He's na fun," she murmured, reaching for her cup.

"That's what I said," tad said as he entered the kitchen. Nain was on her feet, wrapping her arms around him. "Welcome home, Mam."

"Sit, son." She pulled the chair from the table, then sat right beside him, turning back to Tommie. "Tell me about these nightmares."

"They've always happened."

"Even the first night he was born," mam added. "There hasn't been a night he hasn't had a nightmare."

"And the name?"

Mam and tad exchanged looks before mam dropped her head. "Ivy," she whispered.

Tommie couldn't help but sit up straight. All three sets of eyes were back on him.

"Hmmm." Nain tapped her chin. "Have you heard that name before?"

Tommie looked to his parents, who shook their heads.

His nain breathed in deeply and held the air in before she let out a big sigh. "What else can he say?"

"That's all, Mam. He has na other words."

"He only says the name?" She cocked her head to the side, causing the skin on her neck to ripple.

"But never during the day," mam said.

"So at the age of three, he doesn't speak and he doesn't play." She sighed. "Tell me, does he ever smile?"

Tad closed his eyes, and nain nodded.

"I know what's wrong with him."

Tommie looked into her eyes. He could see that she was seeing something flash before hers. *Can she see what I have seen?* he wondered. It was hard to communicate what he was going through. *If she knows, it'll be much easier.*

"What do you see, Mam?" His tad sat forward, clutching his knees for support.

"Have you ever heard that the eyes are windows to the soul?" Mam nodded.

"I see, in his eyes, torment."

They all sat very still for a moment. Tommie wondered if they were all still breathing.

"He's tormented," she added.

"Can we fix it?" Mam reached out and slid Tommie off the table and onto her lap.

Nain shrugged. "He's just a child. What could have possibly put the torment in his eyes?"

"If we knew, we wouldn't have sent for you," mam said, raising her voice, snapping at the old woman. "He's been this way since birth!"

"Juliana!" tad snapped.

"So, the bach came into this world tormented? Poor bach," nain said.

The silent pauses between them played on Tommie's heart. *What's going to happen to me?*

"I'll promise you this," nain said after a moment's quiet. "I won't leave until we fix this."

Tad leaned towards her and wrapped his arms around his own mam. "Thank you," he said. Nain pulled away and smiled at Tommie.

. . .

Tommie ran through the house, stretching his legs. He felt all stiff and sore in the joints for being locked up inside. As the warmth reached his muscles, his mam reached out and grabbed him by the collar.

"Please, Tommie, stop running. It's time to get dressed."

Mam had placed his best clothing across a rack to warm by the fire.

"Are we going somewhere?" Tommie asked, inspecting his clothing.

Mam nodded and placed a hand gently on his shoulder. "You're seven now, which means you're have to be a good bach. Can you do that for me?"

After his mam dressed him, nain pressed Tommie's hair down with the thick brush, but it flicked up at the ends. She humphed before slicking it with a thick paste until it didn't move.

"Very smart," she said, pulling him back to inspect with her fading eyes.

"My hair is all cold now," Tommie said, reaching for his hair, but nain slapped his hand away before he touched it.

"Wait for it to dry; then make sure you wear your hat out in the snow."

Tommie nodded and then turned to face his parents, who were also dressed in their best outfits.

"Now, Tommie," his tad said, getting down to one knee. "Please answer the doctor's questions."

"Why?"

Tad stood up and looked down at him. "Answering a question with another question is rude. Don't do it to the doctor."

"Ydw, Tad"

His tad went to say something else, but was cut off by a firm knock against the door.

"The coach is here," mam exclaimed. "Quickly now, put on your jacket."

Tommie knew what to do. After he buttoned the front of his coat, he placed his hat on and then threaded his fingers into the gloves. It didn't matter how many layers he put on, though; it was cold.

The sunlight had dipped down early in the day, leaving a darkness that seemed to last for days. Lamps lit on each corner of the coach gave out next to no light, but it was enough to help him get inside and snuggle into his mam's side.

"It had to be the coldest of days," mam said as the coachman locked them in.

"It was the only day the doctor had available."

Tommie heard the crack of the whip, and the carriage shuffled forward, leaving home and his nain behind.

The coach went through the small town and reached the doctor's house on the far side of the hills. When they arrived, several men came out to help.

"Come in, sir, madam, the fires are warm."

"Thank you," tad said, giving them his coat as he entered the house.

Tommie absentmindedly copied his tad, but couldn't help but keep his eyes upwards to the ceiling. It was so tall, it seemed several men standing on top of one another still wouldn't be able to reach it.

The walls were dark wood and, every now and then, a bright picture of a fuzzy landscape sat neatly in the middle.

"This way," Tommie's mam insisted.

He followed her into a room where books lined the walls in shelves. By the fire, there were two large seats and a man in one of them.

"Doctor Priddly," the man who had led them into the room, spoke clearly and conscious, as he stood beside the chair. "Your patient has arrived." He bowed his head and left the room.

"Sit, sit," the doctor said, leaving a piece of paper inside a book before resting it on a small table beside him. "I'm just reading Homer. It's my treat after a long day."

"We won't keep you," tad said as he sat in the adjacent chair. Mam stood behind him while Tommie lingered by the fire.

"So, this is the Tommie I've heard about. Come here, bach."

Tommie looked to his parents, who insisted several times that he do as the man told him. He took a step forward, but felt like running for the door.

Doctor Priddly held out a hand, pushing him to hurry.

Tommie took another step, and then his muscles locked in place, holding him too far back.

The doctor reached out, grabbing him by the arm, and Tommie's feet moved beneath him until he stood so close that he smelt the man's breath.

It was hard to know what to do. His instincts said one thing, his brain another. Everything was still all too confusing.

"So, you have bad dreams," the doctor said.

Tommie nodded.

The doctor pushed his glasses up from the tip of his nose and looked Tommie up and down. Then, with two fingers resting on the tip of Tommie's chin, he pushed and pulled him sideways to inspect his head a little closer.

"Sit down now, bach."

Tommie returned to the fire, sat beside it, and looked into the flames.

Behind him, his parents murmured about all that they'd heard from him. They spoke about the nightmares, and the horrors he muttered in his sleep. Each time they said Ivy's name, a shutter ran down his spine. It was much harder hearing about his experiences, as it conjured up the images so easily in his mind.

Better to pretend it never happened then to face it all over again.

"It's terrible," his tad said. "Every night is the same."

"There hasn't been a single night that dreams haven't tormented him," mam said.

"Since birth?" the doctor asked.

"Ydw, and then once he could speak, the name was the only thing for years."

"But he speaks well enough now?" the doctor asked, looking him up and down.

"Now he does, but he is growing, and we hoped this wouldn't have lasted as long as it has."

"It is a concern. Seven years is far too long," the doctor said as he ran a finger along his bottom lip.

There was silence. Tommie wondered if it was a good idea to look over his shoulder and glance at his parents. Their faces would tell him what they were thinking, but did he really want to know?

"Bach?" the doctor asked. "I think I know what the matter is."

"Thank goodness," mam said.

Tommie squirmed where he stood.

"My friends think," mam continued, "that if we don't find a cure, it'll ruin his life."

"Cure?" The doctor shook his head. "I'm not aware of a cure. A good education and a firm hand now and then won't hurt, but a cure?" It was like the doctor then disappeared into his thoughts.

Tommie glanced over his shoulder at his parents. Mam's face was covered in worry while his tad studied the doctor. The man was blank, but Tommie saw right through it. He was hanging onto the doctor's every word.

"Doctor?" tad asked. "What do you think it is?"

Tommie readied himself to run for the door. If the doctor knew the truth about his memories, or even if he had any idea that Tommie's has had another life, what would happen to him? *Has this happened before? Could there be others out there like me?* He didn't think so. *If I'm the only one and the doctor knows, what would my parents think? What would the doctor do to me?* He didn't want to stand around and find out.

"I believe," the doctor said, and then cleared his throat, "that he has a case of an overactive imagination."

Tommie could have burst out laughing, but instead he widened his eyes and glared at his parents. His mam her hands together, clutching them to her chest as she nodded and agreed. His tad's eyes glazed over.

The doctor went on. "Increase his education. Give him more things to think on; that way, his mind won't wander off and create these nightmares."

"We can do that," tad said. "Is there anything else we could do?"

Tommie heard the pleading in his tad's voice. Laced with concern, worried and even a bit of pain, he now sat on the edge of his seat, waiting patiently for the doctor to speak again.

The doctor reached for his book of Homer. "Not at this stage, but if I think of something, I'll write." Flicking through the pages, he landed right in the middle of the book, and readjusted his glasses. Lifting his hand into the air, he clicked his fingers. "I trust you'll find your way home safety."

"Thank you, Doctor." His mam reached for him, and Tommie was glad to be led out of the room and back into the cold winter air.

"Look at your pants!" Mam tsked at herself before disappearing to find her measuring rope.

Tommie looked down. He knew he had grown lately, because now he had no choice but to duck beneath door frames or face smacking his nose.

"Long legs are not a curse," nain said.

Tommie leaned in and gave her a kiss on the cheek,

squeezing his eyes closed. *I really wish she would stop pointing out what is a curse and what isn't. If only she knew...*

"You're a good bach, Tommie, even though it's hard to see."

Tommie laughed. "Are you referring to my acts or your failing eyes?"

She laughed then. "Good question. You answer that."

"If my legs grow any longer, I'll be the tallest bach in the village."

Mam entered the room and tsked again. "You're all grown up now," she said, reaching for his cheek, squeezing too tight.

It took all his will power not to swat her away.

"A man!" She blushed. "Now, Tommie. Stand up straight so I can measure you because I'll make you fresh pants for tomorrow."

Tommie shook his head. "Only *if* you have time, mam."

"I'm not having my only child lose both legs to the cold because I didn't have time."

"You won't be the tallest then," nain added.

After a lengthy period of prodding and poking, Tommie said his goodbyes and left the house.

That winter, during the second half, Tommie arrived home just after dusk and kissed his mam on the check. "Are they sleeping?" he asked.

She squeezed her eyes shut and nodded. The bags under her eyes were puffy and the soft blue scarf across her hair hid the balding spots. "Tommie, it won't be long now." She often reminded Tommie of the lingering presence of death, but Tommie needed no reminder.

It had been weeks since tad and nain had fallen sick. Like the rest of the town, a plague had swept through their home, knocking the majority to their knees.

"They've got time." He squeezed her shoulders and leaned

over into the pot to breathe in the fragrances. Small chunks of meat swished around with the ground vegetables in amongst the dark liquid.

"Can you help them to the table? Dinner is almost ready."

Tommie cocked his head to the side. "Are they well enough?"

"They wanted to come out tonight."

"Not for me!" He shook his head.

"Do as I ask, please."

Tommie nodded and left her by the pot. It was hard leaving her early in the morning to do his work, then returning late when she'd labored so much without any help. His nain easy to move, as she weighed barely anything, but his tad was much harder. With his bulging stomach and poor leg, Tommie had to take the majority of his weight.

After he seated them, Tommie stood by his mam. "Can I help?"

"Sit down, son," she said, squeezing his cheek in between her thumb and index finger before turning back to press out the flat bread.

Resisting the urge to push her away, he turned to the small table behind them and sat beside his nain.

"Who's that?" Nain yelled, and his mam took the towel from her shoulder and flicked it at her to quiet her.

"Nain, it's me," Tommie said, having raised his voice so that she could hear.

"Tommie? Why are you so quiet?"

Tad shook his head. "This sickness…" he paused to catch his breath. "It won't bring back her hearing."

"Or her sight," Tommie added. "But at least you're out of bed." He wondered at what cost. Nain had bedsores and Tad no longer held color in his face. *They shouldn't be out of bed for me.*

"And you're eating!" His mam placed a bowl of stew in front of them. "I thought you'd waste away."

"I have! All except the belly, though," tad said, and laughed, but as he chuckled, his breath labored, sounding hollow in his chest. "All I've wanted is one good meal and tonight I'm going to enjoy it."

Mam smiled at Tommie.

"We don't have to celebrate," Tommie said.

"You broke what?" Nain yelled.

"Cel - e - BRATE!" Mam yelled, sitting down and sighing. "My, my."

"Don't let her get to you, Maude. She's old." Tad sipped his soup and then placed his spoon down. "One-and-twenty today. How's it feel?"

"Like every other day," Tommie said, and his parents chuckled. But Tommie couldn't find the amusement in the joke. Rather, he was filled with an unusual and strange feeling twisting in the pit of his stomach. It burned like acid churning at the base, every now and then rising up to singe his throat.

Don't say her name. He held himself back, not letting the words be blurted out anymore. *I'm no longer a child; I can contain myself.* Even though he still lived with the nightmares, he never let on to his parents. *I've caused them too much pain growing up,, it's not worth reopening the wound. But I never imagined being able to turn twenty-one twice!*

"Stop playing with your food, dear, and eat."

Tommie automatically moved the spoon to his mouth, but his mind was elsewhere. Back in England, out in the country town... he'd had a summer birthday in that life. The vivid memories were always tainted though by the horrific ending.

He shivered.

How can I remember that life when I know everyone else has no memories themselves. Is there something wrong with me? He dropped the spoon into the bowl causing a splat.

"Have you finished?" His mam asked, and he nodded. Sighing at the bowls untouched by his tad and nain, she collected them from the table and moved them to the side.

"Tommie," tad said. "We ain't given you much in this life, but this is something you ought to have."

Tommie's lips pulled at the sides. His heart swelled as he looked to his tad, feeling privileged to receive anything. He had always insisted that his parents not waste resources on silly things, especially when wood often went in low supply and the town's people went hungry. Yet, he did favor his mam's candy, so he never declined that.

Mam handed tad an average-sized box. He smiled as he pushed it across the table towards Tommie.

Tommie took it into his hands and held it there, studying the details. Someone had taken time to craft it nicely, chiseling a grain across the top with a design along the edges.

He thanked his parents for everything they did, then unwrapped the brown box and studied the item before him.

A pile of old worn out sheets of paper with all sorts of markings across them. Stacked in a neat pile, most if not all of the edges beginning to fray.

"You've read every sheet that's come into town, even the ones that were clustered all together." He motioned his hands in front of him, mimicking the shape of a book. "It's taken us a while to collect as many as we have, and now they're all yours."

Tommie looked up and beamed.

"How you've managed to teach yourself to read," his tad continued, "...is beyond me."

It pained Tommie to see his tad torment himself like this, but he could never let on about his previous life. The truth, along with the nightmares, would cause his parents more worry to their already suffering minds.

After their meal, Tommie sat by the fire and, with the warm glow, read his new, dusty papers. His mam hummed her songs while she cleaned the dishes and his tad sat back in the dining chair and lit his pipe. Nain was already back in bed.

The dusty smell of the worn pages wafted into his face each time he moved one and went to the next.

Mam stopped her humming then, and Tommie looked up to see her standing at the window.

"Mam?" Tommie asked.

"Winter solstice today," mam said.

Tommie arched his neck and, from where he was seated, could see the brightest of lights shining through the little square window, cutting a trail through the dark house and illuminating the floor. Mam wiped her hands across her apron.

Tommie watched her carefully as her hands fidgeted and she muttered something incoherent under her breath.

"What's it telling you today, Mam?" Tad asked. He always called her *Mam* around Tommie because his unusual nicknames were reserved for her in private quarters. Tommie had only ever overheard those names when he shouldn't have been listening.

"Full moon," she said under her breath, and Tommie looked up from his pages, intrigued by her tone. She went on. "Oh, unusual, full moon on a winter solstice. That could only mean evil."

"Evil?" Tommie asked.

"Oh, *cachi*," his tad smashed down his fist on the table, and fell into a coughing fit. Mam rushed to his side, rubbing his back.

"We need to get you back into bed," she insisted.

His cough echoed around the small room and eventually he caught his breath. "All that moon speech," he said. "Nothing but cachi."

"You just listen to what you want to hear," his mam returned playfully, extending a crooked finger at him. "But you can't have all the good without the bad." She cocked her head to the side and winked at Tommie.

He smiled back at her. "What evil do you sense?" he asked.

"Don't tell me you believe in that nonsense," his tad interrupted, but Tommie ignored him.

She turned her back and looked out the window, focusing on the moon before shaking her head. "Na idea," she laughed. "I've never been good at astrology. Perhaps if I were born into one of those witches' covens—" Tommie shivered "—then I might'n have something more to say."

"See, I told you. It's all a load of cachi," his tad barked out, and quickly returned to his smoking pipe before Mam hit him across the shoulder with her back hand.

"Quiet, you!" she ordered. "Mark my words. Evil is coming!"

Tommie put the papers back into the box, and helped his tad back to bed.

Early in the morning, just before sunrise, Tommie left for work. Arriving extra early, he pushed open the door to the small shop, feeling nothing but a cold draft. The space was small, but enough room for two desks. One for him and the other for his employer, to do their paper work. The first thing he did, like every morning, was restock the fireplace and light it straight away. While he waited for the warmth to envelope the room, he began to wipe down the desk where last night's soot dusted the surface.

Feeling the warmth, he took off his jacket, hung it in the back corner, and swapped his winter boots for shoes, making it easier to walk around the shop. Tall shelving lined the back wall, with pockets of all sorts of business items. Paper mostly, but there were also quills, ink, ribbon, glues, and anything else needed to write for his job as master of papers.

As he finished his morning duties, he sat beside the fire and ate dried berries, waiting for the day's first customer.

One of the town's oldest members walked in and took off his winter hat. "Master. Thomas."

"Mr. Cadwalladar, how many times have I told you," Tommie began getting to his feet and quickly shutting the door to keep the warmth in, "my name is Tommie, not Thomas."

"Ydw, ydw," he laughed. "Age is getting to me."

Tommie rolled his eyes. Age had nothing to do with Cadwalladar. The man seemed a thousand years old and still had the sharpest mind of all. They sat down at Tommie's desk and Tommie readied his writing materials. "What business do you have today?"

Cadwalladar started noting letters at first, then business contracts afterwards. It was Tommie's job to transcribe them and then take them to the post office, making sure they were delivered to the right place.

"...And, Tommie..." Cadwalladar leaned forward, lowering his voice even though they were the only two in the shop. "Have you heard?"

Tommie cocked his head to the side. "Heard what?"

"Never mind." With that, Cadwalladar slipped coins across the table and turned for the door.

"You're short, Mr. Cadwalladar." Tommie stood.

"Damn mind. Told ya it's slippin'."

"Joke's getting old." Tommie held out his hand, waiting for the right amount.

The rest of the day seemed like a blur. Most people who came in struggled to read the letters they had received. If Mr. Vaugh was in, then he charged them full price, but when he wasn't, then Tommie often let the price slide for those who did not have much. But Mr. Cadwallader was never one short of change.

Most of the town's people couldn't make out the symbols on the pages, and were unable to write their own messages. So Tommie wrote their messages for them, listening in to the secret lives of his town's people.

Old men pleading for the return of their runaway wives;

young men asking for their merchs to wait for them; and newly married couples who'd moved away to start their own lives, writing home to inform families of their new bundle of joy.

Then there were those secret messages that had to be written in a certain way. Tommie hadn't been able to understand it at first, because he was forced to throw out correct sentence form, writing instead a code. He knew who ever would receive the note, would understand the message loud and clear, but Tommie hated to know what he was creating. Perhaps he was enticing war? Or maybe he was writing documents that would eventually undermine shifting political powers?

Tommie shivered. Either way, he didn't know if he was creating mass murder or putting an end to it. But the love interests and messy lives of his fellow townsmen were very rare, and far in-between. More often, he dealt with businessmen yelling at him for not writing fast enough, or neatly enough, and the subject matter was always the same. Money being owed to the greedy men who then argued when they owed Tommie for his services. Too often, it wasn't much—nothing more than the scraps in their pockets for his work.

He envied those men. Powerful. Loud. They knew what they wanted.

Tommie packed up all of his materials and put out the fire. He buttoned his jacket and slipped on his winter boots.

"Where do you think you're going, bach?"

Tommie laughed. "Home, Mr. Vaugh." Slipping his winter hat on and heading for the door, Mr. Vaugh, his employer, put out an arm to stop him.

Sighing, Tommie watched him push his way into the little shop and head straight to his own desk. "Don't go anywhere, Tommie." Mr. Vaugh took off his coat and went to hang it on the hook, but missed it by inches. "I have many things for you to do." He looked to his coat on the floor. He reeked of wheat ale and what he'd most likely poured down his throat until the early hours.

Tommie sighed, but kept his back straight. "What would you like done, sir?"

With his bloodshot eyes, he turned each way and inspected the organized and already pristine shop. Not a speck of dust on any table, not a smudge on any of the windows.

"Urr… Um…"

Mr. Vaugh making sure I know he's the one in charge.

"I must get home," Tommie said.

Tommie quickly slipped out the door and into the cool night air, before Mr. Vaugh added more duties to his already long day.

"You're home." His mam rushed to his side, grabbed him by the arm, and pulled him into his nain's room.

"Is she…" he couldn't finish the sentence.

"Not long," she said. But that was the only thing she ever said when he asked.

With snowflakes littering his jacket, Tommie sat bundled up, watching his nain's labored breaths. He sat there with her hand clutched between his own, whispering stories that she'd told him when he'd been a child, until her chest's rise and fall ceased.

"Goodbye, Nain," he whispered, and kissed her on the forehead.

Outside the door, his mam had fallen asleep in the armchair. He placed a blanket over her. She jolted awake at his touch and he held back his tears.

"I shouldn't have fallen asleep," she said.

"Sleep mam," his voice cracked.

"But—"

He shook his head. "Please mam, sleep. I'll go into town first thing in the morning and have her collected."

She reached up and rested her palm on the side of his cheek.

Then she stood and went to her own room. Tommie restocked the fireplace before heading to bed himself.

As he lay still, looking up at the ceiling, he couldn't help but think of all the death that surrounded him.

Don't think of Ivy. He breathed in and out again. *Don't think of Ivy...*

He fell asleep.

Ivy's hair blew in the wind. She was standing in the summer light, the orange glow brightening her skin. "Tommie..."

"What?" he asked, cocking his head to the side. "But you always call me Thomas."

"Not this time." She smiled and leaned in for a kiss.

He froze. "What do you mean?" He pulled away before she touched him.

"You're no longer Thomas, are you?"

He glared at her words. *This isn't right—what has happened? Am I dreaming? Am I having a premonition?*

She laughed, and the sound of her sweet voice surrounded him like a bubble.

"Tommie..." she said again. "Tommie..." and she leaned in and kissed him.

He sat up and screamed.

Panting, he brought his hands straight to his face, clutching at his hair.

"Tommie?" His mam stood at the door, her aged face showing every wrinkle.

"It's nothing, Mam."

"Nothing?" She shook her head and sat at the end of her bed. "You haven't had those dreams in years."

He had never told her the truth. Those dreams had never left him; they were the same each night. But he had learnt not to scream when he woke up. But this night had been much different. *Something was different.*

"Perhaps it was because of nain?" She looked to the ground, tears wet her face.

"I'll have someone—"

"Na!" she cut him off. "I'll have someone come by. You've got work to do."

He nodded. His work was important to the town, but he didn't want to leave his mam to deal with her pain alone.

"Go, Tommie," she said. "It's nearly sunrise."

He kissed her on the cheek and left her there, hurrying himself to work. Not letting the sadness show, he thought about other things. For the first time in a long time, he let himself think about Ivy.

She had soft, wavy hair. Eyes bright as the sun. He loved the way she walked, in one fluid motion after another. It reminded him of sunflowers in the wind, swaying back and forth, like a dance.

Her hair flung outwards as she spun around and faced him. Her smile beamed outwards, encompassing light between them, reaching down into his chest, making his heart swell.

He took a step forward, and another, until there was no space in between them.

"Ivy," he whispered.

"Tommie," she whispered back.

"Er..." He shook his head. "What?"

She laughed.

He shook his head again, snapping himself from the image in his mind.

Something must have changed!

His imagination often played out memories in his head. But never did they change. They were always the same. The sunshine. The love. The desperate need to go back in time and save her.

His feet stumbled and he stopped.

The cold air whipped up a strong breeze, rattling his bones

to lock him in place. Cold, ice cold, was an understatement. But it was nothing to the pain deep in his soul.

Ivy. He opened his eyes and looked to the sky. The sun was rising, but the thick snow clouds hung low, forcing another darkness across the town.

The pain of his nain's death mixed in with that surrounding Ivy was unbearable. He forced one foot in front of the other and made his way to the shop.

"Mr. Vaugh," Tommie said, pushing open the door, covering his mouth and nose with his mitten-covered hand, and coughing at the plumes of stale, musky vanilla that choked the shop. "Mr. Vaugh!" Tommie kicked the bottom of his shoe, forcing the old man awake.

Mr. Vaugh sat up, coughing and clutching at his chest. "Tommie, bach, you've left the door open. You're letting all the warm air out."

"Just until the smoke clears," Tommie said, leaning down to the smoldering fireplace, fanning it to enliven again.

After a coughing fit, Mr. Vaugh lit another cigar and settled into some reading papers.

"Have you been here all night?"

Nodding, he retrieved a little flask from his desk and pressed it to his lips. The last time Tommie had seen Mr. Vaugh so engrossed in his papers had been just before an uproar with the English. That had resulted in the town being occupied by the military for months, using up their resources and causing a famine. To think he was at it again caused a shiver to run down Tommie's spine. Mr. Vaugh looked up. He, too, had noticed the tension between them.

Something is amiss. Tommie turned away and busied himself, finally closing the door, and began his morning chores.

"Tommie?" Mr. Vaugh said after the store was clean and he had finished his morning routine. "I need you to go to the post office and fetch the mail."

Grabbing his jacket and his boots, Tommie was out the door before the man could request anything more. Mr. Vaugh already had a full stomach of dark alcoholic drinks which often made for a difficult day's work ahead.

The coastal wind was stronger than usual, and the light snow didn't fall to the ground, rather picking up and being swished sideways. He crossed the street in minutes, sidestepping any holes in the ground and staying well clear of the horses.

"Excuse me!" a voice spoke up.

Tommie froze.

He knew that voice. Turning, he looked into eyes that were like the sun. The freezing air around him, somehow gone. The snow that swished by him, somehow cleared. The air around him, somehow gravitating towards her.

Ivy!

"Excuse me," she said again. "Can you please tell me where the boarding rooms are?"

"Rooms?" Tommie's voice broke, but he didn't realize what he'd said. He was stunned, standing on the side of the dirt road in the way of horses, with his mouth hanging open.

She laughed and the sound lifted him up, swirling him around, and he came crashing back down. "Ydw, the boarding rooms."

He looked up and down the street. He knew where they were—he told visitors to the town nearly every week—but for some unknown reason, he couldn't think.

"Er..."

"Good day, sir," she said, and turned away.

"Wait!" He reached out to grab her arm, but stopped himself, thinking better of it.

She turned back around. "Ydw?"

"They are there," he said, pointing down the street and across the other side. "Are you staying long?"

"As long as the town needs me." She bowed her head and left. He watched after her. Each step she took, his heart mimicked the beat. Ba boom, bada boom.

"Are you going to get out of the way?" a man's stern voice asked. "Or should I let the horse kick you?"

Tommie stumbled backwards, out of the way of the oncoming horses, not having realized they'd been waiting to pass.

He clutched the wall of the post office for support until she was out of sight. *Oh my, she's here.* He breathed. *My Ivy is here.*

He regained himself and rushed back to his shop.

"Where's my post?" Mr. Vaugh snapped.

"Oh." He ran his hand across his face. "I forgot."

Mr. Vaugh stood up. "You went to the post office and forgot the post?"

Tommie laughed maniacally.

"You've got into my drinks!" Mr. Vaugh snapped. "Haven't you?"

"Na, na," He shook his head. "There was a merch…" Tommie held his tongue. All of the color drained from his face.

A merch! She's the one in my dream! Is that why my dream changed? After all these years, never had it changed until last night.

His mouth went dry.

"What are you talking about, bach?"

"It's time for me to go home. I need to be with my mam."

"Get the mail first!" the man yelled as the door closed behind him.

Tommie arrived home just after the cart had left with his nain. His mam was standing at the door. "I saw you down the street," she said as he reached the steps.

"I left early," he said. "Today is not the day for working."

"Why?"

Tommie cocked his head to the side, looking his mam up and down. She seemed different, cold even. "Mam! You need me home today. I shouldn't have left to go this morning."

"You left because I told you to leave." She shook her head." Is that the only thing?"

What does she know? Tommie breathed in and out. *Oh, the nightmare! She must think I'm not coping after last night.*

"Come on, there's soup."

Tommie went in and checked on his tad. The man's stomach had all but gone now, and he looked more bone than skin.

"Leave him," his mam said, standing at the door.

"Is everything alright, Mam?"

She sighed and left, and he followed after her.

"Mam?"

"Sit, Tommie, there's soup."

"You already said that." He sat anyway and sipped from a spoon.

"The horseman said a healer arrived in town today."

"That's good news. I'll go in and get him to come and see Tad."

"Na." She clasped her hands together and dropped them into her lap. "Your tad is too sick. It's only a matter of time."

Every fiber in Tommie's bones locked in place. "How can you say that, Mam? He is still here with us, so there is time."

She shook her head. "It's too late." She stood and walked out of the room, leaving Tommie all by himself.

Placing the spoon back on the table, he wondered if he had left his mother alone in the house too often, but he knew better than to press the matter.

That night, he sat beside his ted and cried. "I'm sorry," he whispered. "I don't know how to help you."

Not in this life nor the last. I read so much, and yet I have to sit here hopelessly, and cannot help. Tears swelled in his eyes. *I wish I'd done things differently. I wish I knew what to do to help you.*

His mam came up from behind and placed her hand on his shoulders.

"Let him go," she whispered.

He stood up and left silently, too furious to say anything. It was like Tommie had already lost his entire family.

"Are you listening, bach?"

Tommie opened his eyes and sighed. Mr. Cadwalladar glared back at him. "Ydw, I'm listening."

"You're writing is too slow," he snapped. "And messy!"

"I can use this piece as a draft and rework—"

"Do it right the first time," he cut Tommie off.

"Sure." Tommie held back his desired words, knowing they would cause more problems than anything.

"You don't want me to call your employer, do you?"

Tommie sat up straight. "Would you like me to write that in this letter?"

"Don't be smart, bach."

"Shall we finish?"

Mr. Cadwalladar's nostrils flared. "Like I was saying." He tapped the desk with his ring in a silent demand for Tommie to keep writing. "Plague. Township. Curse. Solution. Problem. Current. Past due."

Tommie put the quill down.

Mr. Cadwalladar glared at the quill, then back to Tommie. "What are—"

It was Tommie who cut him off this time. "You're not starting another battle?"

"I didn't start the last one."

"But you did, and brought the British troops to our town, who stayed for six months eating all our stock. I won't write your war letters."

"This has nothing to do with any of that."

"It doesn't? Plague? Current? What does 'past due' mean?" Tommie looked over the wording again, never able to figure out the code.

"Scribes don't ask questions; they scribe. When you're in my position, then you can ask questions."

Tommie shook his head. "I'm not having you cause any more problems in this town."

Mr. Cadwalladar stood up and glared down at Tommie. "You are a bach *twp*. I'm calling for help. The town is half-dead. The plague is raging and spreading to the rest of the town. We need more resources; I'm calling all the favors in what are owed to me so that the town survives."

"And you cannot write a normal letter for that?"

"The inner workings of what I have going have seen this town prosper. You didn't ask questions then."

Tommie sighed. *I should have.* "A healer arrived in town yesterday—"

Mr. Cadwalladar burst into laughter. "Funny that you mention her."

Cocking his head, Tommie hadn't a clue what he meant.

"Good day, Tommie. Good day." And, like that, he was gone.

Tommie left work early again, hoping to be home before the sun set. As he arrived, the horseman and cart left the house.

"Mam?" he called out.

She took a step out of the house and watched the cart leave their street.

"It was your pa's turn."

Tommie reached out and wrapped his arms around his mam, but she didn't return the hug.

"Mam," he whispered.

"I know Tommie." Her voice was as cold as the air. "It's hard." She pulled away from his grip and went back into the house, going back to her cleaning and cooking like nothing had happened.

In the morning, Tommie woke to a cold house. The fire was out, and no candles were lit.

"Mam?" he called out, but there was no answer. "Mam? Are you here?" He looked into every room, but she wasn't there. He lit the fire so that she had a warm home to come back to, and hoped that wherever she had gone, she wasn't blaming herself.

The fire crackled, and he rubbed his hands together, warming the numbness. Inside his chest, a heavy weight scratched at his breaths.

He coughed, then wheezed and coughed again. He reached for the water and then washed it down, feeling his body demanding more. But as his stomach filled, it did nothing to ease the cough.

Now, it is my turn, he thought, and hoped that his mam didn't catch it, too.

Tommie got into town and opened the store. A small knock at the door made him jump. He turned to see that Ivy was standing there, shivering in the wind.

"Come in," he said, opening it wide.

"Oh my, it's like the air gets colder every day."

He smiled and then turned away to cough again.

"When did that start?" she asked.

"This morning," he breathed out, reaching for Mr. Vaugh's dark drinks for the first time ever.

She tsked at the drink. "That won't do you any good."

"I drank water this morning and it made it worse."

"Did you purify the water?"

He shook his head..

She looked out the window, like she was checking to see if anyone was watching. Then she pulled off her gloves and retrieved something from inside her jacket.

"What's that?"

"I don't have much, but it's so I don't catch the illness of the sick ones." She held it out to him. "Take a mouthful, and it'll clear the cough."

He held it to his nose and sniffed, but there wasn't any aroma to it.

"It's only water. I received it from a priest who purified for me. Now I take it with me and use it along with my healing skills."

He smiled. *She's the healer that has come to town!*

Taking a mouthful, he replaced the lid and handed it back to her. As soon as the liquid poured over the back of his throat, he felt a strange yet mellow sensation deep in his core. Warming, it was like the water spread throughout his body, healing anything it needed to.

"Thank you," he whispered. "Is there something I can do for you?"

"I need a list of supplies written, so that the neighboring healers can send me what I need."

"I can do that."

Just after lunch, Mr. Vaugh walked in.

Tommie looked up from his sheets and stared. It was the first morning that he hadn't stumbled in. That he had cleaned himself, and didn't wear the mask of the dark drinks.

"Tommie, shouldn't you be at home with your mam?"

"Have you seen her?"

He shook his head, slow and labored. "Nope."

Lie.

Tommie stood. "Where have *you* been?"

He was taken aback. "Never you mind," he snapped.

Something's amiss.

The farmer who sat in front of Tommie looked between the two men in their exchange. "Shall I come back?"

Tommie and Mr. Vaugh spoke at the same time.

"Ydw." "Na."

Tommie glared.

"This is na way to treat a customer, Tommie."

"What are you up to?"

First, Mr. Cadwalladar had stopped drinking. Second, his mam disappeared. And third, Mr. Cadwalladar himself had decided he was the savior of this town.

Something doesn't add up, and all this after Ivy showed up...

Muscles burning with fury, stiffening under the pressure, Tommie got up and reached for his jacket. Mr. Paulson, the famer, followed suit, but when Tommie had crossed the room, Mr. Vaugh blocked his way.

"You can't save her," he whispered.

Tommie grabbed Mr. Vaugh by his collar and pushed him into the doorframe.

"Tommie," he warned.

"I have lost my nain, and my tad passed last night. You did not offer me condolences once. Lest you forget what all I did for you when Margaret, your wife, died." Tommie breathed, trying to calm himself. "Now my mam just up and left, and you lied to me when I asked."

"I didn't—"

"I can see the lie in your face." Tommie widened his eyes. "I want to know, why would you be seeing my mam now? What business is it of yours to be near her?"

"Your mam is solving a problem for me."

"What problem?"

"I can't say."

Tommie laughed, but it was a cold laugh.

"She's at Green Bridge."

Tommie gasped. *Is she going to jump?* It was a horrible name for a cliff edge. Beautiful in all types of weather, there were pillars of cliff, suspended out into the ocean, with small natural bridges linking them together. The ocean had once claimed beneath it, leaving nothing but rock suspended across the top.

But it was forever notorious for suicides.

He pushed Mr. Vaugh out of the way and ran out into the street.

"There's something you need to know!" Mr. Vaugh yelled after him, but Tommie didn't stop, his legs pushing him faster down the street.

Crossing the dirt road, Tommie ran to a horse that was tied up at the trough.

"Sorry to whoever owns you, but I need you more."

Tommie hooked his foot into the stirrup and hoisted his right leg over. Holding the reins tight, he pushed his heels into the horse's ribs, signaling it to move along.

With a whinny, the horse obliged. It smelt like wet hay and its breath pillowed from its nose.

The cold air brushed past Tommie. He shivered several times until he became numb. His fingers locked around the reins, and even inside his gloves, they felt like they were turning to ice.

"Come on, bach, let's go!" He wondered if the horse felt his panic, as with each foot forward it felt like they made a lunge into the distance.

Looking over his shoulder, he noted that he was out of the town and leaving it well behind.

Green Bridge was over two miles from town, but even with the horse running as fast as it could, it didn't feel he was moving fast enough. The light trickle of snow slashed against his face. His skin crusted against the wet and the cold, and he could barely see where they were going.

Then, in the distance, he saw a group of people.

He half-relaxed. *People are there with her. They're going to stop her!* He slowed the horse as he approached, jumping off before it came to a proper stop.

"Tommie!" Mr. Cadwalladar left the group and held out his hands in an attempt to slow him or stop him.

"Get out of my way," Tommie snapped.

"That's not going to happen." He reached out, but Tommie sidestepped him and went around him. Being younger and much leaner gave him the opportunity to outrun the man.

Not Mr. Cadwalladar nor anyone else is going to get in my way.

"*Mam!*" Tommie yelled.

"Tommie." He heard her, but couldn't see her. "What are you doing here?"

He pushed his way through the crowd, which reluctantly moved. Edging between people, he made his way forward and realized that his mam wasn't next to the cliff.

"Ivy!" he said.

Hands around him latched onto him, holding him back.

"Tommie." His mam appeared at his side. "You needn't be here, *bach.*"

He couldn't take his eyes off of Ivy. She was bound by the wrist, standing in the wind which caused her dress to flap and her hair to brush out to the side.

"Tommie!" His mam shook him to attention.

"What is going on?"

"You can't be here; it's time to leave." She wrapped her fingers around his wrist and tried to pull him back into the crowd.

The town's priest stood beside Ivy, reading from his book of prayers. Tommie stepped forward, trying to hear what was said, but the wind caught their voices and carried them out into the ocean.

He stepped forward, but the hands that had him pulled him back.

"Tommie, let's go."

"*Na!*" he yelled. "That's Ivy; she's the town's healer."

"We are all well aware of *who* she is." There was an acid tone to her voice. "This is *her* fate."

"Fate?" A shiver ran over him again. *Curse... destiny.* It was all he was ever reminded of.

"Ydw, Tommie. You don't need to be here. Let's go, child."

"Listen to your mam," Mr. Cadwalladar spoke over Tommie's shoulder.

Tommie turned to his mam. "You've done this." It wasn't a question.

"It had to be done."

"Let go of me right now!" he yelled at the people next to him, hitting away their hands.

"The nightmares, Tommie. You've suffered enough. This will free you."

"Free me!" He shook his head, nearly freeing himself as he didn't stop fighting against them. "She's a healer. She will save the rest of the town from the plague!"

"She's plagued your mind for far too long, Tommie," Mr. Cadwallader said.

The other people who didn't have hold of Tommie began to clap. Tommie looked up to Ivy, who was watching Tommie, and she smiled.

The priest unbound her feet and then her hands, and walked her closer to the edge of the cliff.

"Stop this, right now!" He fought harder, people letting go to avoid the pain. He stepped forward, breaking away from the last of the hands that held him back.

His name echoed around him. His mam screamed it over and over again, but he wasn't going to stop. Running up to the ledge, closer to Ivy, he reached out both hands, desperate to have hold of her.

On the very edge of the cliff, Ivy's feet ran out of ground. The priest pressed his knuckles into her ribs, forcing her over.

In that split second, Ivy's body floated outwards. Her feet

flew out into a vertical kick and she collected the priest's robe in the clutches of her fists, holding on with both hands so that he also toppled over the ledge.

Tommie screamed for Ivy.

The crowd behind Tommie screamed for the priest.

Tommie reached the ledge and collapsed to the ground, watching her plummet towards the ground.

They locked eyes for the very last time then, and she reached out with both hands in a last motion of wanting him.

His heart swelled, and he screamed her name.

Then she hit the rocks.

I failed her! Again. He screamed. *I couldn't save her and I've let her die horribly twice.*

The crowd rushed up behind him, clustering around to see for themselves, pushing and shoving with so many bodies desperately wanting to look over.

A nudge too sharp in the middle of his back forced him forward, out into the nothingness.

The air surrounded him.

The screams of the crowd behind him were silenced against the swishing of the air that now raced up and around him.

Tommie looked downwards and plummeted towards Ivy.

The wind rippled against his skin as Ivy came up to meet him.

His body now rested beside hers, and darkness enveloped them both.

SCOTLAND

1658

"*T*amhas! Tamhas!" A shoe hit Tam right in the side of the face. He wobbled from the impact, sat up straight, and glared across the wagon at his *athair*. "Do ya ever listen, son!" the man yelled over his shoulder. "Always got ya head in da damn books! Pass me' back me shoe now, boy!"

Tam rolled his eyes, threw back the shoe, and nestled back into the wagon's side.

"I said," his athair muttered again. "Go and swap with ya brother!"

Tam looked to each of his seven older brothers who were all riding horseback.

Johne and Angus rode up front, while Dauid and Jock followed the cart, and Recherd and Cináed trailed behind. Recherd, the second youngest, bowed his head to his chest and slowly slid to an angle on the back of his horse.

Tam jumped off the wagon, ran to his side, and punched him hard in the leg.

"Ouch!" he yelled out, trying to kick Tam back, aiming for his head, but the horse reared up just in time as Recherd's foot clapped his ear. "What did ya do t'at for?"

"Go sleep in the wagon," Tam said in between his laughs.

Recherd jumped down and ran after the cart.

Taking the reins, Tam hushed the horse until it calmed. He placed one foot in the stirrup and hoisted himself onto the horse's back. With a nudge, they trotted to catch up. Then Tam pulled his book back from beneath his coat and returned to his pages.

"What are ya readin' now?" Dauid, the eldest of them all, coaxed his horse to fall in beside him.

"Chap book," Tam said, holding it out to him.

Driud shook his head. "How do ya read so much?"

Tam shrugged. *I'd read more if I could.*

Jock looked over his shoulder. "T'at little squiggles cause ya brain to bleed."

Tam laughed. He'd once told that to the boys to avoid teaching them to read on the long trips. "Haven't bled yet."

"Ya brain is mush," Cínead added.

"*Sgaoileadh sasannach!*" his athair blurted out from the wagon ahead.

Tam's shoulders went up around his ears as he looked out to the fields, wondering what Pa had seen to set him off.

Sitting beside his athair, Tam's *màthair* smacked him across the leg to deter him from repeating such language, but if soldiers were near, he'd say it in English.

Dauid clicked his tongue and his horse trotted up beside the wagon.

"Athair?" Dauid prodded.

The other boys clustered around, listening in.

"Doon't ya ask for noffin'," Athair snapped.

"It's time we go to Edenburgh," Dauid said with a deep, firm voice.

"No," their athair snapped as he shifted in his seat and then readjusted the reins.

"Athair," Dauid said, demanding eye contact; he was the only son that got away with such a tone. "We've been on the road for too long."

"There's no money left," Jock said.

"And we've visited more towns than any other merchant," Cínead added.

Their athair lifted his chin and jiggled the reins.

"Listen, Dauid Senior, the boys are speakin'," their màthair said, placing a soft, gentle hand on his leg this time.

He lowered his chin and looked deep into her eyes. From where Tam was, he could see a magic wash over him that made him bring down his walls and listen to his sons, but only because his wife willed it so.

"What is it ya want, lad?"

Dauid looked to each of his brothers, finally resting his eyes on Tam.

Tam gave him an encouraging nod.

"We're ready to settle in Edenburgh."

Athair scoffed. "Doon't ask for much then, doo ya?" He shook his head. "Who's gonna pay, huh? For ya little house with na' wheels?"

"We'd get jobs," Johne said.

"And we'd doon't need so many horses," Recherd said, sitting up in the back and stretching out his limbs.

"If we sell the horses, Athair," Dauid leaned in closer, "it'll be more than enough to buy ya and Ma a home."

Athair pulled the reins tight and the wagon came to a complete stop.

All the horses stopped, and the boys looked to one another.

Tam rolled his eyes. *Here we go again.*

"Ya all go to Edenburgh, and I go to Sterling. I've been a merchant all my life and I'd die a merchant."

"Ugh!" They all moaned in unison.

"Look at Màthair," Recherd said.

"Yeah!" Johne cut in. "Her poor legs can't handle anymore!"

"Doon't ya tell me that; I know she has troubles, but the movement helps, it keeps us goin'." Athair spoke strongly and triumphantly, but he lacked the youth and was outnumbered. Sitting on his cart, straight back and tall, he defied the advice of his own sons. But he must have felt defeated as his checks began to take on an unhealthy red.

Tamhas noticed him taking a deep breath and holding it. *He must be out of arguments again.*

"Ya have told us we're goin' to Edenburgh so many times. Now ya change ya mind! Are ya comin' with us or not?" Druid said.

Athair's face reddened darker than a ripe radish.

"Nope, not goin'." Athair crossed his arms and stared at the sign ahead. "Ya go, and me and ya mom stay on the road."

All of the other boys moaned and jumped back on their horses.

Tam hoisted himself up and looked back to his màthair. He watched as she moved closer to his pa, softened her face, and smiled. It was a trick she did to all of them and, before they realized, they'd be doing whatever it was she'd asked.

"It's time for Edenburgh, dear," she said, her musical voice filling the air and causing the boys to quiet and listen in.

"Ugh!" he threw up his hands and stood, turning to jump off the wagon, but she reached over and pulled him back to his seat. He wobbled and fell backwards. The cart protested under his weight.

He hmphed, but she ignored him and put the reins back into his hands, then pointed towards Edenburgh's direction.

From Tam's view, he couldn't see the stern look she was giving him, but Tam saw his athair's wary eyes, thin and straight lips, and flared nostrils.

He sank in his seat, scrunched his face, clenched his jaw, turned the horses towards Edenburgh, and remained silent for the rest of the way. Except, of course, when he yelled out. "Sgaoileadh sasannach!"

The horses' hooves clopped in rhythm against the dirt road. Tam finished his little book about using plants as medicine and tucked it back into his vest. He looked up and noticed something unusual on the horizon.

"What's t'at, Pa?" Tam asked, pointing directly at it.

Johne stood up in his saddle, used his legs to balance himself, and stretched to get a better look.

Their athair didn't answer, but rather grumbled and shuffled in his seat.

"Edenburgh!" Dauid replied in his athair's place.

"We're here?" Tam asked. "Already?"

The others mumbled their excitement, wanting to test out all that Edenburgh had to offer.

"I bet they have lots of *warm* beds," Johne said.

Màthair twisted her body around to look straight at him. "Ya know," she said, "finding a wife would be much better."

All of the boys laughed.

"Better than what?" Angus asked. "Finding one for the night?"

They all burst out in laughter, and the horses stamped their hooves and flicked their ears at all the ruckus.

"We can have a new one every night!" Cínead added.

Tam bit down on his lip when he caught his màthair's eye. She always looked to him differently than the others, expecting more, knowing she'd be pleased with the choices he would make.

His stomach churned.

A flash of images crossed his eyes. Mam in Wales and his mother in England. Two women who'd loved him so dearly, and suffered because he'd disappointed them.

I don't want to hurt a third màthair. I won't!

The boys paired up, planning their adventures. Tam remained quiet by his màthair's side.

"What are ya plans, dear?"

Tam shook his head. "Nothin'." But that wasn't true. *I hope I can find passage to England.* He locked eyes with his màthair and smiled. He knew she didn't believe his lie. *I'll find Ivy in London, I'm sure of it.*

I mightn' have plans for Edenburgh, but I have plans to change everything.

Don't speak of Ivy, don't even whisper her name.

Watch everyone that comes near and figure out what they want.

Tam had learned from his previous mistakes. *Some secrets were better left just that... secret.*

I'll never make that mistake again.

As they passed over the rolling mountains, Edenburgh seemed to swell in their sights as they approached.

Tam couldn't believe a town so big existed.

Closer to the walls, more people were present. Most were on foot, but others had wagons full of stock, with some even spilling over the edges.

Tam's mouth hung wide open. He couldn't believe Scotland had so much stuff, when all they had seen was limited supplies, just enough to feed the towns they'd been in.

They lined up behind other carts, waiting to get through the city gates.

"What's the hold-up?" Athair blurted out.

"I see English soldiers," Tam whispered, leaning to his màthair.

"Sgaoileadh sasa—"

"Shoosh!" His màthair slammed down her hand on his leg. "Not now and not while we stay in Edenburgh."

"Turn around then!" he ordered. "Too many soldiers and too many *blasted English!*"

"Sayin' it in English doon't make it any better," their màthair warned.

Tam agreed. There were tens, if not hundreds, of soldiers lined along the city walls, watching the carts come in and out of the city.

Slowly, they reached the gates and, just before they pulled the horses to a stop, an English soldier waved them through. Confused that they weren't being stopped and thoroughly checked over like usual, Tam quickly tilted towards the soldier, then tapped the back of his heels into the ribs of the horse.

They entered through the tall, stacked-stone gates and were on the other side of the walls in moments. The whole time, Màthair kept a firm grip of Athair's knee, squeezing it tight. It was an attempt to keep him silenced and a way for him to avoid blurting out any profanities. He managed to hold back this time, much to Tam's surprise.

Tam stretched his neck, counting the buildings to be eleven stories high. People littered the streets, rushing one way or the other, not even bothering to move out of the horses' way.

They followed the cart in front, hoping it would come close to the courtyard or someplace they could find a place to stay and house the horses. But instead of watching which way they turned, Tam's eyes remained fixated on all the strange things that were happening around him. High above their heads, open windows had cloth breezing against the wind. Lines linked from one building to another held multiple pieces of clothing. And, every so often, a pish pot's contents was thrown out, showering filth down onto the ground below.

The smell as it splashed across the ground was worse than a pish pot next to an open fireplace. Babes in women's arms screamed as they rushed past. People coughed. Men spat every so often, rolling the flem loudly in the back of their throat before it exited their lips.

Horses flicked their tails and shook, getting the flies off.

Dogs barked beside hungry children. Cats watched from above. Rats ran along roofing edges. Horse manure littered the streets. Men with shovels scrapped it up and threw it onto the back of a wagon.

Tam couldn't believe a place like this existed. Lost in the world of wonders, his horse continued along the road until it reached the courtyard. Dauid pointed to where they could rest the horses.

Tam followed closely behind, listening to the hooves clop loudly against the rocky roads. To his side, Tam passed a carriage. A man dressed in the finest pressed clothing stood beside the door, offering a hand to assist a lady. Behind that man stood another, who held a sign with London written across it.

Giddy in his saddle, Tam could barely hide his excitement. *No more than two seconds in this city and I've found my passage to London.*

He'd never breathed a word to his family about his secret plans. None of them would understand. He looked over his shoulder to his màthair in the wagon behind them. He knew he was going to break her heart. She beamed a smile back to him and he turned away, clutching his nervous stomach.

He didn't think about the carriage after that, but rather focused on selling his horse and accruing enough to take him away from where he was.

I need to get to London to find Ivy. For some reason, I know she's there waiting for me.

Hidden just in the mouth of the alleyway, Tam leaned against the stone building. He pressed his small bag of luggage against his chest. Nervous, his eyes darted up and down the road, searching for familiar faces, but luckily he hadn't come across one.

He had trouble calming his nerves. They were competing between extreme nervousness and excitement.

"Master! Master!" The coachman with a strange and exotic accent stood next to the coach door, holding it open. After he called out to Tam, he gestured for him to get in.

"Oh!" Tam hesitated. Even though he had planned on leaving to find Ivy, he'd never imagined the whole in his chest that formed as he prepared himself to walk away from his loved ones, but one step out into the busy street, he handed the coachman his luggage. Taking one large breath, he climbed into the black carriage.

He sat on the far end, next to the window.

A young lady, finely dressed with buttons and frills going all the way up her neck, smiled at Tam.

"Morn'," he said.

With her hands laced one over the other in her lap, she sat square and nodded.

Tam turned back to the window. On the other side of the street, he saw a woman and instantly became fixated on her dress.

Purple, lilac, and soft white fluffed at her back as she glided from one foot to theother. He wondered whether he would see dresses like that in London, and couldn't take his eyes off the woman who was looking into the shop window.

"Master?" the man yelled through the door. Tam sat straight and glared back at him.

"Madame Rhona," he said to the lady sitting opposite to Tam. "Beg my intrusion. We'll be leavin' when Madame Rose arrives."

"Madame Rose?" Tam asked, the name all too familiar. The air caught in the back of his throat with his realizing that Madame Rose could very well be Miss Rose from England.

His mouth went dry. *Rose. The Rose who accused Ivy... my Ivy... of witchcraft and got her killed!*

"She's my sister," Madame Rhona said. "Always runnin' late."

Tam looked into Rhona's eyes, then averted his own. *This isn't right. I cannot be in a carriage all the way to London with Rose! She'll know who I am!*

How will I avoid her?

He thought of ways to hide his face. *Perhaps holding up books as I read, or placing my hat down and sleeping. I can do that for a few days, can't I?*

He looked out of the window as he nervously waited for Rose's arrival.

Pointing through the carriage window to the woman in lilac, Tam turned back to the coachman. "Is t'at her over there?"

"Na', Master," he said, and then went on about a woman whose athair was prominent in business. However, Tam quickly lost interest.

Deep within him, he felt an urge to jump out of the carriage and run up to her. *Why?* He shook his head, fighting the urge back.

He closed his eyes and breathed. *I'm in the carriage waiting to go to London. I'll know I'll find Ivy there.*

He breathed again but the urge in his stomach had spread throughout his body and it felt more like an urgency now.

I need to speak to that woman before I leave here forever.

He pushed open the door and stepped out into the middle of the road.

"What ar' ya doing, lad?" the coachman yelled.

Ignoring him, Tam rushed past the oncoming carriages to the other side. Slowing as he reached the edge of the road, he went straight up to the glowing mistress and stood beside her, pretending to look in the window of the shop before her.

She turned to him and a soft smile pulled her lips at the edges.

He lost his breath. *Ivy.*

"Ma'am." He tipped his hat and replaced it on his head.

She twisted her body and walked away.

He sighed. *Doesn't she recognize me?*

It was like his heart pulled out of his chest, and he hurried after her. Quickly, he caught up.

"Arh!" she moaned. "Doon't ya not have anythin' better to do than follow me around, me' lad?" She winked over her shoulder and then walked a little faster.

Tam's heart beat faster. *She does remember!* He didn't let her get too far ahead, and stayed on her trail.

I knew she remembered.

How could she not?

That is what she intended, right? All those lifetimes ago, when he'd been due to propose to her, she'd known back then he was all hers. Now, she was living a safe life without him. A bounce in her step showed she was happy and healthy, and for once not the subject of such harsh criticism.

Should I leave her to go on without me? He slowed, wondering if he was the cause of the curse. *Is she safer without me?*

She glanced over her shoulder and they locked eyes.

Every fiber in Tam's body screamed after her. He couldn't let her go even if he wanted to.

Lost in his fantasies, he forgot about his luggage as he followed her down the little alley, behind the shops, and entered a back door to a tall building and began to climb the stairs.

The first, second, and then the third floor passed, and he felt a little dizzy. Perhaps it was being so close to her, or maybe it was the building itself. He had never climbed so many steps before and going up so high burned his legs and made him even more nervous.

She finally stopped on the fourth story and disappeared down a long corridor.

Unclipping a door, she left it open for Tam to enter.

He had to duck his head underneath the frame, and the floor creaked, protesting his weight.

She turned around and faced him, flicking her lilac dress out to the side.

"Ivy." Her name whispered through his lips and she paused to look at him.

Her head turned on an angle, and she studied him for a moment.

The heat radiated beneath his skin. He'd wished for a moment like this, in all his lives—several seconds to be alone with her to tell her how much he had missed her, how much he'd pined over her, and that his entire existence meant nothing to him without her being in it.

But his words wouldn't come; he stood there staring in owe, loving her just like he always had.

She took a step forward and pressed her lips to his.

Surprised, he breathed her in and wrapped an arm around her waist, his other moving up the back of her neck and then pulling her in even closer, squeezing her tightly.

She lifted one leg up, cradling him as she kissed him more hungrily than before.

Tam ran his hand down the side of her, held her softly, and pulled her up onto him.

She tugged at the laces of her fancy dress, opening it at the front. But there were more layers underneath, and she pushed herself away, spun around, and demanded to be unlaced.

He tackled the ribbons, unthreading one after another as they tangled at each end. He let out a roar of frustration and pulled a little clip knife from his vest pocket and ripped the ribbons to shreds.

The dress released her body and she pulled the rest off by herself.

Tam pulled off his own clothes within moments, throwing them all over the apartment as he followed her closer to the bed.

She giggled as he pulled himself on top of her and whispered into her ear. "I've always loved ya."

She pulled back and they locked eyes. She smiled then, and kissed him ferociously for the rest of the day.

Hours later, Tam was well rested and lay with Ivy in his arms. Outside, dusk began to darken the streets, and in the fading light, he twirled one of her soft auburn ringlets around his finger and watched her breathe in and out.

"What ar' ya doin' in Edenburgh?" she asked.

The sound of her voice made his heart pick up its rhythm; it danced around and enveloped him with so much love, passion, and freedom that he felt he could easily lay there in her arms for the rest of eternity.

"I was passing through," he said, laughing at how outrageous his plans were now.

I never needed to go out and find her. She would always show up when I least expected it. She was right here all along, waiting for me to arrive.

Resting his head back on the firm wooden headboard, he watched her as she rolled over, closing the little gap between them, and placed her head on his chest.

"In fact, I was on the stagecoach and then I saw ya," he said. "Got right out; was nearly hit by an oncomin' horse! Stagecoach master yelled at me, but that wasn' goin' to stop me from seeing ya', me lass."

She snuggled her nose into the side of his neck, giving him another chance to kiss her on the forehead.

He had so much to ask her, so much he needed to know, but he didn't want to ruin the moment.

"Was t'at your stomach, lass?" he laughed, and it rumbled again.

"Well, as sweet as you are, you didn't fill me for lunch."

"Should we go for dinner then?" His words had a certain pain to them. His own stomach protested loudly, too, however, his craving for Ivy wasn't satisfied. Scooping her up again, he placed her on top and wouldn't let go.

She giggled, and rolled on top then moaned loudly. Their cool bodies quickly heated with passion.

Tam closed his eyes, losing himself in the moment, but was then startled by a loud bang.

The door opened and a large, tall man ducked under the door frame and yelled at them. "What's all this?"

Ivy pulled herself away from Tam and grabbed the sheets to cover herself.

Tam sat and stared at the half-deranged man.

Much taller than Tam, he waved his hands through the air and paced the room, throwing Ivy's clothes at her before he kicked Tam's about the room.

Tam rolled onto the other side of the bed, got to his feet, and pulled Ivy behind him, trying to protect her.

"James!" she said.

Tam wanted to look over his shoulder at her. She sounded different somehow. But he couldn't take his eyes off the big, ugly, and furious man.

He didn't want her to be hurt—not in this lifetime, not ever.

"I'm sorry," she pleaded.

"Ya did it again, woman!" He stopped the pacing and stared down at her. Fists clench, teeth locked, he slithered his words out. "Ya!" He pointed to Tam. "Ya ne'd to leave."

Tam stood straight and still even though he was stark naked and exposed. "No!"

People from neighboring apartments gathered at the door to watch.

"I'm not goin' to say it again," the ugly beast of a man said. His face turned a darker shade of red. "Get your stuff and get out. This is between me and me wife!"

"Wife?" Tam glanced at Ivy.

She didn't wait for me?

He had waited for her, life after life!

"Yeah, James is me' husband." She didn't look at all sorry, not even ashamed. Rather, Tam took a step back and saw the boredom in her face. He really didn't know what she was playing at.

Is she trying to send me a message?

Did she get a choice in this marriage?

Thoughts flickered through his mind. He didn't care for the details—all that mattered was what was happening now.

Tam turned back to the man and faced him straight-on. "I'm sorry t'at ya married her, but she's not yours anymore."

For a moment there, Tam thought the man was going to agree. Then the man took a deep breath and stormed his way around the bed, marching directly at Tam.

Ivy moved out of the way and ran to the other side of the room, watching from the corner.

The man stopped a step before Tam, and pulled back his big bulky arm and then swung it through the air.

Tam leaned back, just missing the knuckles as they brushed across his forehead. Pushing the half giant in the ribs, he sent the man tumbling sideways so that he buckled over onto the ground.

Using the spare moment, Tam jumped onto the bed and leaped off the end, holding a hand out for Ivy.

"Come with me!" he pleaded.

Ivy looked at Tam's hand, and then back to her fallen husband.

James pushed himself up onto his knees. "T'at's my wife!" he yelled, getting to his feet and lunging at Tam again.

Tam moved fast, running around the room. He jumped up onto the bed, out of reach from their man's arms and down to the other side. The giant man was too slow and his movements were laborious, making it much easier for Tam to get around the room.

"Ivy!" Tam said between breaths. "I'm so sorry for the past," he pleaded with her as he crouched down, just missing a swing and then planting his foot directly into the other man's lower stomach. It gave Tam just a second to cross the room again.

Giggles at the front door only distracted Tam for a moment, but he wasn't there to entertain the watching eyes. He needed Ivy to leave with him.

Ivy couldn't take her eyes off Tam, dancing around her furious husband. Noticing this, James leaned back and roared.

Tam ignored him. "The past is the past and neither of us can change t'at now. And I doon't care t'at ya didn't wait for me, lass. I understand. But we can leave tis place behind and be together. We'd be happy."

The giant puffed his way back and forth, grabbing a firm grip onto Tam's ankle.

Tam twisted his body around and, with his free foot, kicked the giant's hand.

"You'd do that?" she asked.

"No!" the giant blurted out. "She's mine! You're not havin' her!"

Unable to get the beast to let go, Tam wiggled his way around, trying to move. But as the giant moved his grip further up Tam's leg, Tam had less room to get away.

Two extra large fists plummeted down and connected with the side of Tam's face.

For a moment there, Tam only saw blackness. Twinkling white at the edges then refocused him. The beast had pushed him against the wall and hit him with one blow after another.

Tam spat blood out and all over the front of the man's vest.

Ivy emerged from the corner and pushed her husband in the back.

The giant man stumbled backwards and she pushed him again. He grabbed her by the wrist and, with his other hand, slapped her hard.

She didn't scream out in pain, but the people watching from the doorway quickly disappeared, clearly not wanting to see the brutal punishment dished out to an unfaithful wife.

Have they seen this before?

"Doon't ya dare lay a hand on her!" Tam got to his feet, extended a straight index figure, and pointed it at the man's face.

"Tis is *my* wife!" He grabbed hold of her elbow and shook her so violently that the blanket she'd held up dropped to the ground. "You'll never have her again."

With Ivy still in his grip, he dragged her out the door stark naked.

"No! Wait!" Tam yelled after them, but he hesitated at running out the door still naked himself.

He reached for his pants, threading each leg through as he entered the corridor and caught them on the stairs. "How can you do tis!" Tam yelled, trying to reach Ivy. "She's naked!"

The beast pushed her down first and, with his spare hand, held Tam back. "She's *my* wife!" he repeated.

"That doon't allow ya to showcase her to the whole of Edenburgh!"

That stopped the man, and he turned to face Tam again. Red-faced and furious, he leaned in and breathed a foul stench into Tam's face.

Standing tall, Tam glared back.

"I will punish *my* wife how *I* see fit." He turned and dragged Ivy down the windy staircase.

Tam stood frozen in the hallway, listening to Ivy's screams echo in the distance.

Outside in the quiet of the dark streets, small little candles perched high on tall poles, offering enough light for Tam to follow them. The night air chilled his bare chest, and without shoes, he trod in horse dung, the bottom of his heels crunching down on cold, pebbled road.

Ivy can't be any better off, he thought sullenly.

Down several blocks, back to the center of Edenburgh, Ivy's husband forced her along, kicking and screaming.

With each protest, she received another smack, and with each thwack, Tam clenched his fists, steeling the hot rage in his core.

Tam couldn't really see where they were going. There wasn't enough light, and he didn't know the area well enough to predict the location. But once they reached the stairs, Tam saw the courthouse.

He held his breath. This could mean a few things. He'd once heard about a woman being hauled before the assembly by her own husband. They hadn't known what to do with her, so they'd thrown her into a mental institution and granted freedom for the frustrated and lonely husband to re-marry in peace.

That situation didn't bode well for Tam, but it gave him hope.

He didn't know where the nearest in sanitarium was, but if Ivy was to be sent to one, Tam could get her out and marry her himself.

It's a plan, but he was sure to come up with something better. *I'll intercept the carriage with me brothers and kidnap her before she even reaches the institution.* He nodded to himself. *We'll spend the rest of our days as fugitives, but I won't care. Not if it means spending each night in her arms.*

He liked that plan the best.

He ran up the steps and was forced to stop before he reached the door.

"Where'd ya think ya goin' lad?"

"Inside," Tam used his firm voice, the one he often spoke to impersonate his father.

"Not like that, ya not!" The guard looked Tam up and down.

What! This is madness. Ivy is stark naked, and I'm not allowed in without a shirt?

He stepped back down the staircase, trying to see through the ajar door.

"Go on. Get ye', scum."

Tam walked back down the steps and waited nearby, watching carefully, never taking his eyes off the door.

It felt like hours had passed before beast of a husband emerged from inside.

He's alone! Tam stood, scowling after the man as he went back down the road.

Heart hammering against his chest, Tam ran back to the court steps, demanding to know what had happened to Ivy.

"I told ye to get!" the guard said, and behind him, a man of the court emerged, demanding to know what the matter was.

"Ivy, sir." Tam bowed his head. "What happen'd to Ivy?"

"She's in the cells, holdin' till mornin'. Come back then, lad. They'd be a hearin' then."

"Thank ya, sir," Tam said, and he bowed his head and ran all the way home.

The following day, Tam arrived at the courthouse well before the husband did. He had borrowed his brother's best outfit, given that all he owned was in a single suitcase halfway to London, with the remainder of his clothes locked up in Ivy's husband's apartment.

He pulled at his jacket, stole a look at his athair's pocket watch, and slicked his hair with a touch of boot polish he'd borrowed from the kid on the corner.

The husband wore the same slacks he had yesterday, and it seemed like he hadn't bathed in months. The smell wolfed in after him and the assembly of nice, neat men shifted in their seats.

From the back rooms, Ivy came into sight. She wore a brown

hessian cloth that barely covered her body. With her head bowed low, she followed the guard to her seat.

Tam could see the swelling around her jaw, and blue and black bruising around her eye. Her scuffed hair was now knotted, and he saw a slice down her bottom lip.

She is so beautiful.

Tam's heart skipped a beat.

This is the moment! He thought all of the possible things that could happen. *I can save her right now and we could be free.*

The assembly sat in their chairs and the room went quiet. Five men in all, who wore fluffy white hair on top of their own and thick dark cloaks that broadened their shoulders.

"Who here claims her?"

"I do," Tam spoke out, jumping to his feet.

"What?" the husband yelled. "She's my damn wife!"

The assembly spoke amongst themselves and then waited for either man to answer as their leader demanded, "What is the meaning of this?"

"I have come to claim Miss Ivy from her wretched, disgustin' husband." Tam stood tall.

"Husband? That means you are *not* the husband then?"

"Ur... No."

"I'm the husband," James added as spittle dripped from his lips.

The assembly turned back to Tam. "You, sir, cannot claim another man's wife."

The words cut right through Tam's chest.

"Sit down," the council man on the very end ordered.

The people who had gathered and watched from behind all laughed and snickered.

Tam collapsed into his seat defeated, feeling hollow and frightened. He was scared that he'd missed his chance to save Ivy in this life, and scared to go through another dangerous death. He didn't want to spend eternity losing her and watching her die. For once, he just wanted to save her, and in this life, he was going to do it.

Nothing is going to stop me. Not the court or that disgusting husband.

Gathering himself, he looked up and saw Ivy studying him. As they locked eyes, her facial features twisted and she tilted her head slightly to the side, just as she had in the apartment. He smiled at her, and she scrunched her eyebrows together. Her lips remained in a straight line.

"Mr. James Niven." The assembly went on with its proceeding like somehow they were all fated into this moment. "How do you wish to proceed with the punishment of your wife?"

The husband stood again, and he dropped his head in shame. "Sirs, I doon't wish to proceed with punishment."

Tam sat up in his chair expectantly. "The wife tis not a go'd wife. No sons. No bore me an' daughters. She doesn't eve' kep't me bed empty when I away on the trawler."

People behind him gasped.

No, no, no. I have to stop this!

"What do you wish then?" The assembly, all sitting with straight posture, sat there and waited.

Tam wondered what was going to come next. The mental institute? He shifted in his seat. All he needed was to hear those words, and then he'd be out of the courtroom, straight home, convincing his brothers to help out.

"I hand her to ye for punishment, sirs."

The watching people behind him gasped in shock and the entire court assembly nodded in agreement.

"Quiet! Quiet!" the assembly leader yelled out.

The crowd hushed.

Tam sat on the edge of his seat.

The husband lifted his head this time, announcing with

honor, "I hand her to ya, sirs, fine men of the court, to punish her as ya see fit!"

"What?" Tam jumped to his feet and screamed out. "No!" But his words were lost to those of the screaming and cheering crowd.

James lowered his head and walked out of the courthouse, leaving his defenseless wife in the chair to suffer the verbal abuse being thrown at her.

"Quiet!" the assembly leader called out, and everyone eventually settled down, wanting the show to go on. "Put her back in the dungeon so that we can deal with more important matters for now."

And, like that, she was dragged out of sight.

And out of Tam's reach.

Tam stumbled down the courthouse steps and heard his name in the distance.

"Tam!" Dauid yelled, running across the road to Tam's side. Dauid grabbed hold of Tam's arm and pushed him into the nearest alleyway, out of sight from the crowd that filled the courtyard.

Tam slumped against the wall.

"What'cha doin' in there?" Dauid spoke softly, gesturing to the courthouse.

Barely lifting his head from his chest, Tam whispered, "It's Ivy, broth'r. They sent her to the dungeon!" His face fell into his hands and he collapsed to the ground, scuffing up his brother's suit against the brick wall.

"Who's Ivy?" Dauid crouched down next to him and held his shoulders for support. "What've you'd done, lad?"

"I found *my* Ivy," he said. "And she's in trouble." He pulled away from his hands to look to his biggest brother. "Would you help me rescue her?"

For just a moment, Dauid retracted, and then he nodded. Druid was a brother that questioned everything, except when it came to Tam. Thankful, Tam tried to smile, but the hole in his chest didn't feel like he would be able to smile again.

"Only on one condition?"

Tam nodded.

"Doon't take my suit!" he said, hitting him in the arm. "I just bought t'at yesterday and I needed it this morn'." Dauid pulled Tam to his feet. "Arh!" He rolled the word around in the back of his throat. "Ya stole it now. How me goin' to get work now, lad?"

Tam shrugged.

Dauid sighed. "Let's go somewhere; we'd need to plan tis right."

Tam and Dauid found the nearest watering hole, where they remained until the early hours of the next morning.

"Let's get tis straight." Angus placed his fingers firmly on his temples. "We're going to fight the court to save a lass that we've never met."

"Tis is for Tam," Dauid said.

"There's plenty of other lasses!" Angus stood and paced the room.

The brothers hit Angus in the arm, outnumbering him in opinion.

Jock opened the front door, looked out, and then closed it again. "We've only got another couple of minutes. Hurry up."

Tam and Dauid exchanged looks. Within the week that they had been there, Jock had already found himself a lass whose athair had bought them a home, but she hated his brothers and didn't allow him to be there.

"Cínead," Dauid said, pointing a finger at him. "Ya pickpocket the *sasannach* soldiers and find papers. Doon't matter what kind; anythin' will do." He turned to Tam. "Then ya make new papers demandin' the release of Ivy into your custody."

"Tis isn't going to work," Angus said from the far corner.

"Angus, now ya can steal the officer's uniform; Jock, ya help him."

"What about me?" Recherd asked.

"Ye and Johne need to learn the area; best ways in and out."

"Does t'at mean Tam is leavin'?" Angus asked.

Tam exchanged looks with Dauid again, then nodded, dropping his eyes in shame. "I think it's best to get out quick. I've brought back my horse."

Recherd shook his head. "Na, na," he mumbled, lost in thought. "Ye both need to stay here—"

"Not here!" Jock threw up his hands. "My lass will kick me out."

"Na, I meant in Edenburgh! Look at tis place. It's like a maze —na one goin' to find ya."

"That's a good idea." Tam nodded.

"But the horses, we can send out a couple, past the walls so the sgagoileadh sasnnach will follow, while ya and your lady get away," Angus said.

Every brother turned to stare at him.

"What?"

"T'at's the first thing you've said that hasn't been an argument."

"Well, I still think it's stupid. Easier to get a new one, all the trouble this on'es stirred."

Tam rolled his eyes.

"Plan done?" Jock opened the door, insisting they leave.

They got to their feet and left. Tam hung back to thank Jock.

"Just make sure she hasn't got one of those athairs that hold ye balls too tight," Jock said with all seriousness.

Considering who he let her marry... I wouldn't mind giving him a word of my own or two.

"I'll remember t'at," he said, and slipped out the door into the sunlight.

On the morning of the hearing, Tam rose earlier than any of his brothers.

"Couldn't sleep," Dauid said, sitting up.

"Hardly." He shook his head. "Should we go over the plan once more?"

"Na, ye know it, lad."

Tam stretched and readied himself in the English outfit.

"Finally," his màthair said, coming into the room. "I thought ye were going to sleep through the whole plan."

Tam felt her eyes on him, and he even sensed her concern. *This could be the very last time I see her.* He crossed the room and kissed her.

Dauid kicked the others awake. They moaned before getting to their feet and preparing for the day.

"Jock is here; there's already so many people gathered in the court."

"Why?" Tam asked.

She shrugged. "Word went out yeste'day that the court assembly ordered a hearing."

Dauid hung out the window. "Looks like everyone's come in from the farmlands."

"It's not a festival," Tam snapped.

"Ye look horrible dressed as an Englishman," his màthair said, clipping the buttons up on his jacket.

"It's only for today, Ma," he said as he leaned in and kissed her cheek. "I'll see ye after."

She wrapped her arms around him and squeezed him tight. "Ye better, me sonny boy."

He pulled away and rushed through the door, then hurrying down the six stories and out the door. The street was much busier than before, and he struggled to cross without being bumped by an oncoming horse, or having to step out of the way so people could pass by.

He reached the bottom of the court stairs and marched up them. Grabbing hold of the door handle, he attempted to push the door open, but it was locked.

"Can I help ye, soldier?"

Tam turned towards the voice. It was the same soldier who'd told him to scurry off when Tam had tried to enter without a shirt and shoes.

Tam squirmed, hoping the man didn't recognize him. "I'm here on the King's business," he said, trying to sound as English as possible.

"Court closed today; ye have to take it up with them when they go on stage."

"Stage?"

The soldier pointed to the wooden stage in the middle of the large square. People were already standing in front of it, waiting for something to happen.

"When will they be here?"

"By the strike of ten."

"Very well," Tam said, dismounting the steps and disappearing away from the crowd.

He felt the eyes of too many people on him while he walked towards his parents' home. He double-tracked and headed straight back to the courthouse, waiting for the assembly to arrive. But even before he could get close enough, the court was full of people and the already dense crowd had grown even thicker.

Tam pushed his way to the front of the crowd and stood just in front of a platform. Right in the middle of the stage was a strange machine.

What is that?

He glared at it. People around him whispered, pointing to

his uniform, but he shrugged it off. He wasn't there for them.

Right on the strike of ten, several men walked up the side steps and onto the platform. The crowd hushed itself, as if they didn't want to miss a word spoken.

"Bring out the prisoners!" the shortest one with the roundest of stomachs yelled out.

On the furthest side of the courtyard, the courthouse building's doors were opened. A line of prisoners, no more than fifty, were chained at the hands and again at their ankles. They wore links around their necks, connecting them in one long, single file line. Each shuffled one in front of the other until they were all out, facing the crowd, their bonds making for an awkward stance as they squared off at their shoulders.

The crowd screamed and shouted as they threw rotten fruit towards the prisoners.

Tam shifted on his heels. A hand pressed down on his shoulder and he turned to see Dauid behind him.

"We've got tis, right?" he whispered into Tam's ear.

Wanting to nod, because he needed to believe it, Tam could only muster up the nerves to shake his shoulders. His brother's hand squeezed tight, but it didn't make him feel any better.

An entire round cabbage, half black and smelly, zoomed straight over the top of Tam's head.

He turned then, seeing arms arched into the air, projecting rotten tomatoes, bright green potatoes, and cabbages.

Tam jumped, waving his arms in the air, trying to stop anything from reaching Ivy.

"Hey!" A man beside him grabbed him by the coat and shook him. "Ye English don't let us have a'e fun!"

"Let go of me!" Tam pushed him off.

The spoilt food kept coming from each angle—hundreds, if not thousands of items of old food littering the platform. The majority of it came from the tall buildings framing the courtyard.

Ivy tried to bend over, and shield her face to her chest, but a large man dressed in all black forced her to stand tall with a hand clutched around her neck.

"No!" Tam cried out, but his voice was drowned out by the rowdy crowd around him. He couldn't even hear his own voice leave his lips.

Dauid held him back so that Tam didn't crawl onto the platform right then and there to save her.

A bell echoed from the court tower, and the dongs hushed the crowd.

Several other men joined the platform, and Tam instantly recognized the assembly. They wore ruffled jackets and fleecy kilts, in stark contrast to the prisoners who stood in muck-covered rags.

Ivy lifted her head and scanned the crowd. She locked eyes with Tam and her face twisted with surprise.

If it hadn't been for Dauid's hand keeping him in place, Tam would have jumped onto the platform and fought any man who stood in his way to rescue her from those monsters.

The first prisoner stepped forward and his chains were removed. Two men beside him held his arms tight as he walked across the platform and was forced to lay down on a wooden bed. As he lay there, the other men strapped his body down so that he must remain still.

His head poked through a round hole and looked out over the crowd.

Right below him, Tam stood just several feet from the man's suspended head, trying to figure out the contraption.

The wooden piers towered high above them, linking together right at the very top, which held a large, round stone sharpened at the edge.

"We shouldn't be here," Dauid whispered firmly in his ear, but Tam was lost in thought, hoping he could convince them to unlink Ivy from those chains.

Dauid yanked at Tam's clothing, trying to pull him back into the crowd. But Tam fought against his insistent brother.

"What are ye doing?" Tam argued over his shoulder. "We cannot leave her!"

"We need to leave. Now!" Dauid ordered him. "We have no part in tis, ye hear me?"

"What?" Tam turned to his brother and clutched his shirt with both fists. "You promised to stand beside me and save her!"

"Yes, I did, broth'r, but this?" He pointed to the man on the wooden bed.

Following his hand, Tam turned around and looked up, catching a glimpse of the heavy sharp stone slate freefalling downwards and slicing the man's head clean off at the neck.

Blood spattered across the crowd, leaving Tam standing with his mouth open, eyes fixated, unable to catch his breath.

"Tam!"

He heard his name and his body wobbled in place.

The prisoners behind him screamed as they realized their fates.

The crowd roared in approval; some chanted, most clapped, but the majority demanded more.

"Tam!" Dauid pulled Tam backwards again, further away from the platform.

Tam didn't fight back this time, allowing his body to bump from one person to another. People laughed at his face and spat on the ground near his feet.

Still without a proper breathing pattern, Tam was surrounded by his brothers at the side of the building that bordered the square, all of them huddled together on the far side of the crowd. They watched on as the guards brought out more prisoners to line up behind Ivy and another contraption, positioning it side by side with the other so that they could execute more at a time.

"Tis is madness!" Recherd argued.

"We could all get killed for some girl we doon't know!" Angus said.

"Tis is Tam's girl, remember?" That was Dauid's voice breaking over the pack—firm, loyal, and demanding obedience.

"I can't do tis, brother!" Recherd shook his head. "I have a girl of my own to think about!"

"Yeah, Tam, ye're just going to have to get a'other!" Angus said.

A hand clapped over his back just as the crowd screamed out their delight once more.

Every muscle in Tam's body shook. His nerves pulsated down each ligament. Every desire he'd ever felt was nothing compared to the one he experienced now.

This was the moment to save her.

He looked up and watched them unchain the next prisoner. Swallowing down the lump in his throat, he stepped forward.

Out of the crowd, Tam ran around to the edge of the platform, heading towards the steps.

"Stop there!" the soldier demanded, stepping forward and holding his weapon out.

"On the King's orders, I demand ya move out of the way."

The soldier stood tall, then stepped out of the way.

Tam mounted the steps until he stood on the platform.

Thankful as he was for his brothers having his back, Tam needed to do this on his own. He was here to do one thing in this life.

To save the love of his life… unlinke in his many lives before. *This will be the last one, I promise, my sweet Ivy.*

Ivy's chains were taken off.

His body shook, and then he slammed down his foot like he was standing at attention. "I demand, on the King's orders, that the proceedings stop."

The crowd, too rowdy and loud to hear, drowned out Tam's voice.

The assembly waved at the crowd, calling for calm. The screams and shouts stopped. An eerie wave of silence washed over the faces.

"Yes, soldier?"

"I said," Tam cleared his throat, "I demand that these proceedings stop immediately." His English accent had hung on the vowels for too long.

"On whose orders?"

Tam squirmed. "On the King's orders." Tam retrieved his papers from beneath his Sasannech vest.

"What is the meaning of this?" One of the assemblymen eyed Tam suspiciously.

Tam pretended to read from his papers. "This prisoner, Ivy Brùn, is wanted in London for high treason!"

The crowd gasped.

"Is that *so*?" The assemblymen huddled together and quickly parted. "Please produce the proper papers and we will release her immediately into your custody."

Relief washed over Tam as he took several steps forward, grabbing Ivy by the arm.

"The papers?" The assembly member cleared his throat and held out a hand.

"Papers? Oh, ye," he coughed, clearing his accent, and held the papers out for them to take.

The men gathered around, inspecting the small writing.

"Yes, the papers do state that this prisoner is wanted by the Crown for high treason," the tall one who had hold of the scroll said.

"That is a serious crime," the one on the left said.

"Perhaps we should do the King a favor and send her head instead."

"No, that is not necessary," Tam interrupted. "The King

requires the prisoner alive."

"Unlikely," the shorter man said, and then he looked Tam up and down.

"They require…" Tam looked down at his brothers, then back to the men again, "…information from her."

"Very well then," the tallest said. "Unchain the prisoner," he instructed the executioner who was dressed in black. "Release her into his custody."

This is it! I've done it. I've rescued her. Now we just need to get out of here.

"What happened to your accent, lad?" The shortest one stepped forward.

"My accent?" He spoke in a British accent again as he added, "has been subjected to long travels in odd places like this one." He lifted a hand up, gesturing to the nearby buildings.

The council man took another step forward and, without taking his eyes off Tam, gestured to the executioner to stop. "My eyesight," the council man spoke slowly, "is not as bad as your acting. I know who you are!"

"Tam, let's go!" Dauid called from the crowd, but Tam ignored him.

"You," the council man said, pointing a finger right at Tam, "are the evil doings of a young wife. You," he raised his voice so that all of the crowd could hear, "went into a marriage bed and tempted her with your wicked ways. You encouraged her to exit her marriage and, in the very court before the assembly, tried to claim her for your own."

The crowd gasped, murmurs filling the air. Tam shifted his weight. He looked to Ivy, who was still chained, and then back at the men.

"Take him!" the assembly barked, and before Tam could move, two men had come up behind him, grabbing hold of each of his arms.

The tallest of the assembly stood forward at the edge of the platform. He held up a hand and hushed the crowd.

Tam looked to his brothers, who were all huddled together whispering. *They'll have a back-up plan,* he repeated in his mind.

"This young man has come before the assembly, dressed as an English officer, with papers demanding a prisoner's release under the King's orders."

"Crimes!" a person in the far distance yelled, causing an uproar in the audience.

The assemblyman went on, yelling over the top. "What say ye?"

The crowd roared.

Tam fought against the men who held him. His brothers rushed off in each direction, except for Dauid, who stood and tried shouting at Tam.

"What?" Tam yelled back, unable to read his lips.

"Run!"

Twisting his body, the man on his side held his arm with both hands and snapped the bone in two.

The noise ran up his arm and echoed in his ears. Tam screamed out in pain. The man came in closer and fumed in his ear, "No need to fight now, lad."

Tears swelled in his eyes and he bit down on his lip, forcing himself to remain still and not fight again.

The back of the crowd started cheering, and the sound eventually rolled forward; soon enough, the entire court was chanting. "Death. Death. Death."

Tam's mouth went dry.

The assemblymen lined up beside one another and read from a scroll. "You are hereby ordered to the same fate as your contemptuous whore here."

"Death?" Tam yelled, kicking out his legs, trying to wiggle his way free. He saw his brothers at the edge of the stage fighting with men twice their size. His màthair in the neighboring tower was most likely looking down, crying out. He couldn't think of her again. Not now, not ever.

"Yes, death! We will have no more of your evil antics running around our pure city. Nor will we have attempts to stop executions ordered by this assembly. Who do you think you are, lad? Above the law?" The crowd laughed, like he had turned the events into some stage production. "Your death shall be made an example of!" he announced to the crowd, and they clapped in support.

Ivy kicked and screamed.

"Ivy!" Tam yelled, lunging out for her. The men pushed him to the left machine, and Ivy to the right. Forcing them to lay down on their stomachs, the men affixed leather straps to hold them in place. Tam flexed his muscles, but it was no use; they were too tight. First, they'd bound his hands, then his ankles, and finally there'd been a thick strap put across his back.

He turned to Ivy beside him. Her long locks draped down around her face.

She didn't look back at Tam, rather stared out towards the crowd. Cocking her head back, she spat.

Following her trail of sight, Tam saw her beastly husband standing a short distance away. Towering over every man beside him, he was hard to miss. Beside him, a bar maiden wrapped her arms around his bulging stomach.

"Ivy?"

She turned and finally locked eyes with him.

The whole world melted away, like they were the only ones there.

"Remember how much I love ya, and I'm sorry I didn't find you earlier in tis life. I really hope next time we find each other sooner," he told her... and she burst out laughing.

"What makes ya think ya know me?"

Shock hit him right across the face. "Ya remember me, doon't you?"

"From where?"

"All our lives together?" he retorted, waiting for the sick joke to ease up.

She screwed her face up. "Since the shop window? You haven't lived much of a life now, lad." She laughed again.

"Ivy? Ya doon't remember me!" he exclaimed, and then the stone blade crunched its way down between the two wooden planks, smacking into the back of Tam's neck.

The crunch hit, a throbbing against his bones.

Blackness threatened the edges of his sight, his body going numb, but his head remained on his neck. The blade went back up the wooden plank slowly.

His eyes fluttered to the side and noticed Ivy's head in the basket below, a sick grin still held on her lips.

The blade came down once more, straight past the meat, and crunched through the bone.

He didn't feel the rest.

INDIA

1763

"Ivy! Ivy!"

In the other room, *Maa* screamed. She appeared at the door, eyes bright and wild, and raced over to him, scooping him up from his sleeping mat and into her arms.

"Tāmas said his first word," she yelled back towards the door, and several women shuffled into view.

"Did he really?" *Massi* asked.

"What did he say?" *Bhau* added.

His maa turned to him. "Say it again, my clever little Tāmas."

"I—v—y," the word came out slow, rolling off his tongue. He watched his mother's face twist in confusion. She looked to her sisters. They, too, wore the same look as his maa.

"Did he say Ivy?" Bhau asked as Massi stood beside her and nodded.

Tāmas' body started to shake. *What? They know Ivy's name?* Tears clouded his sight.

Did I say her name? A loud, annoying noise rattled his ears. He kicked out his legs, trying to find where the source came from.

His maa exposed her breast, shoving it into his mouth. The

noise disappeared and, soon enough, he was back to sleeping, once again dreaming of Ivy.

Tāmas woke hot, hungry, and thirsty. After feeding, his maa sat him on the floor mat and placed objects in front of him. She returned to a seat nearby and picked up a long, colorful blanket.

"See?" she asked the woman beside her. "There's something wrong with him!"

Massi Vidya walked over and nudged the objects closer to Tāmas. He picked them up, looked at them, and placed them back down.

"Maybe he just doesn't want to play," Vidya said.

"He never plays!" Maa tsked her tongue and kept her eyes on her weaving, creating the longest floor mat with the most intriguing of colors. "All he does is sit there and watch me."

"And you're complaining?" Massi Jyothi shook her head.

Hema picked up her own child from the basket. "Be thankful he isn't screaming all the time." The child in her arms woke and she placed the girl beside little Tāmas. "Rashmi, play with Tāmas," she said.

Tāmas picked up an object in front of him and handed it to the baby. He sat and watched Rashmi play.

Should I pretend to play like her?

She picked up a wooden sculpture and threw it towards him. It hit him in the stomach and he looked down as it fell.

This body is so slow. How many times do I have to go through this?

"See, he can play," Massi Jyothi said.

Maa shrugged her shoulders.

After the downpour, Tāmas ran out with all the other children, splashing in the mud puddles.

"I'll kick mud in your face," Rashmi teased.

"I'd like to see you try!" Tāmas buried his foot deep into the mud and flicked it up into the air. Mud landed straight in the middle of Rashmi's chest.

Arms out wide, she froze and looked to him in shock. "How could you?"

Tāmas ran to her side. "You were going to do it to me first."

"I was teasing!"

"Tāmas!" His name had been screamed from the far distance.

"Is that your maa?"

Shaking his head, he stretched up onto his tiptoes and arched his neck, trying to see who was calling out to him.

"Rashmi!" A voice from a different direction called.

Tāmas and Rashmi locked eyes. "Something's happened," she whispered.

"See you tomorrow?"

"Yep," he said, turning away and running towards the voice that had just called him again.

As he ran down the narrow street, past several homes, he saw massi Vidya waving her arms.

"Tāmas, love."

"Massi, what is it? What is the matter?"

"Tāmas, good child, you must go straight home."

It wasn't her words that worried him, but how she delivered them, which caused a weird shiver to run all over his body.

"*Haan*, yes, Massi." He stepped closer to her, locking his hands with hers. "What has happened, Massi?"

"Another man." She paused to wipe tears from her eyes. "... has gone."

"Gone?"

"Yes, another!" She squeezed Tāmas' hands tight. "Go and tell your mother, and stay there hidden. It's not safe for you out here."

Tāmas turned and ran all the way home. He had never

disobeyed his massi or his bhua, because they were just as important as his maa.

Through the narrow streets, and in between houses, Tāmas didn't slow until he reached home and went straight into his maa's arms.

"Maa," he said, catching his breath. "Another man has gone missing."

"I know, I know," she whispered to him. Every time a man entered the mountains and failed to return, it stirred up the horrid memories of Tāmas losing his father. It wasn't the fact that he was gone, Tāmas had lost fathers before, it lifetimes ago, but this life was different. Not knowing what had happened to him, or the other men, caused a deep pain within him.

Tāmas pulled away from his mother to look at her face. The wrinkles that wrapped around her eyes were filled with tears. She was never one to hide her sadness.

"It's not going to happen to me," Tāmas tried to comfort her, but his words were lost on her.

"Then don't ever go into the forest."

Her words carried weight, and instantly he felt heavy.

He nodded, wondering just how long it would be till he broke that promise.

That night, after the stars covered the sky, Tāmas pretended to be asleep. He felt his maa come in and kiss him goodnight, then tiptoe back out. Once she was gone, Tāmas pulled back the covers and sat up, listening to her movements. Quietly, he hopped out of bed and followed after her.

On the far wall of the house, there sat a home temple with lots of small candles, *diya*, and idols for the gods. She bent down and lit each of the diyas, one by one, whispering her prayers.

He had seen her do this before—a routine in her evening.

Each morning when he woke up, he smelt the smoke of the diya's being blown out.

Leaning out from behind the door frame, Tāmas made sure she didn't know he was there.

For most of the day, she hid her tears from him, but she couldn't hide the red eyes or the puffy bags. She could busy herself with chores around the room and cooking with massi and bhau, but all the distractions in the world would do nothing to ease her sadness.

She sat on the ground with her legs tucked up underneath her. Silent for far too long. "Forgive me," she whispered, "for what I must ask of you." She raised two hands above her head and closed her eyes. "I beg of you to return my husband to his rightful home," she cried. "My poor husband who has only seen the face of his son once. My dear husband that I so poorly miss."

She bowed her head before looking up again. "I ask this of you, and in return will sacrifice myself in any way of your choosing."

Tāmas covered his ears. He hated when his mother's prayers turned to self-sacrifice. *Please don't promise that,* Tāmas repeated in his mind. Turning, he slowly backed away from the door and returned to his sleeping mat. It was the only way he knew how to hold himself back from interrupting her prayers.

He lay staring at the ceiling.

Those men didn't disappear by the hand of a wicked one. He thought about the farmers, and the hunters... the men who went into the forest looking for resources and didn't come out. Then there were the stories that came after their disappearances. Tales of haunted woods, deviant evils, and wicked people.

I don't believe any of that. I don't even know how any of the villagers do. Did those men run away? Is there something in the forest that's much better than our community?

Has someone taken them hostage? Or did they just keep running?

He shook his head.

No one ever speaks about the animals.

When he'd been little, his mam had sat him on the ground while she'd hung the fabrics and beat them with a stick. It made them soft while they dried in the sun. He'd been watching her when, out of the corner of his eye, he'd seen something move.

Watching carefully, he hadn't been able to see what it was. Instead, he'd gotten up and gone towards it. Not getting far, though—his mam *had* scooped him back up and carried him inside.

But he'd needed to see, needed to find out what was in the forest. He'd fought her every step, and as she'd marched towards the house, he'd arched his neck, looking behind them.

Two beaded eyes had stared back at him.

He'd frozen.

A giant cat!

When he'd gotten older, he'd pulled Missa Jyothi aside. "Can I ask you something, Missa?"

"Anything," she'd said, bending down to one knee.

"Are there any cats in the forest?"

She'd thought about it for a moment and then shaken her head. "No, Tãmas, but there are stories of the cheetah."

Tãmas had heard of that animal before. Not in this life, but previously. Thinking hard, he'd tried to remember what their eyes would look like.

"Cheetah is very fast, and very strong."

"Yes, Missa. Is that what took all the men?"

"In this forest?" She'd tsked and shook her head again. "No, no. Men can fight cheetahs. This is the work of a bad thing. Something has hold of our men, and they will fight it until they get to come home."

Tãmas sighed.

A man could fight one, but what if there's several?

Looking back to the ceiling above him, he sighed again.

Four men remained in the village, and he was one of them.

The families with boys had left long ago. But Maa insisted that she wasn't leaving until her husband returned.

Coming of age was something all men waited for. But for Tãmas, it came with dread.

Remembering back to when he'd been in Scotland, and even before that, in Wales and England, he remembered he had once wished for it.

Back then, it had meant freedom. Breaking away from his parents' system of rules and finally being able to make his own choices.

But that had been then.

Now it meant something entirely different.

His mother's prayers had long since stopped mentioning his father; they now focused on him. She would whisper her fears into the night air as he lay awake listening. When he woke in the morning, she was already up, praying again.

The home temple grew larger each year, and now covered the entire room. He walked past quietly and snuck out the door.

"Are you leaving without saying goodbye?" his mam called after him.

He froze, shoulders up around his ears, then turned back to face her.

"Tãmas," she said, and sighed.

"Work awaits, Maa."

She clicked her tongue, kissed him on each cheek, and let him go. "Home early."

"Why?"

She tilted her head. "No questions now. You'll see when you come home." She hurried him off and he fell into a jog, all the way past the community and out to the slopes.

He worked with women who needed to repair their homes

or make them bigger. Tāmas dug into the ground and cut out mud for them to carry back to the village.

After a long day, he strolled home covered in mud, sweat, and dirt.

Maa flicked her hand in the air. "You're all dirty," she said, slapping him in the arm.

He arched his head around the corner, noticing his bhau and massi inside.

"What's going on?"

"Tāmas," she scolded. "Go clean and hurry back."

He turned towards the stream, quickly bathed, and returned to the house. By the time he reached the door, the heat of the day had dried him.

"Tāmas," Massi Jyothi said, crossing the room to embrace him.

"What's going on, Massi? Maa has not told me."

"*Brahma,*" she whispered.

Tāmas had heard of that. His eyes widened when he put two and two together. "The rite of *Brahmana?*" he whispered back, noticing a woman's laugh and giggles in the other room.

She nodded.

Without men in the community to organize marriages, the priest was called in to read horoscopes and help plan a marriage. Lost in thought, Tāmas wondered at what his mother had been up to these last few days. Now he knew.

His maa appeared at the door. "I told you to hurry," she pushed, and then reached out and grabbed him by the wrist, pulling him into the other room.

There in the middle of the room stood Rashmi. She wore bright colors and had her hair twisted down and around her face. Along her eyebrows sat beautiful gems, and she looked to him and smiled.

Oh my, he thought.

"Move, move." Maa dragged him over to stand beside

Rashmi. The priest stood from his chair and came over to hold both of their hands at once.

All the bangles and beads jingled together as Rashmi slipped her hand over his. The priest's hand was cold and clammy.

Under the priest's solid gaze, Tāmas shifted his weight from one foot to the other.

The priest's orange fabrics, layered one over the other, were decorated with patterns, symbols, and beads. He wore a twisted fabric that went around and over his head, hiding most of his white hair. His beard, long and shaggy, had grown down to the base of his stomach in the shape of a point, and he had lightly pressed a white substance to his face.

He closed his eyes and squeezed their hands.

"Spring date," he whispered.

Maa stepped forward, stretching her neck to get closer, to hear better.

The priest let go of their hands and turned to their maas. "The wedding will be held on the second Saturday of Spring."

Maa smiled. Her eyes lit up. "That's in eight weeks," she mused.

"So it is," Tāmas said, but no one took any notice of his tone. The women embraced each other and him, and he stood there watching them.

The next morning, Tāmas stood at the home temple and saw all the offerings. Brightly colored foods, carved idols, and gifts for the gods. *I cannot disappoint another mother.* He sighed.

But Ivy will show. He bowed his head. *Sooner or later, she will find her way to me, just like every other lifetime.*

He slipped out of the house before his mother woke. With all of the excitement from last night, he was well asleep before the massis and the bhaus left.

The community was quiet. The farming women were

walking towards the fields, and an elder was strolling towards the well. He stopped and coughed into a thick piece of cloth.

Tămas watched him carefully.

He heaved for air, and bent over his stick and coughed again.

Rushing over to him, Tămas reached out to hold him up. Along with Tămas, the priest, the doctor, and the elder were the last males in the community.

"Are you alright?" he asked after the man had caught his breath.

"Of course, Tămas," he said, standing up straight. "I'm alright. It's the heavy lung."

"Have you seen the doctor?"

"Yes, many times." He sighed. "But there's no more medicine since the last of the men went into the mountain and didn't return."

"There's no medicine?"

He shook his head. "Don't trouble yourself with such matters, Tămas. The doctor will find a solution." He turned away and continued his walk.

Tămas watched after him. *No medicine, no men, and no answers for anything.* He turned to face the mountain. *How long has this gone on for?*

Standing in the middle of the community, he looked up from the mountain to the mud slopes and back again. *I've done enough digging for now. The community needs the medicine more.*

Walking the long way around the edge of the community, he wanted to avoid home most. Even though his house backed onto the forest, he didn't dare let his mother see what he was up to. It was hard enough avoiding everyone else's eyes, but somehow he managed.

Past the first tree, he stopped and took a deep breath in.

The air was damp and fresh. It chilled his skin and he turned back, wondering if this was a good idea. *What if I don't return? The family is relying on me.* He breathed in and out again. *Wait.*

I'm being silly. There's nothing in this forest. It's all lies for runaway husbands.

Leaving the community behind, Tãmas spent most of the morning trekking up the mountain, up the slopes and through the forest. A white sheet of clouds hung low, touching the tips of the trees. It contrasted the dark, dense tones, hiding the sunshine.

Mist was much stronger here than in the community, and Tãmas struggled to breathe the air into his lungs. *No wonder so many get sick.* He coughed again.

Calculating his moves, Tãmas knew exactly where the roots grew that the doctor required to make the medicine. He'd overheard a conversation when he'd been younger. A group of three men had sat with the doctor and worked out the best way in and out, drawing a map on the dirt ground with a stick.

He'd wanted so much to go with those men, but his mother had forbidden it. He'd even tried to sneak out and run after them, but Massi knew him well, and had already been there waiting.

Now there was a certain skip in his step, embracing his new sense of freedom.

By the time the sun peaked high into the sky, he found the exact plant he needed.

He sighed. *I really didn't think this through.* He looked around to find a strong enough stick, or a flat stone. Something with which to dig out the plant.

After finding some strong, dry wood, Tãmas dug around the plant and tugged at its roots. Soon enough, it let go and was released into his hands.

Laughing at his accomplishment, Tãmas studied the plant.

It had thick petals that were white in the middle and red around the edges. Black and gold dots speckled the inside while its stem was thicker than his wrist. Thick layers of leaves coated the tall stem.

I've seen nothing like this before. Thinking back to all those books he'd read about medicine and plants and horticulture, he wondered if he could breed it. *I need more.* He looked around, searching for more.

The men who'd gone into the forest before had always brought back a handful of the plant's roots, letting the flower flourish in its natural habitat. But with them all gone, Tāmas thought it best to bring it all back. *That way, there's no need to come back in, and the doctor can grow it himself.*

By the time he found four plants, the sun had begun to lower.

Maa's going to wonder where I am. He sighed. *She'll know I didn't work today.* He shook his head.

Looking down at himself, seeing the rich dirt covering his clothing, he wondered if it was best to go straight home.

Strolling back down the mountain, his breaths were labored. He slowed his pace and bent over to cough. The air was thick, and sat on his chest. Heavily, he breathed in and out.

Even though he'd reached manhood, he still hadn't gotten used to the heat. He preferred the thick snow, the dull light in winters, and sitting up late by the fire to read. The heat was something else entirely.

In the distance, he heard a noise. Making his way over to it, he found a small stream trickling down the mountainside. He placed the plants to the side and laid into the stream, letting the water rush over his head and soak his body.

If only this ran closer to the house, I'd lay here every day, even in wet season.

In the water, he closed his eyes. ...*Tāmas*...

He opened his eyes and sat up slightly. "Tāmas!" Very faint, in the distance, he heard his name being called.

Standing, he stepped out of the stream and arched his neck, trying to see where the voice was coming from.

"Tāmmmaaaaassssss!"

"I'm here!" he yelled back.

Collecting up the plants, he headed towards the voice. He didn't walk more than two steps before he saw her.

"Rashmi!" He ran to her. "Are you okay? Are you hurt?"

She shook her head. "Someone saw you enter the forest, so I came looking for you."

He sucked in a breath and held it. "Does Maa know?"

"Luckily for you, it was a child. He accepted my sweets easily enough and promised not to speak."

"Why would you come in here after me?"

"I thought you needed help."

He felt paused by her reaction. *Help?* "Why would you think that?"

"I..." she hesitated. Her eyes dropped to the ground then back to him. Her arms wrapped around herself, like she needed the support. "I was wondering what you were doing in here? *Alone?*"

He held up the plants. "The doctor needs these."

She smiled and let out a large breath, like she had been holding it in all along. "You have no idea just how kind and selfless you are."

"Selfless." He thought on that. "It was the right thing to do for the community. People are unwell. The elderly cannot get over heavy lung without help. What's wrong with finding help?"

She leaned in and wrapped her arms around him. "You're going to be a wonderful husband." She pulled back and smiled.

"It's getting late," he said, and turned towards the community. He felt her eyes on him. He stopped and turned back to her. "Are you coming?"

"You don't want to marry me," she said in a small voice.

He sighed.

Pushing past him, she marched down the mountain, face reddening.

"Rashmi! It's not that I don't want to get married. I just

found out, and it's all of a sudden. My maa didn't even tell me it was happening."

She stopped and turned. "Neither did mine."

He closed the gap between them and leaned in to kiss her forehead. "I don't want to disappoint you," he whispered. "You deserve better than that."

"Disappoint? How can you say that?"

He sighed again. *If Ivy shows up, just like last time and times before that, I am sure to disappoint. There's no way around it.*

"Tāmas, if..." she trailed off.

"I will go through with it and I promise to be the best I can. But if I fail, I'm sorry."

She scrunched her eyebrows together. "You're trying to be selfless again." She shook her head. "You're such a wonderful man, it'll be me who will disappoint. Not you."

He kissed her on the forehead once again, and turned back toward the community.

Down the mountain, Tāmas parted ways with her before reaching the edge of the forest. He didn't want to be seen coming out with Rashmi, and wanted to make sure no one saw him even close to the forest.

If Maa finds out, who knows what she'll turn me into?

Heading straight to the doctor, Tāmas found him out in the garden, clipping at small plants.

"Tāmas, boy, where have you been? The community has been looking for you all day."

"I should have guessed that." He held up the plants. "I knew you needed these."

The doctor held out his hands. "Is that what I think it is?" Analyzing them closely, he gasped. "You've been in the forest, Tāmas."

He nodded.

Holding out his arms, the doctor embraced him. "Your sacrifice could save the entire village."

"Sacrifice?"

"You know the dangers of the forest," he said in a low voice.

"Sure." Tämas shrugged off the remark.

"You've found more than I'll ever need. But there is something I want you to promise me."

Leaning in, Tämas nodded.

"Don't do it again," he said firmly.

Handing the doctor the rest of the plants, so that he could press them into pots, Tämas nodded. "Of course not. That is, unless you kill those ones."

The doctor laughed. "Very well then. I'm guessing that you haven't seen your mother yet."

He shook his head. "I came straight here. What has she done now?"

The doctor tilted his head and glared. "Those are blaming words, Tämas. These are hard times for the community, and you disappear." He walked down to the end of the garden and reached for his bag. "Into the mountains, of all places."

"So you believe in the tales then?"

"Stories are designed to keep us safe. It is how we teach our children to live. Even adults need stories."

Tämas sighed.

The doctor looked Tämas up and down. "What is the alternative? You're not thinking that all of the men in our community up and left their homes, their families, all of their own free will?" He lifted an eyebrow and gazed right into Tämas.

"Not exactly. I only have a hard time believe that there are demons and omens and monsters in the mountains."

"What other possibilities are there?"

"Animals!"

"Don't snap at me, Tämas. You've been in the forest now— did you see something?"

Tāmas shook his head.

"Then you haven't got anything to say on the matter. Go home to your mother; she needs to know you're okay."

Tāmas left, his stomach rumbling. By the time he reached home, the sky was full of stars and rain had begun to drizzle.

"Maa!" Tāmas called out.

She tsked her tongue and appeared in the doorway. "Where have you been?"

"Why were you looking for me?"

"I needed to see you."

That's a lie. Not once she has come looking for me or needed to see me while I've been at work. Not once.

"What's wrong?"

"Sit, sit."

Tāmas crossed his legs next to the home temple, lighting the candles while he listened to his mother speak.

"There's word from the villages. Men are coming to live here soon."

"That's good—how many?"

"Four, I think. Or three and one elder."

"Even better. The community will benefit greatly." Tāmas turned to his mother and eyed her suspiciously. "Out with it?"

She sighed. "There's a girl."

Here we go.

His heart skipped a beat. Anything mentioning Ivy was always surrounded with tension. He had lifetimes to prove it. But this time there was something in his mother's eyes and as she looked into the candle's flame, it sparked.

"Maa?" Massi's voice was heard yelling from outside.

Maa and Tāmas exchanged looks.

"There you are!" Massi stepped through the door and scuffed his hair like he was eight years old again. "Where have *you* been?" She pointed a finger at him.

Dodging the question, he turned back to his maa. "Maa was just about to tell me something about a girl."

"It's nothing, really." Maa shrugged one shoulder.

"Not nothing," Massi snapped. "Tell him." After his maa's prolonged silence, Massi sighed. "The girl has been touched by an omen."

Tãmas froze. *Oh, how she couldn't be closer to the truth.* "Go on," he whispered.

"It's like death touched her at birth. She lacks all the color that a normal person has."

A shiver ran over him. "Is she here?"

"On their way," his maa whispered, not taking her eyes off the light.

"No, no," Massi said. "They already arrived this afternoon."

Ivy is here! She's here. Tãmas got to his feet. Maa and Massi watched him.

"It's late," Tãmas said nervously, "and I still haven't eaten." He disappeared out the door before they could stop him. He reached for the dish his mother had left aside for him and decided to eat it out beneath the stars even though the light drizzle wet his clothing.

Ivy's here and my mother is concerned. I have a bad feeling about this. He placed the weaved plate at the door and began pacing up and down along the forest's edge.

Ivy has returned to me, but I'm promised to another.

How will I be able to speak to her without offending Rashmi and my mother?

Ivy has to know she's in danger.

He stopped and looked to the sky. The rain came down heavier.

I know there's going to be trouble. I see the signs, my mother's concern. Just like my mother back in Wales, she has the same eyes! The same burden in her face!

Tãmas felt that same shiver run over his body.

Oh my. His mouth went dry. *I spoke her name.*

Heart hammering in his chest, his legs ran so fast that they blurred beneath him. *I have to find her, have to warn her. If my mother remembers that I've spoken Ivy's name before, then there isn't much time.*

He ran into the community to find the new men. *If I find them first, they should be with her. She needs to know, and they need to protect her.*

He reached the well and looked around in each direction. Mud huts running all the way up the side of the mountain felt more clustered together than ever.

Ivy! He screamed in his head. *Where are you?*

Looking in each direction, he saw an older man walk by. *A man! One I don't recognize.*

"Excuse me!" He ran towards him. "Wait!"

The man stopped and turned to Tāmas.

"Are you the man who arrived anew, with other strangers?"

"Yes. My three boys and my daughter."

"Is her name Ivy?"

His eyes widened. "How did you know that?"

"I know many things." He shook his head. "You couldn't possibly understand, but you must listen to me. Keep her safe."

The man looked Tāmas up and down. "What do you know?"

"Please believe me. Her safety is important."

"I am her father. I have always kept her safe."

"Good. Then it's best if you take her and leave."

"Are you threatening me, boy?"

He shook his head. "No, no. I would never."

"How do you know it is safer to leave? Is someone coming after her?"

"It's not that…" He held his tongue, looking around, hoping an answer would come to him. "It's… ghosts!"

"Ghosts?" The man looked around, too, trying to see what

Tãmas was seeing. "You see her maa? My wife? She warns us to protect Ivy?"

Tãmas nodded fast, his neck all stiff and rigid. "Yes, I do, and please, do what you should to keep her safe."

"Tell me more," the man said, stepping closer, but Tãmas backed away. He had already said too much.

Turning for home, Tãmas ran all the way, drowning out the old man's cries for him to return.

What have I done? he cried to himself. *Have I made things worse? Have I saved her? Have I said enough to prepare them, or am I overthinking all of this?*

He shook himself as he returned home. *Stupid. Why am I so stupid sometimes?*

"Tãmas!" his maa yelled.

"I need to sleep," he said, leaving her in the other room, heading straight for his floor mat. Tãmas laid down and, as soon as he closed his eyes, he fell into a dream.

"Tãmas," a woman's voice sang to him.

He turned around and she wasn't there.

"Tam!"

He turned back the other way, but still saw nothing. Standing in the middle of an open field, he saw a dark, heavy cloud lingering close to the ground. Rain sprinkled at first, but quickly turned to a downpour.

"Thomas!"

The wind lashed around him, carrying each name he had ever been known by.

"Where are you, Ivy?" he yelled back.

"Come!" she called, her voice barely heard against the whooshing of air.

He ran into the wind, the ground moving beneath him. One foot sprinted out in front of the other, and then he immediately stopped before he fell over a sudden edge.

Backing away, he saw the green field had a cliff. He fell backwards onto his back, heart stammering in his chest as he twisted around and crawled back to the edge.

"Ivy!" he screamed. "Ivy, are you down there?"

"No," she whispered back.

He got up and walked further along, trying to see what was down there, but the clouds were too thick and distorted the view below.

"This doesn't make sense!" he yelled. "Where are you?"

He looked back into the field, noticing that all along the edge was a cliff.

"I'm here."

"Where?"

"Open your eyes."

He blinked, then closed them and opened them again.

He spun around, seeing the green field, the never-ending cliff's edge, but still no Ivy.

"Open your eyes!" his mother snapped.

Tāmas sat up on his floor mat, his mother clutching at his clothes. "Did you sleep all night in wet clothes?"

Shivering, he got to his feet. "Doesn't matter."

"It does. You nearly slept all day."

He stretched his arms and went into the other room. The home temple had seemed to grow even further, and a small dish of vegetables and rice sat waiting for Tāmas.

"You woke me early," he said, pinching the greens with his two fingers and placing them into his mouth.

"Early is better than late."

He eyed her suspiciously.

"The mud will be soft today. Heavy rain all night."

He hummed to agree, finishing the last of the food. "Stay inside today, Maa. The water in the air isn't good for your chest."

She clicked her tongue at him again, then shooed him

towards the door. "My grown man, time for work." She pushed him out the house.

He stood for a moment and glared over his shoulder. Running his tongue across his teeth, to make sure he didn't have food stuck there, he made his way down to the community, towards the slopes.

Mam had been right; the mud was much softer and easier to dig out. He worked for many hours, until the first of the women showed up to take the bricks.

By high sun, bhua came into his sight.

"Tāmas," she said, holding out her arms.

He leaned in to embrace her, but she backed away. "No, no. There's no need to put mud all down my dress. You'll ruin the colors."

"Are you here for bricks?"

"No, the doctor wanted me to find you. He needs you to do something for him."

"Of course, what is it?"

"He needs to you go to Yukhsom and get medicine for Pallavi's baby."

"Pallavi?" He had known her when they'd been growing up. Unaware that she was with child, his heart grew heavy to know the baby was unwell.

"You remember her?"

He nodded. "When do I go?"

"Now. The child might not live through the night."

"But Yukhsom is two days' walk!"

"Take the donkey, Tāmas—it'll help with the trip."

He kissed his bhua on the cheek and, without washing his hands or bathing, ran towards the fenced field.

Clicking his tongue, he called out until the donkey ran straight to him. "Come on, boy, we're going for a long walk."

He scuffed the animal's mane, then threw up and over his leg, softly giving him a tap to go.

. . .

Going down the mountain, Tămas got off the donkey and walked beside him. The terrain was steep and the donkey's hooves often slipped.

The further they got down the mountain, the fiercer Tămas's muscles burned. His mouth had dried and he didn't know where the closest river or stream was.

The donkey threw up his nose, making a *heehawk sound* to stop. "We've got to keep going, boy. The baby needs medicine."

Tămas froze.

"Baby?" *Baby!* He turned and looked back up the mountain. The trees had hidden the community, and if it hadn't been for the farmers clearing the forest for the fields, he wouldn't have been able to see it.

"How could I have been so stupid!" he said to the donkey as he turned it around. "There's no baby. They've sent me out of town! I would have known if there were a new baby! Because there are no men. I'm the last of the men and the only one about to marry."

The donkey kicked up his leg and slammed it into the ground, just missing Tămas's foot by an inch.

Tămas let him go and began to run up the mountain. The donkey followed behind.

Bhau! He cursed. *How could you? You're family and you tricked me.*

The humidity was too thick and his breaths instantly became labored. The donkey behind him slowed their pace, but still they continued to climb upward. The mountain got steeper, but that wasn't going to hold him back. The pain in his legs was nothing compared to what Ivy had gone through in their last lives. He never wanted to see it happen again.

"Tămas!" a man's voice screamed from above.

He stopped running and glared.

"Tămas, hurry!"

Running faster than before, Tămas saw the old man from the

night before. Heading straight to him, he grabbed hold of his shoulders.

"You were right—they have my daughter."

"Where?"

"They took her and I couldn't keep up. I lost them!" he cried.

Tãmas left him there and ran back towards the community. Not a single person was around. He ran into homes, into gardens, and out into the fields.

No one.

He gasped.

The doctor! Running straight to the garden, knowing he would be there, Tãmas screamed upon finding him gone, too.

Bending over to catch his breath, to gather his thoughts, to figure out what to do, he wondered what his maa would have done.

Taken her into the forest.

He thought back.

Never go into the forest, Tãmas. Her words rang through his mind. *But I saw you, Mam, leaving the forest,* he had said to her. *No, child, you saw wrong.*

He stood up straight.

"I know where they are!" He ran back out of the doctor's garden and up past his home. Straight through the dense bushes, he jumped over logs, around thick trees, and side-stepped bushes.

He felt movement around him, knowing he had captured the attention of the fast animals nearby.

Looking up, he saw birds flying in the opposite direction, zooming past him to get out of the area.

"*Maa!*" he yelled as his feet blurred beneath him.

Up ahead, he saw the bright colors of the women's dresses. He reached them and found the community gathered together.

"My son, of course you have come." Maa came to his side and held onto his arm.

He brushed her off and pushed through the crowd. "What have you done?" He stepped forward and saw Ivy tied to a tree, swollen black and blue. A young man resembling Ivy's father, stood at her side, while two others were dead at her feet.

"Tāmas, you should be heading to Yukhsom, getting medicine," Bhua said.

Closing the gap between them, Tāmas reached up and ran a hand over her face. *She's dead.*

His insides were nothing but hollow.

Pressing a hand to her face, he closed his eyes.

"You did this to her?" he whispered.

"Step away now," Maa ordered.

Ivy's eyelids flickered opened. Her cracked and bleeding lips moved slightly.

"Ivy?" he asked.

"So you do know this girl?" Rashmi asked, stepping forward but still keeping her distance.

"No," Tāmas said, unable to take his eyes off of Ivy. "But how could you do this to her?"

"It was what needed to be done," his maa said.

He turned to her then. "You did this?" He stepped closer to her. "You murder an innocent girl because she has no color!"

His maa squinted her eyes. She took a step forward and latched onto him, digging her nails into his skin.

"Your father went into the forest and disappeared. All the men of this community went into the forest and disappeared! You woke screaming as a child and said a name! Her name!" She pointed straight at Ivy. "You are the last man, Tāmas, and the day you went into the forest was the day she came."

He turned, looking over his shoulder, and saw her lips move. *If I can get these people out of here now, if I can calm my mother down and show her how wrong she is, then I still have time to save her. I can get her out of here.*

He looked back to his maa. "This isn't you," he said calmly. "And we still have time to make things right."

"I've been waiting for your father your entire life. He's gone." Tears swelled in her eyes.

"There are animals in the forests. Large ones; massive cats. I've seen them. They can work together to bring down many men at a time. Why have you never thought of that?"

She shook her head. "Why do you defend her?"

Rashmi stepped forward. "I want to know the answer to that, too."

Tãmas froze. He'd known this was going to happen. *I wish her father had listened to me now. Why didn't he take her and leave?*

"This is not right." He faced Rashmi. "I would defend you. Or you," he said, pointing to others standing around and listening. "Who is she?" He shrugged. "Just a girl that you all have attempted to murder."

He crossed the space between them.

"Wait, Tãmas!" his maa yelled.

He stopped and turned to face her. "*No.*"

"No!" she stepped back. "You defy me, your own mother. I am your flesh and blood, and she is the curse that has plagued us all."

"Curse?" He shook his head. *They have no idea what a curse is.*

"With her death." His maa raised her voice so that all who stood around them could hear. "With her death, we will free the men from the forest."

His maa picked up a large rock from her feet. Rashmi did the same.

Tãmas held up his hands out wide, stepping back. "Stop—this isn't right! She's just a girl."

"You knew the omen, Tãmas. You have said the words yourself, even as a child!"

He shook his head, standing in front of Ivy to protect her.

"Tãmas!" Rashmi said, holding out her hand for him to come

to her. "Come, let's leave here together."

He looked her up and down, then eyed Ivy from over his shoulder.

"Help me," she whispered, her voice crackling.

"I won't let you do this to her. I will stop you all—" Tămas lost his words.

First, the noise rattled in his ears, and then his knees wobbled. As he fell downwards, he realized that someone had hit him on the back of the head. The ground came up to meet him. Slowly, his eyes fluttered.

He opened his eyes. The first thing he saw was Ivy's dirty feet, bound and limp, blood spiraling down the top of her feet, dripping off the toes.

He blinked slowly, looking up at her.

Rocks, large and solid, pelted her body. She moved ever so slightly as each one hit.

Then she didn't move at all.

Her right eye hung open, the left one swollen shut. Looking into them, Tămas could tell that she had left him behind.

A rock larger than a goat's head slammed into Ivy's stomach and fell straight on top of Tămas' head.

Darkness was a gift.

GERMANY

1829

*D*eep in the mountains of Germany, Mr. and Mrs. Jagar had welcomed their third child just as morning had broken. Mrs. Jagar had needed the sleep, so the midwives left the baby in the arms of the *vater*, surrounded by the two older children who couldn't help but poke and tug at the baby's ear.

"What ya'l call it, Papa?" little Martha asked.

"Him!"

"Him?" The boy's face twisted in confusion. "You cannot call it *him*."

"Their vater let out a big belly laugh and the children stood watching their vater closely, unable to see the funny side.

"Children?" their *mutter* called out, and they trotted into her bedroom.

"Stop calling the baby *it*, Junior," their vater muttered as he followed them in.

"Well, I'm not going to call it *him*. What a silly name!"

"*Him?*" Mutter tilted her head in confusion, exactly as the children had done.

Vater rolled his eyes. "The baby is not called *it*, or *him*, or

173

anything else for that matter." He held out the baby to his tired wife and she snuggled the sleeping *junge* against her chest.

"Have you not chosen a name then?" she asked.

"What with these two chattering away in my ears, I haven't had two moments of peace! How do you put up with these rascals all day?" He gently tugged on Junior's ear.

Both children pounced on top of their vater, pushing him towards the end of the bed.

"Thomas," their father finally said.

"Ah, that's lovely, dear."

"Isn't that *Opa*'s name?" Martha straightened her back, expecting an immediate answer.

Both her mutter and vater nodded.

"Can I call him 'Tommi'?" Junior asked.

Mutter's eyebrows bunched, showing she wasn't keen. But from that moment onwards, the baby was never called Thomas.

It wasn't long after Tommi's birth that Mutter and Vater welcomed a set of twins. Twins were a handful in their own right, but these two were particularly troublesome. Vater had a separate room downstairs to conduct his business. With people coming and going, the twins kept their mutter upstairs pulling her hair out.

Junior and Martha often remained in the garden during the summer months, and when the snow fell to the ground, they sat silently at their vater's feet, beside the fire reading any material their vater could get his hands on. But no matter how many hours they remained studying, they couldn't keep up with Tommi.

"Born one and thirty, that child," his mutter said every time he did something not of his age. "To think, he's only eight, but it's like speaking to an adult stuck in a child's body." She shook her head, then looked at the twins ripping pages out of old books.

Tommi often remained quiet, but that was because there was too much noise already in the house. Down the road, there was another family in a house of the same size as theirs. Those children were always polite and kind, and never spoke unless spoken to. Tommi didn't like that. He doubted he'd have been allowed to read if he'd been born into that family. But he did enjoy the quiet there.

"Tommi?" Vater yelled from the other room.

Tommi walked into the office and saw an older gentleman sitting on the visitor's seat.

"Close the door, Tommi."

Tommi had never been allowed in his vater's office while he worked with customers. He closed the door and walked over to the other visitor's chair, standing beside it.

The man had white hair with a crowning bald patch on top.

"Good evening, Tommi. I am Doctor Ernest Von Krebs." The doctor extended his hand for Tommi to shake.

Tommi took his hand and shook it like he was supposed to. "It's a pleasure, Doctor."

The doctor sat back in his chair and laughed.

As much as Tommi tried, he struggled to be a normal child. And even though he understood he was different, he knew there was one thing he should never do.

Never speak Ivy's name.

He shivered at the thought.

"What would you like to be when you grow up?" The doctor asked.

Tommi looked to his vater. Selling insurance wasn't appealing. He saw his older brother following in his vater's footsteps, too, so that gave him wriggle room to branch out. But he still didn't want to upset his vater.

"I like reading about the healing practices, and how plants help fix ailments."

"Yes, very good. Do you know what that profession is called?"

"Healer."

"Close. How about a doctor?"

Tommi thought about it. He understood that the history books were wrong. He'd lived through the earlier times to see exactly what the writers had made up. Dabbling in doctors' medical books, he'd wondered just how much they'd made up to create a fuller body of knowledge. He questioned everything now.

"Is that something you would like to be?"

"If I can learn something, and share that knowledge so that other people can learn, too, then yes. I'd like to be a doctor."

"Very good. Is learning something you like to do."

He nodded. "But sometimes," he hesitated, "the books seem to—"

Doctor Krebs laughed. "Disagree?"

"Yes, and then it's hard to understand."

"Think of it as a conversation, Tommi. Sometimes, those conversations turn into arguments." He smiled. "It is very impressive that you can see that at your age."

Tommi turned back to his vater.

"Go and play now," Vater said, smiling.

He got up, shook Doctor Kreb's hand, and left the room. On the other side of the door, Tommi pressed his ear to the door and listened in. His vater used a low voice, most likely suspecting he was there listening.

He sighed, unable to hear the conversation.

Later that night at the dinner table, his mutter cried. "He's too young," she said, taking her napkin to wipe away her tears.

"What is she talking about, Papa?" Martha asked.

Vater inhaled deeply, puffing out his chest, and looked to each of his children before finally resting his eyes on Tommi.

"Tommi," he said in a slow voice, "that doctor has offered you an apprenticeship."

"To become a doctor?" Junior asked.

"Yes," Vater said. "He's been looking for someone to pass on his knowledge to, and while he was in town, our own doctor told him how advance Tommi is in his education."

"I'm a good reader," Martha added.

Tommi smiled at her.

Vater nodded. "It'll require a lot of travelling around Germany, Tommi."

The doctor's words from earlier in the day ran through his mind like an echo. *"And visiting patients that local doctors can no longer treat."*

They need my help. He looked to vater, then his mutter, and back to his dinner plate. *This is my time to go out into the world and help those who need me.*

He sighed.

But my family needs me, too. Tears formed in his eyes, but he pinched the bridge of his nose to try and hold them back.

Mutter burst into tears again, covering her face with both hands.

Vater stood and went to her side, squeezing her by the shoulders.

"When do I leave?" Tommi asked in a small voice, not wanting to upset them any further.

"Are you sure this *is* what you want?" Vater asked.

Tommi nodded slowly, then went to his mother's side and cuddled into her. "Think of all the people I can heal." He smiled. "And I promise I'll write all the time and I'll come home again, sometime in the future."

I wish I didn't promise that.

Her eyes lit up. "Really?" With trembling lips, she gave him a hopeful smile. He just hoped he could fulfil the promise.

"Yes, really, really." The lie tasted bitter on his tongue.

"You better write to me, too, Tommi." His sister pouted.

"Of course." He smiled.

Several days later, Tommi folded what little clothing he owned and tied it with string. He walked down the staircase holding it in his hands just like a package.

"Do you not have a bag, Tommi?" the doctor asked.

Tommi shook his head.

"Fair enough. You can have one of mine."

Tommi handed the doctor his clothing and watched him disappear out the door, letting Tommi have a moment to say his goodbyes.

"Come home whenever you can," his mutter said, trying desperately to hold back her tears. She failed miserably as the red rings around her eyes glowed darker, but Tommi knew that, the moment he left, she'd cry for days.

"Of course, Mama."

"Make your Papa proud son." His vater stood tall behind the family, pretending to be strong.

Tommi pushed through his siblings, reaching for him. He wrapped his arms around the man and squeezed him tight.

"Make sure you write to me. I want to know all the things that are happening here."

Tommi hugged each of his siblings and walked out of the house.

The carriage waiting for him was nothing like the ones he had seen go by in the past. They'd had open tops or thick fabrics held up by strong poles. This one was made of wood that had been shined so much it glowed. A little window on the door had a curtain hung inside, and there were two extra-large wheels on the back, two smaller ones at the front.

As Tommi walked down the pathway and got closer, it was like the carriage got bigger.

Two draft horses were ready to go, and the horseman tipped the top of his hat and gave Tommi a nod.

The doctor opened the wooden door and pointed to the metal step that hung low. Tommi slipped his foot onto the step, held the sides of the door, and hoisted himself up.

Inside the carriage were two bench seats covered with stacks of books. He stepped through the narrow space, maneuvering around several bags on the floor. On the left side, facing forwards, there was a large gap. On the right, a small gap just big enough for Tommi to sit in.

At least it's next to a window.

As he sat, he noticed just how many bags the doctor owned. They crowded his feet, giving him a sense of being caged in.

The stacks of books lined the walls. Tommi ran his eyes over them. He had always wanted to collect so many books.

"Wave goodbye to your family, Tommi."

Tommi pulled back the curtain and stuck his arm out. Martha and Junior ran down the road, chasing after him. *I'll miss you*, he thought, unable to say the words out loud.

He sat back in the seat and closed the curtain. He closed his eyes, unable to look back. Seeing his parents standing at the door, watching after him, had put a dull ache right in the middle of his heart.

Why do I always have to hurt my family? Each life, he'd had a new and wonderful family, but an empty place in his heart for those who he'd loved previously. He'd let them down and was then left to remember, unable to go back and change anything.

He pulled the curtain back again, needing the fresh air.

Leaving is the right thing to do.

Biting down on his nails, he thought of reasons why.

I need to do the right thing this time and I'm going out into the world to do it. I need to be away from my family, away from people I hurt the most.

Flashes of his maa back in India crossed his mind. He bit down on his nails even harder.

If I'm not home, then I can't upset another mother.

"Leaving home is hard, Tommi," the doctor said, breaking the silence between them.

"Yes, Doctor Kreb," he said in a small voice.

"Please, just call me Doc, just like Asher does."

Tommi nodded. "Who is Asher?"

"The coachman." Doc winked and then returned to his book, laying it across his lap.

The carriage wasn't fast, but it felt like it flew past his hometown. As the brick road ended and turned into a dirt track, the *clickity-clop* of the horses' hooves quieted, kicking dust up into the air.

"And you are..." he hesitated. The thinking wore on his face. "Eight?" Doc asked.

"Yes, sir." Tommi didn't pull away from the window. He hadn't been this far out of town before, and wondered whether he'd ever return.

I promised, though.

His head felt full. A cloud in his mind grew bigger, causing a ringing in his ears. The new heaviness put weight on his neck, cramping up the left side.

I haven't kept a single one of my promises. Not in India or Scotland. Flashes of *Màthair* and the tall building he'd left her in crossed his mind. The dull heartache grew wider across his chest. *And in Wales!* His *Mam* and her face as she'd stood on the edge of that cliff, with the high winds lashing against her pale skin, that torment in her eyes. *And in England.* He sighed. *The worst of them all. A promise I didn't even get to tell Ivy. My Ivy! And she still doesn't know.*

The ache spread across the rest of his torso, tightening his muscles.

He breathed in and held it.

"I'm going to keep a log book." Doc's words snapped Tommi out of thought.

He looked up and saw Doc balancing a small inkpot between his knees and a clean book across his lap. In between his hand and the page was a thin cloth. As Doc moved his quill across the page, the cloth stayed with his hand, protecting the page.

I'll write to Papa and suggest he do the same. He sighed at the thought of the gentle man. All too often, Tommi had stayed up late, helping him fill out his books.

"What is the log book for?" he asked.

"To keep track of all the things you've learnt. That way, I'll know not to repeat myself and force us both into madness."

Tommi laughed. "Very well." It was a good idea, but Tommi couldn't have sounded more deflated.

He pressed his head back against the wall and looked out to the luscious greenery and rolling landscape. If the dark green trees hadn't clouded the sights, they would have been vibrant green rolling hills.

Breathing in, he felt a touch of winter in the air. He enjoyed the snow, but wondered how he was going to cope on the road.

As he got lost in thought, the carriage began to slow. Poking his head out the window, Tommi saw a family on foot up ahead, pushing a wagon towards town. They stepped off to the side and let Doc's carriage through.

Three older people walked ahead while a young girl with a woven basket on her back walked behind them.

Tommi locked eyes with her.

Round, jaded eyes looked back at Tommi.

A shiver ran through him, shattering the ache in his chest.

He stared at her and she stopped walking to stare back.

I know her! He breathed, trying to think, trying to understand. *Rashmi! It's Rashmi, my promised one.* His mouth hung open. *Is she coming for me, too? Is she trying to find me, as well?*

The carriage continued on and he stuck his head out further so he didn't lose eye contact.

Have I done the right thing by leaving? Am I supposed to be on the road?

She faded out of view, but Tommi could still see her outline staring after him.

He sat back down and felt the weight of his decision. *Why is Rashmi coming into town? If she's coming back for a second chance, maybe I am meant to marry her.*

All the thinking hurt his little head.

His body wasn't ready for this. He was still just a child, after all. *Only in body.* He sighed. *Not in spirit and certainly not in mind.*

"It's a long journey to the next town," Doc said. He leaned over and held out a book. "And there's only so many hours before we lose the light."

Tommi nodded and opened the cover. He settled into the thick lines, trying to turn off his mind and relax into the information in front of him.

Tommi grew fast, but his reading progressed faster. He had read every book that Doc owned soon enough, then catalogued the entire carriage into a logical order, swapping those that weren't needed for newer books.

"I don't know how you do it," Doc said.

"Do what?"

"Retain all that information."

"Well, how do you do it?"

"I don't. I read and re-read the same book. I understand the concepts, and I can apply them just like any doctor, but you, Tommi, you retain the arguments by exact author, and the counter-arguments, too, and you see what information all the writers are missing."

"Is that a bad thing?"

"No, not bad." He sipped his water. "Bloody amazing."

Tommi sat back and smirked. Even though he felt he'd learnt a lot, he knew he still had so much more to learn.

Traveling from one town to another, Tommi and Doc gained quite a reputation. They received letters at each post, asking or begging for their assistance. People who were desperate for help turned to them when their local doctors continued to fail, or when unknown diseases occurred. All too often, people offered up their life's savings, but Doc always refused. He only needed enough for a full stomach and to keep the horses healthy. That's why Tommi never left his side. There wasn't a better doctor out there.

Late one night, Tommi sat in his room listening to the tavern below. He had burnt through three candles, and had a fourth waiting.

Sleep, he mused, *is for the dead*. He sighed, wishing it were true, but the last several weeks, sleep had been torture.

He'd wake clutching at his mouth, trying to hold back a scream. Sipping boiled valerian root to relax himself; getting blind drunk to distract himself. Even sleeping by day and remaining awake at night so that the sunshine sent him nice dreams. But that didn't work, either.

There were no remedies for nightmares that had stained the soul.

He was on his last idea.

Sleep deprivation.

Can't have nightmares if I don't sleep at all.

He laughed, manically, clutching at his sides as he lost his resolve.

A *bang* on the wall from the next room quickly quieted him down. And he pulled the flask from his bedside table and sipped from it.

He got up then, paced the room, and decided to risk the cold night air. By the time he returned to his room, he collapsed by the fire, heating the tip of his bright red nose.

"Get up, *junge*."

Tommi moaned. A foot in his side hit him hard, forcing him to roll onto his back. He moaned again. Cracking an eyelid open slightly, he looked up and saw the coachman leaning over him.

"Go away, Asher."

"Breakfast, junge."

"No breakfast. Go away. Let me die."

"Was that you making all that racket last night? Woke me too many times." He stepped over Tommi and took a poker, stabbing at the logs in the fireplace. "If ya don't get up, junge, I'll brand ya in the arse."

Tommi sighed. He widened his tired, dried eyes and pushed himself up into sitting position. Giving Asher a glare through his eyebrows, he watched as the coachman extended his hand to help him to his feet.

"Doctor's waiting now."

"Fine," he said, aiming for the door. "And you stink worse than the pigs."

Tommi laughed. "The whisky will do that."

Down in the tavern, Doc picked at his food.

Tommi slipped into the seat across from him and sank his face into his hands.

"Long night?"

"Even kept me up," Asher said as he sat beside Tommi.

"These nightmares need to stop," Tommi mumbled.

"Perhaps we should discuss them," Doc said, putting down his paper.

"No!" Tommi snapped. "No need—they'll go away on their

own." They never had previously, but he had learned to live with them.

But I didn't have a single one until now. He looked at his plate. Eggs, bread, and mushrooms. *Why have they started now?*

"What's the date?" Tommi asked, pushing the yolk to the side.

"March 9th." Doc sat up straight. "Happy *geburtstag*, Tommi."

Asher clutched Tommi's shoulder and shook him gently.

"*Dankeschön.*"

A shiver ran over his body. *Another thing! My birthday. Ten and seven again.* The air caught in his throat. *It's not the place that matters, it's the time. How didn't I realize that this was going to occur? Ivy's close.*

"Where are we headed now?"

"Coswig."

"Coswig? Coswig," Tommi mumbled under his breath. "Why does that sound familiar?"

"Most likely because we've been receiving letters from the local doctor and half of the community for nearly six years."

Tommi shook his head.

Asher leaned in. "Railway."

"Oh!" Sitting up straight, he smiled. "Perhaps we could ride the train."

Doc rolled his eyes. "You both look like children."

Tommi smiled wider, and Asher did the same.

"Fine." Doc returned to his paper. "But *after* we treat the patient."

The road to Coswig was long. The wind rocked the carriage, blew out the candles, and knocked books off the top of their stacks, scattering them across the floor.

"Arh," Tommi moaned. "This wind is going to disturb my catalogue."

"Never mind that. How am I going to read without candlelight?"

Tommi shook his head. In all their travels, wind came and went. But it was like this one was following them across Germany.

"We should have come sooner," Doc said, having lowered his voice.

"Perhaps," Tommi answered as he picked up the books and replaced them in the correct order. "But we saw as many patients as we could while on our way."

"Too many people need our help."

"Yes, it's a shame that we cannot see them all."

"Perhaps I should open a school."

"For doctors? There are already schools for that."

"Yes, but with the knowledge you and I have gained, we could help those doctors understand more."

Tommi sighed. "It's a good idea."

"You're lying."

"I'm tired, and going to use this opportunity to close my eyes."

Doc returned to the curtain, trying to clip it closed. Daylight was for reading, night for sleeping. He had drilled that into Tommi's head more than anything. But Tommi still favored naps. It helped him read faster in the afternoon.

Before he knew it, he was fast asleep.

Crackling. Popping. Hissing.

The smell of wood, crisping before ignition.

Tommi ran through the woods, looking for the sun.

"Why is it so dark?" he yelled out, but to who?

He stopped and turned.

"Where has the sun gone?" He twisted in each way. "Why is it so dark?"

The sky was black. There were no stars. There were no lights.

The sounds of heat echoed in his mind.

The wind whipped around him, carrying with it an utterance of a whimper.

"Ivy!" he said, still looking into the darkness, trying to find her. "Ivy!"

Tommi sat up, Doc was in his face.

"What's wrong with you?"

Pushing him off, Tommi fell from his seat and landed on the floor. Several books poked him in the back.

"You didn't catch anything back at that town, did you?"

Tommi pushed open the door, leaned out, and was sick all over the ground. It tasted like burnt coals and smelled just as strong up his nose. "Nightmares," he said, leaning back in and wiping his mouth with his sleeve.

"That's contagious?"

"You better hope not."

Doc laughed.

He pushed himself back up onto the bench seat and leaned into the pile of books for support. *What was that dream?*

He shook his head, not wanting to bring on another.

Was it a warning? Am I the one causing the curse? He hated that it existed. *I plan each life to do good, to help others, to break Ivy from the curse, but why? Oh, why? Does she suffer. Why can't I save her? Why do I end up causing her death?*

He breathed in and out.

This isn't fair!

He wanted to scream at the world. To curse all the profanities he could think of in every single language. He wanted to go to sleep and never wake again.

As soon as he closed his eyes, Ivy's face flashed across his mind again.

Shoving the door open once more, he lost what remained from his stomach.

. . .

Tommi rode up top with Asher for the afternoon. The wind was easier to put up with when books didn't open and close, the curtain didn't unclip itself and hit him in the face, and he couldn't hear Doc cursing every couple of minutes.

The sun peaked out from behind the fluffy clouds and warmed his dry skin. When the clouds covered it again, the wind felt much colder.

"How much further do you think town is?"

"Hard to say." Asher was a man of few words, but out on the road, he did sing a loud song.

Tommi sighed. "Do you ever get bored up here?"

"Bored?" He shook his head. "Look at the places we've seen. Every day is different. How you both sit inside the carriage with the curtains drawn, ah, that would make me bored."

"Really? But we read."

"Arh, not for me. The three of us do important work, but I have no need for the books."

Tommi paused. He'd never thought of Asher as being just as important as Doc and himself, but after a moment he realized something. *Without Asher, we wouldn't have reached the patients who needed us the most.*

"Do ya hear that?"

Tommi cocked his head slightly to the west.

Asher pulled the reins, causing the horses to come to a stop.

"Have we arrived?" Doc yelled out.

An aaawhhhooooooo sound was carried in the wind.

"What is that?"

"You hear it, too?" Asher stood up and looked in the direction he thought it was coming from.

"If we're not there, why have we stopped!" Doc slammed open the door and climbed out. "What's that noise?" he asked, looking about.

"It's like a kettle noise?" Asher suggested.

"But in the sky?" Tommi said. They all looked up, searching.

Hoooooooo.

"Is it coming closer?" Doc asked.

"Wait! I know what it is!" Tommi waved his hand for Doc to get back into the carriage. "It's the steam train!"

Asher gasped and flicked the reins. The horses lunged forward.

"Wait!" Doc screamed.

Asher halted the horses once more.

Doc climbed up to join the others as Asher flicked the reins.

The horses raced along the track, shaking the carriage violently. Tommi could hear the books falling inside the carriage and Doc yelled at Asher to slow down.

Asher looked to Tommi, who shook his head. "We've got to see this train."

"There will be another train! They come back and forth!"

Asher's smile widened.

The road seemed to widen as they got closer to Coswig, but there was no sight of the train. Asher slowed the horses to a steady trot to stop Doc from complaining. If Tommi had had the reins, he'd have been screaming all the way.

The carriage climbed up and over a hill, and just as they reached the crest, Coswig came into view. The town was small, but there were plenty of people about. Buildings were clustered together, and more were being built at different stages.

Asher knocked on the top of the carriage. Doc poked his head out the window. "That can't be Coswig!" he moaned.

"Why not?" Tommi cocked his head.

"Last time we were here, there was a church and a stable."

"And a pub," Asher added.

"I don't remember this place," Tommi said.

"Well before you joined us, Tommi." Doc said, getting back into the carriage.

Tommi leaned into Asher's side. "I don't see any train."

"What does a train look like?"

Tommi shrugged. "I guess if it makes that sound, we'll know we've found it."

They rolled into town and Tommi asked the first person he saw about the train.

"Already left," he said, holding his hat to his chest.

"When will it be back?"

"It'll be back in one week."

"A week!" Tommi shook his head.

Tommi turned to Doc. "Looks like we're staying a week."

The man sighed. "No, we're not. Three days maximum. Go get us a room, Tommi. Fix the horses, Asher. Oh, and, Tommi!"

"Yes?" He paused and turned.

"Don't tell them we're staying a week."

The following morning, Tommi was up and ready. "Have you got everything?"

"Yes, Tommi."

The carriage headed out of town, into nearby farming land, and stopped outside a cottage.

"Are we in the flattest part of Germany?" Tommi opened the door and stepped out.

"Seems like it," Doc said, leaning out and handing Tommi the medicine bags.

"I like the mountainside," Asher said, helping with the bags.

"There really is something magical about the mountains," Tommi said.

"Magic!" Doc shook his head. "Don't start with all that again."

"Come on, Doc," Tommi said, picking up the bags and falling into stride beside him. "You can feel it when we're there."

"Stop. Please stop it right now."

Tommi nodded as he ignored Asher's laughter behind him. They walked to the door and knocked. Within moments, the door opened and a man looked both Tommi and Doc over.

"Thank you for coming, Doctor."

"We are sorry that it's taken us this long to get here."

"Please come in." He held open the door. "My daughter is sleeping, but I can wake her."

"No, don't bother." Doc placed his bags on the floor and took out items to place on the table. "There's things we can discuss first before there's any need to wake her."

Tommi looked around the room. Crocheted blankets covered an armchair. A cross-stitch hung on the wall. He also noticed a clean fireplace with the door wide open, and windows letting in the summer breeze.

He breathed in the air and felt the peace in this home. They didn't have much, but it was perfect.

"What do you do for trade?"

"I work the cows, sir."

"And your wife?" Doc asked.

"Forgive me," he said slowly. "She passed after childbirth."

"My apologies. Tell me about your daughter."

"She's been sick since birth, and the local doctor doesn't know why. She's sixteen and can't get out of bed."

"And treatments?"

"Local doc did everything he could; even wrote to all the other doctors in the country asking for help."

"Yes, we received earlier letters," Tommi said. "But it was difficult to determine what to think when the doctor wasn't sure himself. That's why, on your letter, we came."

"Thank you," he said. "I worry, though… she's very sick."

Doc turned to Tommi and nodded. "Please show me where she is so I can examine her. Tommi here will have some more questions."

"First door on your left." The man pointed down the corridor.

Doc disappeared, leaving Tommi alone with her vater. The *man* watched after him, shifting his weight from one foot to the other.

"Doctor Krebs is a good man," Tommi said. "He will do an examination, and then I'll go and do mine. Then we will discuss our findings together and come up with a plan."

The vater wiped a tear from his eye. "I'm grateful that you've come, I am, truly grateful."

"Is there anything else you can tell me? What she doesn't eat? Things that make her even more sick?"

The vater shook his head. Then, instantly, he was on his feet. "There is something." He disappeared into another room and was gone for just a short while. On returning, he came back in with his hands full of little pieces of paper.

Laying them out onto the table, he sat back down and began flattening them out.

Tommi picked one up and read it.

"I don't do the letters or the paper numbers," the vater said. "But each time Doc came, he gave me one of these. Said it was important that I had a record of why he came, just in case we needed other doctors."

"That's a good idea," Tommi said, trying to squint his eyes and read the tiny little words squashed one line above another. "But why is the paper so small?"

"The doctor can't afford lots of paper," he said. "It comes from the other side of the country."

"Well, there's a good business if you wanted one," Tommi said.

"No, sir, the cows need me."

Doc came into the room then and nodded for Tommi to do his assessment.

"Sir," Tommi said. "Do you mind if I take these notes and read them tonight?"

"No, of course, please take them. They're no use to me when I don't know letters and paper numbers."

"Very good of you." Tommi collected them up, placed them into his bag, and turned for the corridor. On the left-hand side, the door had been left wide open.

He stepped through and saw a four-poster bed with long white sheets draped down, covering his view of the patient.

Even with the window wide open and letting in the freshness of spring, the smell of sickness was thick. *Cancer.*

He turned his back to the bed and placed his bag on the dresser. Opening it and pulling out little vials and bottles of ointments, he listened carefully to her labored breaths.

He pulled two brown onions from his bag, cut them in half, and set each piece in a separate corner of the room. Although he'd only read one of the many notes, something had sparked his interest and he wanted to test how fresh the air really was.

Returning to his bag, he pulled out his notebook and quill, and opened the inkpot.

"You were always so serious," she whispered.

Tommi froze, his shoulders rigid and stiff. It was like her voice danced around him, causing all the little hairs on the back of his arms to stand up.

Slowly, he turned and took in her face.

Round yet drawn out, she looked like a piece of straw.

Ivy.

He gasped. She had been suffering for a great length of time.

"I've been wondering when you'd show up," she said with her labored breaths.

He cocked his head to the side. "You've been waiting?"

"Much longer than I would have liked." A half-teasing smile pulled at the corner of her mouth.

Taking a step closer to her, he stopped again. "Waiting for me?" He pointed to his chest. "Or for the doctor?"

She smiled again. "You, Thomas." The sound of her voice saying his name sent tingles all over his body. "I've been waiting for you for many lives."

Closing the distance between them, he stood looking down at her, melting into her eyes.

She reached for his hand. He retracted his own, however, scared to touch her.

"It's okay," she said. "I'm not contagious."

He took a deep breath and sat down on the edge of the bed. "No, it's not that." He swallowed his pride and wrapped both his hands around hers. "You remember," he whispered.

She nodded. "I'm sorry for what I have done. I can see all the pain I have caused you." She paused. "...And the world," she whispered.

"You have caused?" He shook his head and squeezed her hand tighter. "How can you say that? You were put to death so young! Each and every time." He breathed in and then back out, trying to calm himself. "I'm the one that couldn't save you. I should have been the one to stop it all, but in some lives I caused it. I said your name as a baby, and those people, my family, remembered!"

She looked deep into his eyes and smiled. "Think, Thomas. Think back to England."

The heat flashed in his mind. "How could I forget?"

"Tell me," she whispered.

The shiver from before returned, but this time with a violent aftershock. "I heard you were in trouble. My mother came to find me. I was out in the forest chopping wood and she came on horseback. She told me to get to your house immediately because she'd heard that you were in danger somehow. She gave me the horse and I left her in the woods alone.

"I rode straight to your cottage and found it empty. I saw the tracks in the grass out the back and followed them." The memory was a piercing ache in his head. He didn't want to think about it, but pressed on. "Seeing you tied up. The f-flames."

She placed her hand on his leg. "It's okay, Thomas."

He shook his head. "I couldn't stop it."

"You weren't meant to."

"How can you say that!" His whispers were firm, strong. "I was promised to marry you and I couldn't save you."

"Is that all you remember?"

He nodded.

"What about the words I spoke? When I asked you to cover your ears?"

Tommi thought back. Even though it was lifetimes ago, it still felt like yesterday.

He took a moment for the images to flash across his mind. "You were on fire," he said, the word catching in the back of his throat. He swallowed it down like a ball of nerves. "You were speaking and it was like something more than words was coming out of you."

"You saw that?"

"Yes, like waves in the air. Up and down. And your voice went right through me."

"I'm so sorry." She pressed her boney fingers to her eyes.

He leaned in closer, clutching her hand to his chest. "None of this was ever your fault, and you have suffered. You're still suffering."

"No, Thomas, you don't understand. I am the one cursed the world. I've caused all the darkness and the destruction. It's me who had us killed over and over."

He shook his head, unable to understand.

She rolled her head to the side of the pillow, looking towards the door. "Let him see," she whispered.

He followed her trail of sight and saw nothing there. "Who

are you speaking to?" Just as he'd finished his last word, though, a rush of light charged at him. He froze in place, yet felt like he was falling.

Letting go of her hand, he stood. Images, one after another, flashed in his mind. His eyelids fluttered violently and every hair on his body buzzed and tingled.

When it was over, he nearly collapsed to the ground. Sitting down on the floor for support, he reached up to take her hand again, resting on his knees and laying his face on the pillow.

"Ivy," he whispered. "What was that?"

"The truth. Do you see now?"

"I ... I ... don't understand."

"Tommi!" Doc called from the other room.

"Go now, but can you come back again?"

"I'm not leaving you," he whispered.

She smiled and her eyes closed. "Come back when you understand," she whispered.

He got to his feet and collected up his medical supplies. Holding up a vial, he shook it before coming back to her side.

"Take this before you sleep. Just sip it each time you need it. It'll take away the pain."

She sipped from the vial and he replaced the cork, leaving it on the table beside her bed.

"I will return." He pressed his lips to her forehead, then collected his bag and left.

Doc and Ivy's vater were waiting at the table. Doc stood as Tommi came into view.

"I will return in the morning," Tommi told her vater. "I have supplies back in my room that will help ease her discomfort."

"I'd like that," the vater said.

Tommi followed Doc out of the house and walked side by side with him to the carriage.

"You know it's cancer, right?"

"Yes." Tommi felt a tightness in his throat. Doc's tone was clear. She wouldn't survive for much longer.

"Very well. I'll converse with the local doctor to see what knowledge I can supply him."

Tommi rode in silence, looking out the window all the way back to the town. Once they were there, he locked himself in his room and collapsed to the ground.

Ivy. He cried. Crawling towards his bed, he climbed in and curled up fully clothed. *What was all of that?* He thought about how the light had rushed at him, and within an instant, so much information had entered his brain.

Trying to think of it in pieces, he focused on just one thing.

A baby's cry.

The sound rang in his head. Irene had been younger in that vision than she'd been when Thomas had met Ivy. She'd looked just like Ivy. Naked on the old wooden table, two women surrounding her. She'd screamed out her pain, clutching the table's edge. Knees bent, her round stomach moving until a baby appeared between her legs.

A midwife had held the girl in her hands. A spirit had entered her body, and the one standing over it had bent down and kissed the child.

Then it had disappeared.

Thomas sat up in bed. It was the middle of the night, and he was drenched in sweat. He crossed the room and opened the window, allowing the night air to cool him down.

Why am I supposed to see her birth? It doesn't make sense.

The following morning, he rose before Doc and got Asher to drop him at Ivy's house.

"Go back to town," Tommi said. "I'll walk back."

Asher tipped his hat and set the horses back to town. Tommi turned towards the house and knocked on the door.

He waited, but couldn't hear any movement in the house.

His heart picked up its pace and he pushed open the door.

"Ivy!" he yelled out.

No answer.

Rushing down the corridor, he stopped at her door.

"Thomas?" she whispered.

He sighed with relief and went to her side. "I didn't hear anything…" He couldn't finish the sentence.

"Father is with the cows for most of the day," she said weakly.

"I dreamt of your birth last night."

She smiled. "They helped you see." She rolled her head to the other side, looking back at the door. "Thank you," she whispered.

"I don't understand. Who are you talking to?"

"Spirits. They gave me this life to see and to know."

"Is that why you can remember?"

She nodded.

"Will you remember in the next life?"

She shook her head ever so gently.

"What! Why not?" he snapped.

"Sit, Thomas. You can see now. Think about the images they showed you."

"Um." He thought about the mother and how much pain she'd been going through. Then the baby's screams had been loud, surrounding him, like when Ivy's said his name. "The spirit," he whispered.

"Yes."

"Is that who you are speaking to now?" He looked towards the door, hoping to see it for himself.

"No. I speak to the earth's spirits, who stay with me in life always. They are the ones who granted me the sight. But without that spirit that you saw, without that kiss—"

He cut her off. "It's a blessing."

"I have no blessing in this life."

He thought about it for a moment. "But... but what about these spirits? What do they do? Why can't they bless you and heal you when they gave you the sight?"

"They shouldn't have done that. They intervened."

"And you suffer because of it?"

"Calm down, Thomas." She held out her hand. He took it and sat back down. "Close your eyes."

He did, and in the blackness behind his eyelids, he saw a bright light in the shape of a man walking up to him. He then felt a firm hand press to his shoulder.

"What is that?" he asked.

"They said that it was time for me to see."

Images flashed in front of him, just like they did when he was sleeping. He saw Ivy in this life, being born. The spirits were watching over her, helping her enter the body as it exited her mother.

But there were other spirits involved. They looked and waited for as long as they could before they pressed their own mouths to her forehead and kissed her all at once.

The baby screamed as she accepted the knowledge the spirits had given to her.

"Why this life?" he asked. "Why not try in all the other ones?"

"Everything aligned with my birth in England. On the spring equinox and a full moon, I was born to a witch." She shook her head. "The spirits knew that I could accept the information now, but without the kiss, I was..." she trailed off into her mind.

"What is it?"

"I don't deserve the blessing, Thomas."

"Don't say that."

"But I don't. I never have. That is the gift of this life. To see all the wrongs I have caused to happen to others." She paused and, after a moment of silence, she added, "you have no idea the pain I've caused."

Tommi shook his head. "I see the pain, but it's the pain that you've been put through."

"Thomas, open your eyes. The spirits have given you sight and you still do not see."

"See what?"

"I'm caught on a wheel, to go around and around, one life after another, playing the same game of pain and torture. But it isn't just me that suffers. It's all those people that I forced to be stuck on this wheel with me."

The heat zapped his mind. His body shook. "You said words that still have an effect today, even after all these years?"

She nodded. "The curse."

He remembered now. The curse that she'd spoken when he'd thought she had already burned to death.

"The spirits call me a diamon, Thomas. I should have given people a destiny, and instead I destined them to pain and torture. What type of person am I?"

"Don't think that way, Ivy. We have to keep our focus on the curse. Maybe this is exactly what this life is allowing us to do."

"I don't think so."

He got up and began pacing the room. "Sure. We can think this through and work out how to break the curse."

"Break it? Thomas, remember the words said?"

He shook his head. He remembered how he'd felt when the waves he'd seen had floated through the air and wrapped around him. He remembered the way it had stung, when they'd gone right through him as each word she'd spoken had pierced harder into his body. He remembered the heat that had expanded from her and hit him harder than he could even have imagined.

She was chanting something soft, underneath her breath.

"An anchor," he said, the memory becoming stronger. He sat down again, holding her hand.

She explained, "A curse is not just the words spoken; it's also the words that surround them and the in-between. It starts with the white space and it's the intention that cements them into existence."

"I don't understand."

"The words you heard were only half of it. What I actually did was curse each and every one of those people to feel my pain, to experience my torture of that life in every life they lived from then onwards. One after another, never living peacefully. But not only that; also the children that they have, their descendants, will suffer, too. What did they deserve to endure that? Why should they suffer?"

Tommi felt sick.

"Can't you see it in the world? The pain, the war, the horror? Horrible things are happening in the world because of me. No longer do evil acts hide under the cloak of darkness; now, they're done in the middle of day."

"We can make things right."

"Thomas! When I made that curse, I was able to use the power of the planet. I felt it spread like a plague and it wrapped around the entire planet."

He sighed. *The entire planet?* The shiver returned.

"And all for what? Because they wanted to burn me alive? Me? One person in one lifetime so long ago, and now the world has to suffer time and time again."

Tommi got to his feet and crossed the room. He needed time to think, time to digest it all. Even after so long, getting these answers that he had asked for throughout his lives... they were harder to hear than he imagined.

There's no relief. He sighed. *How can we save so many people?*

He turned to her and her eyes drooped. "You're tired."

"Yes. But I don't want to sleep anymore. Not while you're here."

"I'll wait."

He kissed her on the cheek and watched her sleep.

. . .

"Thomas?"

Tommi got to his feet when he heard Ivy call from her bedroom. He rushed straight in and smiled. "I'm here."

"I was afraid you left."

He shook his head. "I never seem to get enough time with you. I'm not choosing to leave early."

She smiled and it touched her eyes, but then she closed them for what seemed too long.

He was by her side immediately, feeling her forehead. Encouraging her to drink water, he watched as she sipped it slowly, struggling to swallow.

"I need you to promise me something," she said.

He kneeled beside her, leaning towards her to be closer. "Anything."

"Leave and don't come back."

He cocked his head to the side. "What? How can you say that?"

"Go and find someone to love. Live your life and forget me."

He shook his head.

"You've helped so many people. It's time to live for yourself."

Tears clouded his sight. He shook his head again. "How can there be anyone else?"

"I do not deserve your eternal love."

He lifted her weak hand and pressed it to his lips. "You do. You always have, but we get so very little time together, it's not fair that I don't get to say it. Ivy, I have always loved you and it's my love that will put an end to this curse. Hate has followed you for far too long, and it's going to be stamped out by my love."

"I feel that the hate in the world is multiplying."

He shook his head.

"Love conquers all, even the hate."

She shook her head. "You want to sacrifice your soul for me. It isn't right." She closed her eyes again, her breathing shallow.

He leaned into his bag and retrieved fresh lavender, placing some beside her on the pillow.

"Ivy?"

She whispered, "I wasn't strong enough to hold the bubble?" Her words were soft.

He looked around the room. "Bubble? What bubble?"

"That day, in England. I put a bubble around you so you wouldn't be affected by the curse." She paused, breathing in and out. He listened to her chest, realizing she was barely getting any air in. "But when I ignited the flames, the bubble burst and I couldn't protect you."

"Don't trouble yourself with that now."

"I'm sorry," she whispered, and breathed in one more time. It was like she held her breath and didn't let it out.

"Ivy?" he asked, shaking her. "Ivy, wake up!" He shook her again.

Clutching her face in his hands, he whispered her name. "I love you."

The spirit mightn't have blessed you, but I do. He pressed his lips to each of her eyelids.

"Come back to me," he whispered, placing her hands across her chest.

Tommi sat on the front step with his face in his hands. The sun had moved across the sky before he'd even thought of moving.

A noise at the back of the house caught his attention. He walked around and saw Ivy's vater taking unsaddling his horse.

"Oh my, you nearly gave me a heart attack. It's, err, Tommi, right?"

"Yes, sir." Tommi walked to his side and placed a hand on his shoulder gently. "She passed at noontime, sir."

A. A. WARNE

The saddle dropped out of the man's hands. The horse side-stepped away. The man's eyes were as hollow as death itself.

"I'm sorry," he whispered, trying to hold his own tears back.

"You were supposed to help," the vater said. "You're here to heal her."

"The sickness went right through her body." Tommi took a step back, giving the man space. "There is no cure for what she had, but I sat with her all morning and took away her pain."

The father wobbled where he stood, then pushed his way into the house, screaming out her name.

Tears streamed down his already wet face as Tommi listened after him. Leaving him to his pain, Tommi tended to the horse; he finished pulling off the saddle blanket and found its feed. He then collected his bag by the front door and walked back to town.

It took him all night, and by the time he arrived, it was morning. Up in his room, he cleaned himself with the bucket of water and put on fresh clothing. Then he found Asher out in the stable, raking hay.

"Can you drive me back to the house?"

"You look like shit," Asher said.

"Doesn't matter." Tommi shrugged. "I need to return."

"Very well, sir."

There was one thing Tommi could rely on of Asher. The man never asked questions, no matter how outlandish Tommi's requests were.

As he stood by the road, waiting for Asher to bring around the carriage, Tommi watched how people walked by laughing to one another and living their lives. He looked up to the sun and wanted to curse the day. How could it rise and set and keep on going when he was suffering, when Ivy could no longer feel sunlight on her face, or drink in the warmth of life?

The pain made him delirious.

"Sir!" Asher's voice snapped Tommi to attention.

Nodding, he climbed in.

He rested his head on the back of the seat and closed his eyes. He didn't open them until he was back at the house.

"What time do I pick you up?"

"Don't. I'll walk again."

"But, sir, tis not a short walk."

"I know."

The vater came out and met him at the door. "No point you coming around now."

"Excuse me, sir, but I would like to dig her grave."

"That's my job," he snapped. "Not yours."

"May I assist you?"

For a moment, he considered it. And then he agreed. Together, they went into the bush, near the river, where another grave sat by the oak tree.

"Tis my wife, and my dearest Ivy must lay beside her. I will join them one day, too."

Tommi thought that was nice. Loving, even.

They dug until high sun, then drank from the nearby river. They kept digging until the hole was so deep that they had to climb out of it.

"That'll do," the vater said.

Huffing and puffing at their efforts, they returned to the house, wrapped Ivy in her white sheets, laid her neatly into the wagon, and then walked the horse back to the trees by the river.

Tommi climbed into the hole and the vater passed Ivy down, ever so gently. He laid her down and climbed back out.

Standing beside the grave, they bowed their heads. Tommi squeezed his eyes shut.

I'm sorry I've failed you again. Tommi thought of things to promise her, but held back. *I can't promise you anything, but I know this. I know I'm going to fight for you. I will break that curse and you will live free from pain and free with love.*

Even if I have to sacrifice myself to achieve it.

Consider it done.

The vater picked up the shovel and began to push the dirt into the hole.

Tommi went to his side. "You've done enough today, sir."

The vater straightened his back.

"Take the horse back," Tommi told him. "I'll do the rest."

He nodded and turned his back. Tommi watched after him until he was out of sight. Then he sat by the grave and retrieved something from his pocket.

A vial of ingredients that he had once mixed together, long ago, but never spoken about.

He'd given it once to a suffering animal and it had worked within minutes. Now, Tommi pressed it to his own lips, feeling the burn go over the back of his throat and down to his stomach.

Climbing down, he pushed Ivy to the side and lay down beside her on her right.

"This is my first promise to you," he said. "I'm coming with you."

His eyes fluttered as his breaths went out of rhythm with his heart. The beating in his chest slowed, and his mind flashed images across his eyes.

Ivy waiting for him in the sunlight.

"I'm coming," he said, and the air weighed him down.

The darkness entered his body and pulled him to a place where he could no longer breathe.

AMERICA

1941

"*T*amsin?" A liquid voice surrounded him. "Tamsin, my sweet little baby, wake up."

Tamsin opened her eyes, blinking to nothing but white. Confused, she heard the sound of a cry, somehow instinctively knowing it was her own, and she then felt a mother's love wrap around her and the cries soothed into another deep sleep.

"Tamsin!" her mother yelled. "How many times have I told you? Young ladies do not play with their food!"

Tamsin looked up, angry and annoyed. She did not like being told what she could or couldn't do. She was a good child, just like before, like many times before. But in this life, it was much different. She had limitations.

"Tamsin!" her grey-haired mother yelled through the door. "Tamsin, for the love of all good things, please open the door!"

Tamsin pressed both her palms against the pantry door, holding it in place so her mother couldn't get in.

Her stomach growled, rattling the rest of her body. Bones protruded from her skin and her muscles were weak, but she had enough strength to hold the door, if not for long.

"If I have to drive into town and get the policeman, so help me, I will! You know they take wretched children like you to jail first and then they hand them out back of the church so God can punish 'em."

Tamsin twisted around and pressed her back to the door, sliding down and sitting on the ground.

"You hear me, child?"

She had walked away. Slamming drawers and bashing something metal like a knife or a spoon against the sink.

Tamsin used the opportunity to lean forward and grab a container. The pantry often sat empty and, if it wasn't full with flour or salts, it had nothing in it at all. Leaning back against the door, she felt her mother bash at the door again.

"I'm going to get them now. And they're going to take you away. Away from here now. They'll put you in a home full of wicked kids."

If only! Then maybe I might get some food.

Tamsin listened, but there was only silence. Quietly, she pulled back the lid and slipped her hand into the darkness, feeling its contents.

A powdery substance slid between her fingers and she shoved them it into her mouth, tasting a custard.

Outside, the car roared to life.

Tamsin waited patiently for it to leave, but it sat idling.

Bang! "You unlock this door this instant!" she screamed.

Pressing her fingers back into the container to coat them with the sticky substance, Tamsin heard the footsteps march out the door and the car switch off.

She sighed. *I wish she would get the police; then I could tell them all the things she does to me.* She slumped at the thought of how things had progressed. Trapped in the middle of nowhere, Tamsin was never allowed to leave the house.

"Strange men are out there," her mother had once told her. "And if God wills it, then we will leave." Tamsin often watched her mother drive away into a nearby town, and she used the opportunities to look for food.

There was always food coming from somewhere, but it was locked away, hidden from Tamsin's reach. The pantry offered a sad result of different flours, but Tamsin took whatever she could get.

Her stomach rumbled again. She'd gotten used to the pain long ago, but the noise often got louder than her thoughts.

Getting to her feet, she pushed her toes up against the door, and with both hands, reached for more containers.

Tugging at the lids, it took all her energy to get them off. She breathed in the dull fragrance and often poked a finger into one to taste if it was eatable.

Always the same. She sighed. Tamsin settled on the sugar pot. *Why does she have to be so cruel?*

She thought back to India, when her *mam* had often punished her when she hadn't done as she was told. She'd kept such a short leash on her, but never once had she gone hungry.

This is life so different. The sugar grains melted on her tongue, sending a buzzing feeling right throughout her mouth. *Things could be so much worse.* She thought back to the day her mother had driven her father to the train station. Tamsin had shaken as the car had gone out of view.

"Three days," he'd said, placing the Bible in front of her. "This is the only book you read. It is the only book that matters."

Tamsin had nodded. She never disagreed. She'd taken the book to her room and waited for him to go, knowing he'd return, but that had been years ago.

In the pantry, Tamsin wondered what had become of the

man. *Did he get a taste of freedom? Or see that the world isn't cruel and a punishment?*

She felt the shiver run over her. *If I didn't have so many lives, I might have believed them. I might not have been able to understand that the world isn't full of death and torture. The torture is right here.*

Tamsin stood tall. *Why am I the one hiding in here, when they're the ones that are wrong?*

She replaced the lid and put the sugar container back on the pantry shelf. *Don't make a mess. Replace it like I haven't touched it. Because I didn't touch it!* she reminded herself.

It's fine, it's okay. She won't find out.

Her hands rattled. The bones of her knuckles accidently tapped against the door. She pressed an ear against the wood, hoping to hear where her mother was.

Is she on the other side waiting for me to come out?

The sugar had reached her stomach, and she felt all kinds of new energy running through her veins.

This is it. I'm going to leave. Why haven't I thought of this before? She breathed in and out, and then held her breath. *But what if she catches me? What if... where will I go?*

Tamsin didn't know this land. From the house, all she could see were green fields. Not a single person had come to the house, and she hadn't seen anyone walk by.

What if I don't know the language? If I see someone, will they understand me? They'll bring me straight back here. They'll take me to my mother... The thought sickened her.

She shook her head. *I have to do this. And if they bring me back... No. I won't let them.*

Slowly, she pulled the door back to open it. With her face pressed against the frame, one eye out and both hands ready to slam it shut, she looked out.

The kitchen was empty.

The window sat wide open and the breeze was flicking up the curtains, blowing them across the sink.

She opened the door wider, letting her ears do the wandering. Throughout the house, it was quiet. Outside, she heard the *chip, clip* of the pegs.

She's outside. This is it! Move your butt, Tamsin! she told herself, but her feet didn't move.

I am Thomas and Tam, and I am Tãmas and I am a man. I can do this. I will do this and I will become what I am meant to be in this life.

I can't do any of that from inside this pantry. Move a foot now, she snapped at herself, and her body listened. She stepped out into the kitchen and quietly clipped the door behind her.

Her hands shook by her side. Her teeth rattled as her jaw bounced up and down, crunching her teeth together.

Remaining close to the wall, and avoiding any soft spots on the floor, she tiptoed down the corridor, trying not to creak the floorboards. Slipping into her room, she grabbed her coat and then climbed out the window.

Falling to the ground, she felt a noise left her lips. Quickly gathering herself, she crawled underneath the house, hiding behind a pillar, clutching onto her coat.

Waiting to see if her mother had heard, she shook violently as her nerves tensed in her body and relaxed momentarily, only to make her shake harder.

Please don't come and find me. Tears swelled in her eyes. *I don't want to be here anymore. I want to go.*

If time hadn't passed, she'd go back to India, or Germany, or even Wales. *I want to go home.*

Clip, clip. The pegs were easy to hear. Crawling back out from beneath the house, Tamsin stood tall and looked out to the field before her. With her mother on the other side of the house, she might have just enough time to make it to the crest and out of sight, that is if her mother doesn't come around the side of the house.

She slid her arms into her jacket and buttoned up the first button. One foot extended out in front of her and she pushed off the ground, extending her legs. She had run many times, but never in this life. Her body felt awkward and didn't know what to do.

Pushing her limits, she ran faster.

The grass was dry, and prickled the bottom of her feet, but she had to ignore the pain. *It's nothing compared to what she'll do to me if she finds me out here.* She kept running, and the wind whooshed through her hair and flicked it backwards.

Her mouth quickly dried, but that didn't stop her, either. *Nothing is going to stop me!* She kept going, running faster, feeling the energy pulsate through her muscles. The crest was close... and then she reached it.

Stopping, she looked beyond it and saw nothing but more fields. Empty and dull green. No houses, and no trees but a few spread out here and there. Not even a town.

Which way am I supposed to go?

Looking back to the house, she saw it looked like a speck. Seeing her mother walk towards the car, Tamsin dropped to the ground and rolled down the other side of the crest.

Did she see me? She jumped to her feet and set her eyes onto the nearest tree. It seemed to be miles away. *Is she driving to come and get me? Will she run me over?*

The panic made her body move faster than she could have imagined. The pain in her feet was no longer felt. The adrenaline ignored it, letting her run even faster, sprinting to the point that both her legs extended out and only one foot at a time touched the ground. The longer her stride, the faster she ran.

In a matter of minutes, she crossed the field and got closer to the tree. Breathing heavily, she sucked in air, forcing it into her lungs, and she kept going. The tree was no wider than her and had next to no leaves on top. She reached it and slid behind it, catching her breath.

Buckled over, she felt her lungs expand and deflate. Her stomach ached harder.

Clutching at her chest, she felt the sweat drip off her beneath her coat.

Peaking her head around the tree to look back at the crest, Tamsin froze.

She's not there! Shaking her head, she managed to get her breath back. *But if she saw me, she would have caught up.*

Looking around, she wondered if she was coming towards her from another direction. Letting her ears reach for any sound, she listened for the car.

Nothing.

She could have jumped with joy, but knew she still didn't have long.

Snapping her head in each direction, she looked out, planning her next direction. Seeing a tree on the horizon, she pushed off, falling into a sprint.

The sun baked down on her, and the sweat made her feel like she was covered in water. The coat might not have been a good idea, but she knew leaving it now would only show which direction she'd gone in.

The pounding of her feet hitting the ground sent thudding up into her ears.

She reached the horizon just as the sun began to lower.

I made it. She breathed out, buckling over to the ground. Coughing and panting, she couldn't get enough air into her. Heaving for more, her lungs inhaled, sounding like she was wheezing.

She lifted her head and looked around. More fields with trees every now and then. *How far does this land go?* She sighed.

Pushing herself up to sit, she placed her head between her two bony knees and felt her stomach lunge. Leaning out, she vomited up all the powdery substance she'd eaten back at the house. Struggling to come up, the vile burnt the back of her throat, and she heaved again.

Crawling away from the mess, she tried to stand, but her body collapsed to the ground again.

Weak! She moaned. *I'm so weak. This body isn't going to make it.* The nearby tree offered a little comfort for the heat of the sun. When the sun finally lowered beyond edge of the far fields, the air instantly cooled.

Shivering beneath her coat, she felt the water covering her body now soaking back into her skin.

Slumping against the tree, Tamsin let her eyes shut.

Tamsin snapped open her eyes to pitch blackness.

I fell asleep! She looked around, noticing something in the far distance. A light moving through the trees, coming straight for her.

Mother! She was on her feet, inching herself back around the tree, desperate to hid.

If I keep running, she'll find me out in the field. Tamsin looked up to the sky. The stars were littered right across it, but there was no moon.

Too much light to move. She looked towards the cluster of trees on the far end of the paddock. But the car was driving along the other side, shining light in between. *Should I stay or run?* She looked in all the other directions. *What if there's more?* Then she saw, on the other side, three cars driving along a road.

They're not here for me. They're not. My mother doesn't know this many people. And she would never let me come anywhere close to them, for risk that I might say something.

Tamsin began to shake again. She didn't know what to do.

Instead, she didn't do anything. She pressed herself closer to the tree and hoped her coat wouldn't be seen by the lights.

The cars from the other side drove up and around the cluster of trees, joining the lone car. Together they shone lights, brightening the entire region.

They're going to find me. They're going to find me!

A noise above her made her arch her neck and look up. There, a blue bird chirped quietly as it looked down at her.

As they locked eyes, a wave of relaxation washed over her. *Who are you?* Tamsin thought. She breathed easier and felt tired again. "Am I safe here?" Tamsin whispered.

The cars sped up and drove off in the other direction.

She slumped to the ground again, and looked up and smiled. "Thank you."

Closing her eyes, she collapsed once more, letting sleep take her instantly.

Tamsin woke to a honking noise.

She jumped to her feet as a car drove off the road, across the paddock, aiming directly towards her.

It honked again, and again.

She turned and ran in the opposite direction, back towards her mother's house.

"Wait!" a man's voice screamed out to her, but she didn't listen.

He's come to take me back to that wicked mother!

She ran even faster. The top button of her coat came loose, and the jacket, much too big for her body, fell down her arms. She let it go, letting it fly from her body. The weight now gone, let her move even faster. But there was no use outrunning the car. It over took her and slid out to the side, stopping right before her.

The man who had yelled out to her, now jumped out of the car and held up both his hands.

Tasmin didn't move, in fear that he'd chase her down, just like her mother had once done the previous times she had run away.

The golden-colored hair man, placed his arms out wide, palms flat, and walked around the front of the car.

As he got closer, Tamsin could see his bronze-colored eyes.

"It's okay," he said loudly, over the idling engine. "I'm not going to hurt you."

Tamsin panted, trying to catch her breath. *Is it any use to keep running?*

"What do you want?" she asked, the panic in her voice noticeable.

"Are you the gal they've been lookin' for, ma'am?"

Tamsin shrugged. *Did my mother send him? Would he take her straight back to her?* She watched as his eyes wandered down her body and back up again. *Is he one of those men that she warned me about?*

"Those are some heavy bruises you got there."

Tamsin pulled at her sleeves, wishing they went down further.

"I'm Isaac." He stepped closer, but Tamsin stepped back. "And I'm not from around here." He paused. "I promise I won't hurt you. And I know you'd rather have me just drive away and pretend I didn't see ya, but by the look of you, you're hurt and need help." He pressed his hand to his heart. "I can help."

Tamsin soaked in his words. There was something so familiar about him and yet she knew she had never seen him before.

His bronze eyes were different, like they contained an entire world. The way he stood, tall and proud, all while being so warm and inviting.

Her heart skipped a beat.

She knows him. *But how?*

Thinking his name on repeat in her mind, *Isaac...* she paused. *Is this Ivy?* "Excuse me Mr?"

"Yes, ma'am."

"What's going to happen now? Are you going to take me home?"

"Is that where you want to go?" He scrunched his eyebrows together and cocked his head slightly to the left.

That has to be Ivy! She had done that so many times before. She shook her head.

"Is there some place I can take you? Where do you want to go?" he asked slowly, and took another step forward.

"I can't go back to my mother's house."

"Is that your home?"

She hesitated, then nodded."

He breathed in and held the breath. "Tell you what," he said. "I was just finished packing my trunk yesterday and was about to leave town when I heard you were out missing. So, I thought I'd spend another night to help out. But seeing you here like this…" He gestured to her arms first, then her legs, but avoided her face. She couldn't see the damage that had been done, but she always felt it. "Well, that's not right." He shook his head.

Tamsin struggled to read him. *What is he thinking?*

"You know what, I'm gonna to take you with me."

Tamsin's hands shook.

"Would you like to come see America with me? I don't know where I'm goin'. I just drive on that open road and stop wherever it leads me." he said, moving his hand out towards the sky. "Then I find towns like this one and stop off for a few days. I earn my keep and then hit the road again."

It sounded adventurous, and reminded her so much of Germany. She smiled.

"But I can't offer you a home, I only have my car." He looked to the ground as if in disappointment, but then connected with her eyes again. "But I will promise you that I'll never touch you. Not once." Holding up his hands like he was surrendering, he then pressed his fist to his heart. "On my life, I promise you that."

She was silence for a moment. "Why?"

"Why? Cause that—" he pointed to the bruising, the cuts, the marks, and the skin that could no longer hold its right color, "—that ain't right. You deserve better than that."

She shivered again.

"Will you come with me?"

Tamsin lost her breath. Quickly eyeing her surroundings, she looked back at him. "How did you know I was here?"

"I saw you last night," he said quietly. "I was with the other cars that were out searching." He pointed to the cluster of trees. "But I could see the panic in you. You were hidin'. You weren't lost. I know that feeling..." he trailed off, like he'd entered his thoughts. "I thought I'd come back when the search was over."

"Over?"

He nodded. "Your mother said you wouldn't last the night. I knew that wasn't right either." He walked to the car and leaned in, grabbing something wrapped in paper, and held up a canteen.

Tamsin took a step forward and stopped.

"If you don't want to come with me, that's fine. I get it. But take these." He closed the distance between them, but stopped when he got too close, holding the items out for her to take. "You look hungry, and you need water. These nights might be cold, but the days will dry you out real quick."

She reached out and took the water first. Pressing it to her lips, she let the water pour into her mouth and disappear into her body to reach her stomach.

Dry heaving suddenly from something entering her body, she stood up straight again only once she'd gotten her breath back, and took another mouthful. "Thank you," she said.

He handed her some wrapped food and a green apple. "Good day to you, ma'am." He tipped his hat and went to the other side of the vehicle.

"Wait!" She said, and he paused. "I'll come."

He smiled, walked back around the other side of his car, and held open the passenger door.

Hesitantly, she slid in and clicked her bony ankles together.

He slammed the door shut and she jumped, taking in the sights of the car. The softness under her bottom; the lines that ran across the door. She had never been in her mother's car before, let alone in someone else's.

She turned to see where he had gone then, and saw him at least a yard away in the paddock. He was running back towards the car, with her jacket in his hands. He held it up, panting as he got back his breath. "Can't forget this," he said, climbing in, and throwing it across the back seat.

He handed it to her and she covered herself with it. He sat beside her, and then he clicked the car into gear and it moved forward.

Holding onto the seat with both hands, she couldn't believe how quickly the car took off.

This is so much faster than the horses, she thought, thinking back to her previous lives. Then that had her thinking about trains, and just how fast that would be like.

The paddock was flat, but the car seemed to hit every bump. They bobbled up and down, swaying sideways when he turned.

"We'll be back on the road in a minute," he said, and she lowered herself down in the seat. "Where to?"

She looked at him, confused.

"Where should we go to?"

She shrugged. "Germany?"

He burst out laughing, clutching onto the wheel for support. "Germany! Of all places." He shook his head. "What type of answer is that? How old are you?"

"Fourteen."

He squinted at her in the corner of his eyes. "You don't look like a day over eight."

She squeezed the green apple in her hands, wanting to eat it, but the water swished in her stomach, making her feel sick.

"Doesn't matter though. Pick somewhere else."

"Not Germany?"

He laughed again. "We're at war and they're our enemy. Didn't you know that?"

War with Germany? But... but... it's so peaceful! She looked outside. *What type of place is this if they can declare war against a peaceful country?*

"I meant, what part of America would you like to go?"

"But the war?"

"It's okay, it hasn't reached inland." He looked to her for a moment longer than she would have liked. "Did you know about the war?"

She shook head.

"The world war?"

"The entire world?" Her hand went to her mouth, covering it.

He nodded.

Her stomach sank. *How could the entire world be at war with itself?* She thought about her family in different parts, picking up weapons and fighting with people from across the ocean. *Now I'm thankful that they too have gone.*

The car reached the road and he pulled up the hand break.

"That way—" he pointed left, "—leads to the town. We can drive through and keep going. Or, that way, we won't hit a town for at least a couple of days."

Her face softened and the corners of her lips pulled to the side.

"I don't have much food, but we can make it last."

She nodded.

He put down the break and the car lunged forward, turning towards the right

. . .

It was like Isaac had endless energy, driving throughout the day and most of the night. He slept on the backseat for less than an hour and then kept on driving.

Tamsin slept, but struggled to relax. She generally had one eye open and jumped at every noise.

Relax, she told herself. But her body couldn't. The night sky was gentle against her eyes, but the sun was starting to lighten it softly.

Tamsin rolled her head and looked to Isaac. His hands held the steering wheel tightly, and his breathing was steady. The long drive was starting to take a toll on his face, with bags under his eyes beginning to darken.

Is this really my Ivy? She wondered. There was something so familiar that she couldn't ignore, but having little contact with Ivy in all the previous lives, it was hard to remember.

It didn't help that this body was struggling. It took a toll on her mind and memory.

She breathed in and out, forcing herself to think back.

Ivy and I were always the same age, but now we're not? Why is he so much older than I am? And why does he have a different name?

Tamsin had a different name in every life. He was often named after a previous family member, or just a name his family loved, but strangely enough, it always started with a 'T'. But for Ivy, it was always the same.

Until now. She thought about the weirdness to it. But she couldn't deny the presence between them. It was an undeniable feeling that pulled her towards him.

This has to be Ivy. She smiled. *Has she come to save me this time?.*

"You want to sleep on the back seat?" he asked.

She shook her head.

He pulled over to the side of the road and turned the car off. Up ahead, the sun began to peak over the horizon, lighting up the land in front of them.

He got out and went to the boot, pulling something red and round out. Struggling to open the door, she used all her strength to push it open.

"Sir, what is that?" she asked, standing back and watching him press it into the side of the car.

"Petrol," he said. "You know, it's what the car runs on."

She nodded, pretending to understand.

"This is my last can. I filled the car a few times while you were sleeping, but if we don't find a station soon, then we'll be walking. Can I ask you something?"

Her shoulders went up, preparing herself.

"Please don't call me 'sir.' That's my father's title."

"My apologies, master." She lowered her head.

"Master?" He shook his head.

She hesitated, struggling to form words. Knowing she wasn't allowed to speak as freely as when she'd been a man, she nervously bobbed from one foot to another, waiting for his reaction. "If you are not a sir or a master, then what should I call you?"

"Isaac."

"Oh, but I mustn't! It's not proper."

He laughed. The sound was so loud and vibrant that she felt it vibrate right through her body. "Proper?" he asked between laughs. "Are you one of those religious folks? You know... the ones that have to behave in certain ways and are forbidden to do pretty much anything."

She went silent.

"I don't mean to offend." He shook the red container before putting it down onto the ground and replacing the lid. "You talk a little different from the rest of the townsfolk. I'm just tryin' to work you out."

"I'm not sure," she said. "I don't know the rest of the town folk."

He looked at her then. A sadness washed over his eyes.

"But everybody was out lookin' for you."

She was taken aback. "For me?"

"You didn't know them?"

She shook her head.

"Well, we'll have to change that, too."

She smiled.

A couple more days passed before they finally stopped at a town.

"Is this the one?" she asked, opening her eyes and yawning.

"Well, that depends, darl'. You want a small town or a big city?"

Her eyes lit up but all she could answer with was a shrug.

He got out and opened the door for her.

She had her coat buttoned all the way up before she got out of the car. Then she lifted the collar up and around her neck.

He walked close to her, but he didn't touch her. When another person walked too close, he leaned out an arm, making sure that they went around.

She smiled as they connected eyes.

He leaned in to whisper, "Are you alright?"

"Yes. Thank you."

My mother would never find me this far from home. She doesn't even know what direction I've come in. But no matter how far away she was, the nerves didn't subside.

The town was no bigger than the one back in Wales. A long road ran through with a dozen cars parked alongside it, and a horse and carriage rolled passed but the driver didn't acknowledge their presence. Instead he looked ahead, like she wasn't even there.. The clicks and clacks of the hooves bounced off the shop windows, echoing all the way around.

I've missed that sound. She breathed the horses in, smelling the sweat and heat radiating off of them. Flies stuck to their skin, and she saw the horses had something black covering their eyes from the side, blocking most of their view.

"Tamsin," Isaac said from behind her.

She turned to see him pointing inside a shop window. There were clustered items lining the walls, chairs in the middle, and fabrics rolled on the other side.

"It's all the things we need to make a home."

"A home?"

He nodded. "You've really struggled this last couple of days in the car. Let's stop the driving and stay here for a while."

"Stay?" She looked around.

"No one will find us here," he whispered. He pushed open the door and held it for her to enter.

Looking at all the things that went right up to the roof, Tamsin wondered what she could trade to own some of these things.

"Are there any houses available?" Isaac asked the man behind the counter. Their voices blurred into the background as Tamsin lost herself in the colored fabrics, remembering India and how all the woman dressed.

She looked down at her own coat. Dull and boring. Grey and horrible. It was nothing like the bright shawls, the fancy coats, and the beads.

Isaac was by her side. "The man has a room for us for the night. We can get cleaned up and then go out to a house on the far edge of town in the mornin'. Can you read?"

She cocked her head, surprised at the question. Then she nodded.

"Here," he said, holding out a paper. "It's so you can read what's going on in the world."

"A *zeitung*," she said.

He shook his head. "A what?"

She caught herself. She didn't know the English world for it.

"A newspaper," he said.

She smiled and looked it over. Back in Germany, they were a large piece of paper with printing on both sides. This was many papers put together. *It's amazing that so much news has come from around the world.* She wondered if she'd be able to understand all of the languages inside the pages.

That night, Isaac sent for food to be eaten in the rooms. He asked for a room be set up with two separate beds and a table at the end.

"I didn't know if you'd want to be in the room alone. I can still change—"

"I don't want to be alone," she said, cutting him off.

A tall man carried in a tray and placed two plates on each side of the table and a bowl in the middle. The smell quickly enveloped the room and Tasmin's mouth watered.

The man left, banging the door shut behind them.

She sat quickly at the table and clutched her hands together, waiting for Isaac to say a prayer.

"It's just us," he said. "Eat when you're ready."

He picked up his cutlery and began eating. She watched how he skipped his prayer and began placing the food into his mouth.

But that isn't how we eat meals here. She didn't have time to think about it, however, rather skipping the prayer herself, grabbed the fork to shoved the food straight into her mouth.

One mouthful swallowed, by the time she chewed the second, her stomach was already full. She looked to the plate full of food, and envied Isaac able to eat more.

"We should of eaten better on the road," he said.

"But we didn't have a lot of food," she said.

"Still. I could have caught something and cooked it."

She glared at him. "There was enough."

The only thing missing on Tamsin's plate were the heads off the broccoli.

"You're not hungry?"

She shook her head. "It's... not that."

"You're not used to eating, are you?"

How did he know? She looked down at herself, realizing just how skinny she was.

She didn't leave the table until he was finished, and then she crawled into bed and slept solidly until morning.

When she woke, a newspaper was waiting for her on the table, next to a bowl of fruit and a note.

"Sleep, rest, and relax. I'll come for you when everything is sorted."

Ivy is so different in this life. She thought about the idea that perhaps Ivy had been meant to be a man all along, and he a woman. *What changed?* She took a moment to think about it, but nothing came to her. It was like being caught on a wheel that never ended. *But now that something has changed, does that mean there's no wheel now?*

She slumped in the chair, thinking of all the different lives they'd gone through, the horrors they'd endured, and the pain and suffering everyone went through. It caused a shiver to run over her body.

Isaac came for her just before lunch. "Are you hungry?"

She shook her head. She wasn't use to so much food. It was only a week ago and she dreamed about having something to eat. Now all the food in front of her, made her sick. She sat at the table and watched him eat a large portion of meat and two vegetables on the side. Her stomach twisted. It yearned to be full, but it had to get use to working the way it should.

She breathed in, savoring the fragrances, knowing it'll take time.

"We're allowed to lease the house for a few months, and then they'll let us buy it."

Don't people make houses? "Buy a house?"

He nodded. "I have to go to the mill tomorrow and work. The owner of the house said if I stay with them long enough, then I can buy it."

She looked around the room. "What do I do?"

"What do you want to do?"

I want to read and grow my own plants, make medicine and heal the sick.

"Read."

He nodded, finishing off the last of his food. "There's books down the road. You can borrow them, and there's some you can buy."

She smiled. *Leaving with him was the right thing to do.*

Isaac packed up what little things they owned and drove out to their house. Right on the very end of the street, before the riverbank, stood a small cottage-like house. It had large square windows with yellow fabrics in them.

"I think it needs to be painted blue," he said, opening the car door for her.

She got out and looked up and down the street. There were barely eight houses before it reached the end of the main road.

"This is the edge of town," she said in a small voice.

"Yep. Furthest house there is, except the farming houses. But I knew you didn't want that."

The idea of a farming house sounded nice too. Anything away from her mother finding where she was, sounded perfect.

She walked inside and breathed in the stale air. Cracking open the windows, letting the breeze come in, she wondered who'd lived there before.

"I'll make some furniture."

She nodded, hoping they wouldn't have to sleep on the floor for too long.

"And we'll get a dog."

She smiled. "Sounds lovely."

. . .

Isaac did everything he'd promised, except for the dog. Every time a dog came near Tamsin, it barked at her non-stop.

"Maybe we'll get a cat instead."

She nodded.

As the days passed, Tamsin ate a little more each day.

One afternoon, Isaac came through the door and called out her name. She stood in the doorway, concerned at his volume.

"Won't the neighbors hear you?" she said.

"Look!" He crossed the room and held out a little brown package. "Now we have a home, we can have rations. Look—they gave us chocolate."

She held up the dark piece of flat food and studied it. It softened underneath her fingers. "What is it?" she asked, scrunching up her nose.

He took it back, broke a piece off, and placed it into his mouth.

She watched him roll it over his tongue and then smile.

"You'll never know," he said, "unless you try it."

She copied him, but with a much smaller piece. The moment it hit her tongue, she recognized the sugar instantly. But the bitter sweetness quickly took over.

"This is ..." she rolled it around her mouth.

"Delicious!" he finished the sentence for her.

She rolled it around her mouth again and again, then asked for more.

"Would you like to go to church tomorrow?"

"Church?" She felt all stiff in the joints. *My mother goes to Church every Sunday.* Tamsin had never attended in this life. Previous ones, she attended as much as her family did. But never in this life.

Would my mother be there? She shivered at the thought.

"We don't have to if you don't want to, but it might be good for you to meet some people."

She nodded and shoved more chocolate into her mouth.

"Are you alright?" Isaac leaned into Tamsin and whispered as they entered the church.

She nodded, but it felt stiff. Reaching for him, she held onto his arm. He placed a hand softly over her fingers and looked down at her to smile.

"My boss believes you are my daughter."

She looked up at him, as they stopped in line, waiting for people to take their seats.

"I didn't correct him," he added.

She nodded. *A father! That seemed fitting given all that he had done for her.*

Inside the church, Tamsin looked around and studied the tall ceilings, the colored glass, and the wooden seats.

It's so different from the bricks in Wales, and the little wooden room in England.

He held out his hand and gestured for her to sit.

"You first," she whispered.

He sat down and Tamsin moved in next to him. Everyone else settled into nearby seats and the door behind them closed.

The priest walked down the aisle and stood at the podium, and then he began to read from his book.

The door opened again and closed with a bang.

Tamsin froze. *Is that my mother?* She didn't dare turn to look.

"Can I sit here?" warm liquid voice enveloped her.

Tamsin slowly turned and looked straight into the man's eyes. She inched closer to Isaac, and the man sat down.

"Are you sure you are alright?" Isaac whispered into her ear so that no one else heard.

Her neck too stiff to move, she wobbled her head up and down, causing all types of pain to run through her chest.

Tamsin moved her neck to the side, looking at the man who'd sat down.

The curvature of his nose was similar, along with the shape of his ears.

Her heart sped up and beat in her chest at a rapid rate, faster than she had ever experienced.

That has to be Ivy. Her mouth went dry. *He looks exactly like her!*

She then moved her eyes to the opposite side and looked at Isaac. *If Ivy just sat down, then why did I think Isaac was Ivy?*

She breathed in and out, slowly and stiffly.

The priest read his message and led the congregation in songs. Then, once he blew out the candles, he walked down the aisle and opened the doors.

The man beside her was the first one out.

Tamsin stood, clutching at her chest.

"Let's stand out in the garden," Isaac said by her side. "We can meet some new people."

She nodded and followed him out, but in the sunshine she remained quiet, looking for where the man had gone.

"Tamsin, there's my employer. Let me introduce you to him."

Tamsin did as asked, trying to put Ivy in the back of her head.

The week was uneventful. Isaac left for work early and returned home with new materials to make furniture. She sat and often read to him until they ran out of light, then she'd light as many candles around her, and continued going.

"Do you know," she began, "that house over there has electricity?"

"Yes, I know, and I've asked for this house to be wired up. But it won't be until next month."

"A month?"

"They ran out of materials and are waiting for them to come in. This was the last street in the whole town."

"Does it take a long time?"

"I don't know." He banged the hammer down on a nail, then stood up the frame he'd been working on. "I did see a town all lit up a couple of years ago, but that was close to a city. Out here, it would take longer."

"How many places have you been?"

"I never counted."

"Where is your real home?"

He laughed. "You're full of questions tonight." He looked at the book on her lap. "You don't want to keep reading?"

She shook her head. "I want to know who you are."

He put down the tools and crossed his legs. "I left when I was fourteen. My mother died and my brother had been posted to the war. My father didn't leave his room, and I was afraid of what he would do once he did."

"Your mother died?"

He nodded. "She wore bruises like yours. So did I." He turned back to the frame, adding another piece to it.

"My father told the doctor that she had a sickness." He shook his head. "And the doctor believed him."

Tamsin had nearly been a doctor herself, back in Germany. Even back then, she would never have believed that. But that had been before she'd known what people did to create such bruising.

"See, I've ruined the moment. It's better when you read."

She turned back to the book and searched for where she'd gotten up to. "The different accidents of life," she read, "are not so changeable as the feelings of human nature…"

. . .

231

Friday was spent at the very edge of the garden, finishing the end of her book. She placed it down beside her and looked up to the trees.

A bluebird flew in and landed on the branch, gathering with others.

She stood and watched; it had a piece of twig in its beak, collecting it up with others.

"Tamsin?"

She twisted and saw Isaac at the back door.

Collecting her book, she hurried up the dirt path and saw him slumped against the doorframe.

"What have you done?" She called out to him as she ran across the garden, reaching out to him.

He took a step back, inching away from her hand.

"Let me help you," she said, clutching onto him.

She slipped her arm underneath his and helped him into the front room. His warmth radiated into her and she took note of his clammy complexion. Sweat dripped from his hair, down around his face, and his breathing seemed rapid.

"Have you hurt yourself?" she asked as she helped him to the cushions.

He shook his head. "I didn't feel right all morning and, after I ate, I collapsed."

"We need to take you to a doctor."

"No, I need sleep."

She sighed. Looking him over, feeling his temperature, listening to his heart rate, she could see all the signs. "Have you cut yourself?"

"Not today... but I did last week."

"Show me."

He lifted up his shirt, and she saw a tiny graze across his back. Around the skin, it had turned purple, and blue veins were raised to the surface, spidering out.

"It's septic."

"It'll be fine. I just need to sleep it off."

"You're not fine, and if we don't get the right medicine, you'll die."

He laughed but it was a slow, labored laugh. "It's a tiny cut. I can't die from this."

She pinched her lips together. *You're already half-dead.* "I'll go and get a doctor," she said flatly.

She fetched some water and placed it by his head. Making sure he was comfortable, she left him alone and hurried into town.

A little blue bird followed her along the tree line and she wondered why it had returned now. *Are you trying to tell me something?* She kicked up her heels, hurrying. *I wonder who you are and why you're watching over me.*

Reaching town, she looked for the first person she could find to ask where the doctor would be. Up ahead, she saw a woman with a small child. Rushing towards them, she all jumped onto the road when a man stepped out of a shop.

She stopped and glared.

"Miss!" he said, taking his hat off and bowing his head.

Tamsin recognized him instantly. The man at the church who sat beside her, her looked just like her Ivy in the previous life, but she too had changed so much in this life.

From the front-on, though, and in such close proximity, Tamsin no longer could mistake those eyes, the slender nose, the energy about her... him.

Ivy. My Ivy. There's no denying it.

"Can I help you?" he asked, looking her up and down.

"I'm looking for a doctor."

He replaced his hat. "One for animals?"

She shook her head.

"Then you want Doctor Wallace."

"Wallace?" She followed where he pointed to the end of the

street, past the church and on the left, to the first house in sight. "There?"

He nodded. "Would you like me to walk you?"

She took a step back. Her heart skipped a beat. *There isn't anything I've wanted more than to be by your side... no matter where or when or...*

"Miss?" he stepped forward.

She needed to hurry and be back to Isaac before he got any worse. "I'll be fine, thank you." She turned and paused before walking off. "Can I have your name?"

"Ian."

She smiled. *Ivy is an Ian. It suits her.*

She hurried down the street and into the doctor's office. Doctor Wallace drove her home and treated Isaac on the floor.

"My wife and I did the same thing when we first married," the doctor said as he looked around the house. "Except we already had twin boys and my father-in-law insisted that he make everything." He pulled instruments that Tamsin had never seen from his bag and placed them beside Isaac's head. "Which was a good thing," the doctor went on. "Because I'm good with needles, not a hammer and nails." He laughed, and so did Isaac.

"Why isn't your wife here attending you?"

Isaac and Tamsin locked eyes.

"It is just myself and my daughter."

Doctor Wallace nodded. He continued on pilling out little bottles of liquid, lining them up on the floor.

Medicine has changed. Tamsin watched him carefully, assessing his different medical approach. Where are this doctor's herbs and oils?

She sighed in confusion, but didn't take her eyes off him for an instant.

"Now stay still," Wallace said, placing the needle into his patient's muscle and injecting a brown liquid.

"What is that?" she asked.

"This—" he held up the syringe, "—is a needle. You would have had a few of these when you were a child."

Tamsin held back her eye roll. "I meant, what is *in* the needle?"

"Just a little medicine to make him feel better." He rubbed Isaac's arm.

"What is it made from?" she insisted.

Wallace laughed. "Full of questions this one."

Isaac nodded. "She is. Humor her."

"Very well." Wallace collected up his bottles and syringe, placing it back in his bag. "Morphine is the best treatment for any illness. It takes away the pain and puts the patient in ease."

"Morphine?" She twisted her head. *That sounds an awful lot like morphium.*

"I've heard of it before," Isaac reassured her.

"How does it kill the infection?"

"Never mind that dear, your father needs some rest."

"Thank you, Doctor," Isaac said.

"Rest. Drink plenty of water. Stay away from the whisky and, Isaac, no work for a couple of days, if you can, make it a full week."

Tamsin showed him out and closed the door behind him. After watching him drive off, she turned and inspected the incision.

"What's the matter?" Isaac whispered.

"The doctor is no good."

He laughed.

"This is not a laughing matter. He gave you morphine."

"And?"

"He didn't mention anything about the infection."

"But I feel really good," Isaac smiled.

Tamsin shook her head. "No, that's not good. Morphium is a pain killer, it does nothing to heal you."

"He said morphine."

"That's what I said," she snapped. "And besides, what doctor doesn't even clean the wound?"

"You know a lot about doctors."

"He didn't even take your temperature."

"But I feel great."

"Of course, you do." She sighed, thinking of the healing things she could do with what very little they had. "Do you have whisky?"

"There's not much left." He pointed to a small box on the other side of the room. "Wait. The doctor said no whisky—"

She cut him off. "Forget that doctor." Reaching for the bottle, she removed the lid and sniffed it. The stench was thick, hitting her nostrils like a burn. Instantly pulling it away, she replaced the lid and put it to the side. Lifting his shirt again, she inspected the wound.

"What are you doing?" he asked.

"That wound needs fixing. It's already entered your bloodstream, but I have methods of extracting it."

"Tamsin?" He went to sit up.

"Stay still," she snapped, and he laid back down as he was told.

She boiled a pot of water and slipped in two large spoons and a butter knife. They boiled for over ten minutes while she washed her hands and fingernails. Going to the bedroom, she retrieved a towel and his belt.

Then she poured out the hot water and placed one of the spoons onto the direct flame of the gas stove.

The other two, she used to cut and scrap the puss away from his cut.

"Bite down on the belt," she said.

"How do you know how to do this?" he asked, mumbling around the belt.

"Can you please trust me?" She inspected the wound again. As it oozed, she scraped more puss and cleaned the skin. The blood seemed clotted, but once she took away the muck, it ran red.

She threw all the utensils into the sink and clicked the stove off.

"Drink this," she said, holding out the whisky.

He sipped it.

"Drink it all," she said.

"I'm not a good drunk."

She laughed. "You'll pass out from the pain."

"Bottoms up."

Wrapping her hand in the towel, she picked up the spoon, carried it straight over and pressed it to the wound.

He screamed an almighty bellow as the skin beneath her hand sizzled. Lifting it off, she then threw that into the sink and sat beside him, listening to his breaths well after he'd passed out.

Isaac woke a day later when the doctor arrived.

Tamsin let him in reluctantly, and he put down his oversized bag and put on his glasses.

"I see you had a rough night," he said.

The bags beneath Isaac's eyes sat dark and heavy.

"He hasn't had enough fluids."

"You need to make sure he drinks," he said, using an accusing tone.

Tamsin rolled her eyes and crouched down, watching everything he did.

"What have you done here?" The doctor pointed at the wound.

"I cleaned it and cauterized it."

His mouth fell open. "You're not a doctor! You should never—"

"He wouldn't have lasted the night."

The doctor shook his head. "I'll give you another injection, but please, miss, it's best you leave the healing practices to me."

Tamsin got to her feet and waited by the window, hoping he'd leave faster than before.

"What was all that about?" Isaac asked as the doctor's car drove away.

"I don't think he's a real doctor."

"But how would you know that?"

She shrugged.

The following day, Tamsin asked Isaac for some money to buy food. He gave her the last he had and she walked to the town's main street.

I know if I buy herbs, I can crush them and make a paste. Hopefully, they have the right stuff, and that way I can get the toxins out of his blood and he'll feel better.

As she thought about all the different herbs she needed, she looked up to see a man leaning up against a fence.

She stopped and wondered what to do. *Do I cross the road? Do I speak to him?* She'd never been so nervous around someone before, other than when she'd seen him previously.

"Mr. Ian."

He laughed.

"No need to call me mister. Ian is just fine."

She nodded, but held back from a curtsy like her mother had taught her. Everything her mother had said seemed like a lie.

"Good day to you," she said, and turned on her heels.

"Can I walk with you?"

She nodded.

"Thank you, Miss Tamsin."

"No need for the Miss," she teased, "Tamsin is just fine."

He laughed.

They walked beside one another, and she looked up to him, noticing his height, his age, his demeanor. *So much has changed. And yet his eyes were just as bright. He must be at least twenty-one.*

She smiled. *Was he waiting for me? Does he remember me?* She didn't think so.

"Are you well?" he went on.

Scrunching her eyebrows together, she looked him up and down.

"You went to the doctor's the other day."

"Oh, it's for my..." she hesitated, "father. He's unwell."

"Is he good to you?" He stopped and she stopped, too. They faced each other and she felt more nervous than she ever had.

"What ever do you mean?" Tamsin guarded herself, she didn't know what to make of his abrupt question.

"You wear this coat," he pulled at the collar and she stepped back, clutching it closed again. "It's much too hot and humid." He took his eyes off of her and looked to the treetops. She felt the gaze lift off of her, like a weight releasing. "It's like you've got something to hide," he added.

Tamsin looked around, seeing that the main road was still several house lengths away. "Good day to you, sir." She picked up her pace.

"I'm sorry," he said, pacing after her. "Please forgive me. I'm trying not to be rude."

"I like this coat, and no, I'm not hiding anything. Isaac is a good man." She continued to walk and he fell into stride beside her.

"Isaac?"

"I meant, my father." She continued to walk, but not as fast as before. As he fell into step beside her, she thought of all ways to start a conversation but also wanted to avoid any slip ups. There was so much she wanted to ask before in the previous lives, but knowing Ian couldn't remember, she decided to keep it to small talk. "Where have you come from?"

"The secrets of the mystery man," he laughed. "Nowhere exciting. I travel through, sightseeing mostly."

"I hear there is a war going on," she said. "You'd do more sightseeing if you were to join the troops."

"Psst," he clicked his tongue. "And get a bullet through the head while I'm at it?"

Tamsin stopped walking and looked at him. "You're a deserter?"

"Shhh." He stepped forward, held her arm, and looked around to see if anyone had heard. "Not so loud."

Tamsin laughed. "So, you are!" She stood back in awe.

"So? Wouldn't you if you had no interest in fighting another's war?"

"By the sounds of it, it seems to be everyone's war. The entire planet's!"

He took a big breath in. "Smart, aren't you?"

"Tell me something, Mr. Ian. What happens to a man who deserts when the authorities find him?"

"Are you planning on dobbin' me in?"

"Oh no," she said, clutching her chest. "Please, forgive me. That wasn't my intention. I just have a curious mind."

He stood watching her carefully. Tamsin felt his eyes all over her, and it made her nervous. "Very well," he said. "Depends on what state you're in. Some states lock you in prison; others will hang you. Heard there are even states that line you up with all the other deserters and shoot you in the head one by one."

Tamsin nodded.

Ian burst out laughing. "For a woman, you took that information very well."

"Oh." She looked around, confused. "How was I supposed to take it?"

"Not like a man," he said.

"A man?" she half-squealed, her voice high-pitched.

He laughed again. "So matter-of-factly," he explained.

She laughed, nervous once more.

They began walking towards the main road, still several houses away. "Why are you out this early?"

"My father." She coughed, half with nerves and half suspecting that she had caught something from her fake father. "He is very sick and I haven't what I need to heal him."

"None of the shops are open yet."

"I know, but I must wait until they does."

He smiled.

"Do you have employment to attend?"

Slowly, he nodded. "I sure do."

A nervous feeling washed over her. As they reached the end of the road, she wondered if she'd ever see him again.

He paused and faced her, stepping closer.

She took a step back, but the brick wall behind her, the side of the shop, stopped her from going any further.

"What are you doing?" she asked.

"What I should have done the first time I saw you." He pressed his lips against hers.

She pushed her hands into his chest and he leaned back.

"I'm sorry," he said.

"Don't be," she said, trying to regain her breath.

He leaned in again, and she pressed her palm to his chest, stopping him abruptly.

"Now I'm sorry," she whispered, their foreheads pressed together. His hands on her hips, squeezed tightly. His breath brushing against her cheeks.

"Why?"

"Because I can't let you do that again."

He took a step back, and instantly she regretted her words. Knowing Isaac was at home, very sick and waiting for her to return, she couldn't run off with this man now. Not after all Isaac had done for her.

"Will I see you again?" he asked.

She shrugged her shoulders, not wanting to promise

anything. Turning away then, she headed down the main road towards the particular shop she needed. Every step she took, she felt his gaze on her back and used all her strength not to turn around and run back into his arms.

Reaching the the store, she stood waiting, keeping her eyes on the ground, forcing herself not to search for him again.

Isaac was awake when she returned home with her arms full of fresh vegetables.

"Are we expecting people over for dinner?" he asked.

She corked her head to the side, curious as to what he meant.

"You've brought enough food to feed the street."

She laughed. "We will eat next to none of this. I'll make a paste and set it over your skin. It'll make you feel tired, but it'll draw all the sickness out."

He smiled. "You amaze me."

The air caught in the back of her throat.

"You do," he said, sitting up.

She didn't waste any time, boiling water and preparing the herbs. Often mumbling to herself, she thought back to her previous lives where she worked with herbs often. *The right mixture will draw it out faster, but there's so much missing.* She tried to think of alternatives, but didn't see those at the shop either. It had been too long since she made her last medicine paste, wishing she had a book to work from. A loud knock at the door made her jump.

"Miss. Tamsin," Doctor Wallace said. "How's he doing today?"

"Doctor," she opened the door. "I wasn't expecting you."

"I must visit my patient to see how he's doing. Arh, still on the floor." He shook his head.

"I just laid back down," Isaac said.

"Good, so you're on the mend then."

"He doesn't look it," Tamsin added, returning to her mixture.

"Soup is good for the soul, they say."

Tamsin couldn't help hear the mocking tone to his voice.

"She's not making soup," Isaac said. "She's making medicine."

The doctor laughed, and then leaned in and smelled the mixture. "Medicine is for chemists. Not wives." He moved back towards Isaac and retrieved a syringe and a medicine bottle. "You know," he said as he leaned closer to Isaac. "They used to kill woman who made medicine. Accused them of being witches."

"Actually," Tamsin spoke up, "woman used to be the healers, and men accused them of different things, killing them for their own reasons."

"What's got into you?" Isaac asked.

The doctor whispered something, then added, "women, huh?"

After he left, Tamsin continued with her mixture. It took the rest of the day and into the evening. Isaac slept off and on, only waking for sips of water.

"You're still at it?" he asked with a croaky voice.

"It'll be done soon enough."

"Have you eaten?"

She nodded and held up a celery stick. She knew it wasn't much, but her stomach was still getting use to having as much food as she wanted.

Celery tastes so different here. I don't remember it being so crisp back in England. She sighed. The thought of England tingled her senses. Her mind raced.

"Is Ivy a man's name?" she asked out loud, quickly covering her mouth when she realized she'd spoken aloud.

Isaac sat up and, after moment of silence, he spoke. "Yes, but I knew a boy named Ivy growing up. Why do you ask?"

Tamsin wiped her hands down the front of her dress, trying to think of an answer. "It was in the paper this morning.

It said Mr. Ivy Thomason. I didn't know that was a man's name."

He nodded. "What about him?"

She shrugged her shoulders.

"What was the article about?" he insisted. "Must have been good if you remembered his name."

"Oh," she laughed, trying to hide her discomfort. "Didn't read it. Was stuck on the unusual name." She turned away and lit more candles, lighting the place up.

After a bathroom break and a full stomach of water, Isaac laid down and Tamsin covered him in a thick, green paste.

"It tingles."

"That's not a good sign."

"Didn't you make it right?"

She scoffed. "No, it means you're sicker than you realize." She shook her head. "I'll make more tomorrow."

Covering his chest, stomach, face, neck, arms, and legs, she only finished after he was fast asleep.

Three days and nights later, and he was back to normal.

"See," the doctor said, "my medicine works!"

Tamsin's shoulders went up and around her ears. She could have thrown the hot pot right across the room, landing it right between his eyes.

"Is that right?" Tasmin asked.

The doctor helped Isaac to his feet and they shook hands. "Thank you so much, Doctor. I feel amazing."

"Very good. I'm glad to have done my job. Make sure you stop by my office with payment once you've started working again."

"Very well Doctor, thank you once again."

Tamsin stood beside Isaac and watched Doctor Wallace enter his car and drive down the road. Once he was out of sight, Tamsin nearly screamed.

"Payment!" Tamsin clenched her teeth. "He wants a payment for what?"

"Keep your voice down!" Isaac crossed the room and placed his lips against her forehead.

She froze, and he didn't pull back. Instead, he wrapped his arms around her and squeezed her tight.

"I know it wasn't the doctor who helped me," he whispered. "You saved my life."

She pulled away.

"I owe my daughter my life." He smiled, and the warmth of the first day he met her, returned to his sunken eyes.

She turned and faced the sink, conscious of the small space between them.

"You don't owe me anything," she said. "You got me out of that town and saved my life. Now we are even."

He laughed. "Is that what this is about?"

She shook her head.

"What day is it?" he asked with his voice picking up pace.

"Monday."

"Oh, so I was only sick a couple of days?"

She laughed. "Try over a week."

He nodded. "Felt about right. How about we go to the pictures tomorrow night?"

"Can we afford—"

He held up a hand. "Of course."

Tamsin washed her dress and her coat down in the nearby river. She wore one of Isaac's many shirts to cover herself, so that if anyone came near, they wouldn't see the discoloring of her skin.

The bruising was stubborn, but had changed to a yellow around the edges. For years, patches of blue and black were so big, that entire sections of her body had no natural skin color. Back when she was still living with her mother, she wasn't surprised if the damage never healed. Now, it was only a matter of time until there was no evidence at all, like it had never happened. But for Tamsin, memories never fade. And she was glad that part was over.

The stream was fresh and extra cold, dancing between her toes. Small fish swam up and quickly took off when she moved.

Pulling her dress out, she squeezed all the wetness out and flung it over her shoulder, picking up a large stick and heading back to the house. There, she held it up over a frame Isaac had made for a chair and, as the sun dried it, she beat it with a stick.

By the time Isaac arrived home, the dress was dried and she was ready.

"Pictures tonight," he said with such excitement that she laughed.

He came in close and picked her up off the floor and swinging her around, only then placing her back down again.

She stumbled backwards, pushing an arm out for him to stop.

"I'm sorry," he said.

I know he means well, but my body is broken. I don't know if I can do this. She smiled, but it didn't reach his eyes.

He walked back out to the car and she watched after him.

Closing her eyes, she regretted her actions. *Have I offended him?* She opened her eyes again and he was back at the door, with a single yellow sunflower.

"I saw this on the way home," he said, handing it to her. "And I thought of you."

"It's massive!" She held it, seeing it took up both her hands.

"Make sure you don't take it outside, though."

"Why not?"

"Whoever I stole it from won't be happy."

Tamsin clutched her chest and then laughed.

"Ready to go?"

She quickly placed the stem in a small cup of water and it instantly fell over.

"It is a big flower," he laughed, reaching for a breakfast bowl.

Laying the flower down, so that the end just touched the water, Tamsin turned, blew out the candles, and left the house.

The pictures were nothing she could ever have imagined. In all her times, the idea that people could have taken photos and film from around the world and then sit somewhere to watch it unfold like this fascinated her.

Imagine if I took a photo of every year in each life... I wonder how many photographs I'd have.

She laughed and linked arms with Isaac as they left.

He looked to her with soft, loving eyes and smiled.

She smiled back, but feared that the expression didn't reach her eyes.

Outside, in the foyer of the theater, many people gathered to talk.

"I'm just popping into the bathroom," she said. She left his side and was back within minutes, but Isaac wasn't where she'd left him.

She stood waiting. *Perhaps he went to the bathroom himself?* She waited for another ten minutes and decided it wasn't possible. Walking out of the foyer and into the night air, she looked up and down the street, noticing Isaac standing with a group of men.

They broke their huddle when she walked closer to them.

"Miss," one said, tilting his hat.

"Are you ready to go?" Isaac asked, walking closer to her and then taking her to the car.

"Who were those men?" she whispered.

"Just locals. Nothing to worry about."

Worried? She wasn't worried until he said that, then instantly she knew something had been said. She saw it in their posture, sensed it in the air. There was always a stench that lingered in the air when conflict was happening.

"Can you tell me what's going on?"

"Well," he eventually broke the silence. "One of them was Brian, and I work with him. The other one was his friend and the far one was *his* friend."

"Okay."

Isaac opened her car door. She slid in and he slammed it, making her jump. As he walked around the front of the car, his cheeks were red.

He climbed in and slammed his door too.

"Are they friends of yours?" She asked him in a small voice, not wanting to push but desperate to know what had occurred.

"Sure," he said, shrugging his shoulders. "Please Tamsin, there is nothing to worry about."

"You do seem upset."

He took a deep breath in and held it. "There's a man in town that did something wrong. I don't agree how it was handled." He backed the car our and hit the gas too hard, causing her head to hit the seat behind her. "Can we leave it at that, please?"

She nodded, watching the darkness zoom past the window.

The next morning, well before sunrise, Tamsin woke to the sound of Isaac's car.

She sat up and peaked through the window, desperate to know where he was going.

He still had another day off of work, and he wasn't even in his work outfit. The events of the night before flickered through her mind.

Breathe, Tamsin. Doesn't mean something is happening. Just because Ivy is in town, that doesn't mean this is about her... him. Or, could it be?

She paced the room.

And I have to call her Ian! Not Ivy! "Arhh..." *she moaned out her frustrations.*

Quickly getting dressed, she wasn't going to sit around and wait to find out. Tamsin hurried along the street and into town. *Nothing is happening. I'm going for a nice walk while the weather is nice.*

What if someone asks me why I'm out so early? She squeezed the coat closed with both hands. Because I like the dark, yes that is what I'll say to them.

No. She shook her head. That won't work.

I know. 'It's none of your business, and you wouldn't question me if I was a man, so why would you now?'

They'd slap me in the face.

Being a woman was much harder than he'd imagined.

Tamsin made it to the main street. Pressing herself up against the wall, she looked both ways and saw nothing.

No one was around, and only a single vehicle drove along the street and out of town.

No one here. And only one car moving. She looked again and noticed six cars parked up the far end of the road, including Isaac's.

This isn't good. A shiver ran over her. She slipped off her shoes and held them in her hand. With the new advantage of not making any sound, she ran across the street and pressed herself up against the wall again. Hoping that no one had seen her.

Breathe, Tamsin, breathe!

She walked along the shopfront and froze.

A sound echoed out, like someone had been hit.

She moved quicker until she reached the alleyway, and then she stopped and listened.

"I had a brother who was posted and sent overseas," an angry voice said.

"Good for you!" Ian's voice said.

Tamsin gasped.

"And he was killed," the angry voice added.

"Who gives you the right to avoid your duty?" a different voice entirely said.

Tamsin recognized it instantly.

Isaac!

She heaved in and out, clutching her shoes to her chest until her knuckles when white. *I didn't save your life Isaac only for you to hurt my Ivy! How could you?* Tears swelled in her eyes. *How am I going to stop these men while I'm small, and still weak, and haven't healed, myself? Will they even listen to me?*

Would Isaac stop for me?

She stepped out of her hiding spot and into the alleyway. Instantly her eyes landed on Ian and she froze.

Tied up with his arms behind his back, he had more blood on his skin then he had blood in his body.

His eye was swollen, his lip fat, and his ear was half hanging from his head.

He lifted his head and locked eyes with Tamsin.

"Men, good men, die every day, and you…" one of the men beside him, holding a baseball bat covered in blood, paused his rant, stepped slightly away and backhanded Ian across the face, "you aren't a good man, and you get to stay here and live your live!"

"That's not fair!" another one on the opposite side, yelled at Ian.

Isaac stepped in and hit Ian across the face.

Tamsin stepped forward. All the nerves in her body had told her not to. Her muscles screamed at her to stop. But it was like her feet moved on their own and she gravitated towards him, towards Ian, *her* Ian.

"You're not going to get away with this," the one with the bloody bat said, raising it up over his head.

"No!" Tamsin yelled out, running towards him.

"Tamsin!" Isaac looked up and stepped forward.

The man in front of Tamsin swung around with a hand out in front of him and smacked her across the face.

Tamsin lifted up off the ground and was flung to the side. Her head collided with something hard and she felt herself wobble, then crash down to the ground.

With one eye open she saw Isaac running straight towards her.

"Tamsin!" Isaac cried, as he reached her, picked her up, cradling her in his arms.

She opened her eyes at looked to Ian.

Covered in blood, he could barely lift his head. The angry man beside him lifted the bat once again, and brought it down, forcefully colliding against the crown of Ian's head. He slumped and a thick line of blood oozed from his mouth.

She closed her eyes and then opened them again. She felt nothing.

"Tamsin, why are you here?" Isaac cried over her.

"Get her to the doctor!" a voice nearby yelled.

She closed her eyes again. When she opened them, she saw the building above her brightened by the light, slowly moving away.

"Stay with me!" Isaac yelled. "I need you!" he cried.

She felt her arms dropped down and behind her, but they were numb, hollow even.

She opened her eyes and saw Isaac's bright red face looking down at her.

"Hey," his voice cracked. "How are you feeling?"

Her bottom lip had cracked open, and she whispered.

He pressed his ear to her lips and she said it again. "Ian?"

He pulled away, his eyes widening, and he glared at her. He shook his head.

She closed her eyes, no longer feeling the need to open them again.

UNDERWATER CITY

2097

*T*amati's mother carried him on her hip as she walked through the cold, grey tunnels towards the meeting hall.

The room was buzzing with people as she crossed the rows of tables and sat down at the same one she did every other day.

"Tamati!" Two fingers reached across the table and squeezed his plump cheek tight.

He opened his mouth, twisted his head, and sank his teeth deep into the woman's hand.

"Ouch!" she screamed, pulling it away.

"Every time you do that, he bites!" his mother snapped.

"Teach your child to stop doing that, Mary," Denelle said in an accusing tone. Her vibrant orange hair, fuzzing out in each direction.

"You want to touch his face, then you're the idiot that gets bitten."

"He's not a dog," she snapped.

"Just stop. Watch him for me, will ya?" She pushed his little body across the table towards the fuzzy-orange-haired woman.

He scrunched his eyebrows together and exposed his teeth.

"You're a little vampire, aren't you?" She held up a carrot stick for him to take.

He reached for it and she shoved it into her own mouth, quicker than lightning.

"Ha!" she laughed. "You're going to have to be quicker than that!"

"Are you teasing him again?" his mother snapped. "Give me back my baby!"

He was swung around, and stopped facing the tray of food. He didn't know what this place was, but they always had bright vegetables that were never cooked and he hadn't seen the sun shine once.

If the sun doesn't shine here, then how do the vegetables grow?

He planned on asking that when he developed a full voice and words.

"See, look at him? You can tell he's always thinking."

Mother sighed. "*I'm* always thinking."

"Still nothing?"

She shook her head.

Tamati watched her carefully.

"How can there be no word? It's been a year."

"Longer than a year; he's already eighteen months."

"Oh."

"Yeah, oh. At the very least, they could tell me he is dead."

"They won't do that if he isn't."

"Sure, sure." His mother ran her hands over her tired face. "So, if he's alive, then why hasn't he come home? He's not out fighting the war. He's transporting resources, and that doesn't take a year!"

"He did go through a war zone."

She sighed again.

"Eat," Denelle insisted.

"I'm too tired."

"I said you were tired yesterday and you denied it."

"For once, could you not lecture me? It's like having Mom back in my ear again."

"Let me take wiggleworm for the day. Let you rest and catch up on a few things."

"What? You?" She shook her head and handed him more food. "He'll come back with a missing toe or you'll somehow grow a third arm out of his chest."

"Pfft. Kids love me."

"Kids love to torture you." She pointed a carrot stick at her. "There's a big difference."

"Fine. But stop whining. Get your butt up to the control center and find out what's happening up there."

His mom rolled her eyes. "How many times have I told you, Denelle? We're not privy to that information."

"But your husband hasn't returned from his mission. You have a right to know where he is."

"Think about it like this. All of us—" she pointed to the many people around the crowded room, "—come from every corner of the globe. What would happen if we were told that one country was holding another one hostage, or war crimes were being waged, or that one country was winning and another one wasn't? It would disrupt our way of life down here. It'd ruin our chance for peace and it could tear down our entire community and flood all the ones around us. Peace is what keeps us safe."

"People have a right to know."

She sighed, then spoke very slowly. "And knowledge is power, right?"

"Yeah." She nodded and her bright fuzzy hair bounced around.

"So, *if* all of us—" she made a circular motion with one finger, "—knew what was going on up there, then there would be a war going on down here, too."

"Oh." She nodded like she agreed.

Tamati kept picking food off the tray and eating it.

. . .

Tamati sat in the classroom writing out his math.

"Remember to carry the four and then add it..." the teacher trailed off.

Tamati looked to the door and saw the principal pointing at him through the window.

"Tamati," his teacher said. "Gather your things and I'll see you tomorrow."

He did as he was told and rushed out the door.

His mother, with puffy red rings around her eyes, gathered him into her arms. She pulled away and kissed him on the forehead.

"It's your father, Tamati." She wiped away her tears.

He had been preparing for this moment ever since he could remember in this life.

"He's come home," she said.

"Home?"

She nodded, unable to speak.

The principal bent down to his level and spoke slowly. "Your father is in the hospital. He is unwell and might not survive. Go and be with him. Go and meet your father, Tamati."

He nodded and took his mother's hand.

Rushing through the school, they pushed open the doors and ran out into the open.

"How do we get to the hospital?"

"I only know the train." She pointed up above them. A tube ran across the top of the school and disappeared into a nearby building. They were numerous, going in all different directions.

"Which one?"

"I don't know, but we will find out when we get to the top." She pressed a button and they stepped into the lift. It bounced off the ground and stopped when it reached the platform.

His mother had hold of his shoulders because, even though

he been in the tubes many times, he couldn't stand still, and the instant sickness he felt made the dizziness worse.

"No time for stairs; we have to hurry."

He sighed, letting her drag him through the maze and onto the train that a guard pointed to.

"Do you want to sit?" she asked.

He nodded. It helped with the movement. He hadn't had time to get used to a car in the last life. In this one, he still couldn't get his head around the idea that they were living beneath the ocean.

I hope there isn't a next life. He sighed. *It's getting harder to understand and adapt.*

He missed the old times when life had been simple. Here, it was fast, and everyone rushed through their days, packing more in.

But, most of all, he missed the sunshine on his face.

"This is it." His mother stood and he slipped his hand into hers.

They stepped out of the train and stood in the hospital foyer.

"Yes, please!" the man behind the counter yelled for them to come forward.

"I've been told my husband is here."

"Name?"

"Miko Rodger."

"Yes, here we are." He pressed a button and a bell rang twice. "Follow this man." He handed something to him. "He will assist you to his room."

"Thank you," she said and, most likely without knowing, squeezed Tamati's hand.

"Take the stairs?" she whispered, leaning in to him.

He shook his head. *I'm not willing to wait any longer.*

Tamati leaned into his mother for support as the lift took them all the way up, high into the building. The man stepped out, and they followed him until he stopped in front of a door and gestured for them to go in.

"Stay here for a moment," she said, kissing him on the forehead.

Tamati stood outside and watched his mother walk in. She pressed both of her hands to her mouth and then disappeared behind a curtain.

All kinds of nerves stirred within him. The shiver ran across his skin. His stomach rolled, flipping like a tick caught in a trap. And he shifted his weight from one foot to another, feeling the urge to run.

I can't remember this man at all. He worried that the man wasn't going to like him. As he thought back to his earliest memory, he couldn't help but think to the father he'd had in America. *I was glad he went away. Is this one going to be the same?*

He shivered again.

But what if he is like the one in Germany or in Wales? He'd had so many fathers, and he'd had so many lives without them.

This man, I don't remember at all.

"Tamati?" his mother's voice called out.

He took a big deep breath in and stepped towards the curtain. The room was full of light, and he held up a hand to shield his eyes. Feeling his mother's arms wrap around him, he went forward as she pulled him closer to the bed.

He opened his eyes and saw a man. With the same facial features as he saw when he looked in the mirror, but he was all wrong.

Twisted slightly to the side, he was propped up by blocks so that he didn't lay flat.

Tamati gasped.

"It's okay, son," the man's voice said. "I'm not in pain."

"It's nice to meet you," Tamati whispered.

"We've met before, and you both spewed and peed on me."

Tamati laughed.

"It was the greatest moment of my life."

His mother burst into tears.

Tamati looked him over. Half of his body had been burnt. The skin exposed the flesh underneath and it looked more painful than Tamati could stomach. He looked up to the man's face and they locked eyes.

But the man only had the one, as the burning had consumed his entire left side, leaving him without an ear and half a head of hair.

"What happened?" Tamati whispered.

"I went to the surface to collect supplies for the city like always. The city needed fuel mostly because the solar was running low. When we got there, the fuel was already gone and we were taken captive."

His mother sobbed louder. "We had no idea."

"No one did. It happened so fast, we didn't even have time to message it in."

"Where did they take you?" Tamati sat down beside him, but was reluctant to take his hand.

"At first, they took us far away. Could have been the other side of the world, I'm not sure. We were locked in a cage for years, but we were all together." He drifted off into his thoughts.

"How did you escape?"

"Tamati!" his mother snapped.

"No, Mary, he should know." He looked to Tamati. "We didn't escape. They came for us and gave us a choice. We could fight with them or they would kill us."

Tamati gasped. *What type of war is this?*

"I wanted a chance to see you again, so I decided to fight." He shook his head and tears formed in his eyes. "Turns out, we went to fight against my own people. Once I found out, I made a pact with the others to escape, and that's when they did this." He gestured to his burnt body.

"How?" Tamati whispered, barely able to speak.

"It was some kind of bomb that had different effects at certain distances. It completely disintegrated a huge hole in the ground and everything in it. But I was standing the furthest away. That's why it only affected half of me."

As he gazed at his father's wounds, memories from his years of study as a doctor resurfaced and the old desire to help the sick kicked in. Standing, he collected a pair of gloves, and inspected the wounds closer. He lifted the scabs on the skin. "If we remove the scabs and dress your skin with natural herbs, hmmm… I'll have to think carefully on a concoction, but I could get it back to near normal. There will be scarring, of course." He stood straight and then noticed his error.

His father squinted his eyes. "You've learned that at your age?"

He shook his head. "I like to read."

"You're not using your father as a guinea pig, Tamati. He's in pain and the doctors can heal him."

Tamati sat back down, pulled off the gloves, and flicked them across the sterile room. They landed neatly in an open bin.

"Sure," he said, trying to mask his annoyance. *What do I know anyway? I've spent lifetimes reading nothing but biology, microbiology, and natural medicine. And this lifetime, all of that has been dismissed, like their knowledge is the only knowledge, with their little machines that they hover over a body and beeps telling them what's wrong and what to do about it.*

He slumped in his chair as his parents talked among themselves.

The dismissal of his knowledge hurt deeper than he realized. It reminded him of the middle ages. Ridiculous period," he sighed, *"when people forgot the medical advancements of the Ancient Greeks, Egyptians and the Romans, that propelled them ahead of their time. And all for what? The idea that seeing a naked body was too alarming?*

He sighed again.

"Tamati!" his mother snapped. *"Sit up straight and stop being so rude."*

He did as he was told, wishing that for one lifetime he could skip the child stage and remain an adult. He shivered again. *I don't wish for another life at all.*

He sat back in his chair and remained quiet as his mother told his father all the things he'd done growing up.

It was several years before his father was discharged from the hospital and returned home. Tamati walked through the door and found him trying to sit down at the table. He was too stiff and sore to move properly.

"Here's my son!" His father beamed, pointing across the room, apparently halfway through a conversation about him again.

"Hello there," a strange woman said, and then disappeared back into the guest room.

"Who is that? And why is she here?" Tamati sat down, smiling back at his father.

"She's a nurse and she's setting up a few things for me, so I can rest better."

Tamati rolled his eyes. "The best thing is for more movement, not less."

"How do you know these things?"

He shrugged. "I know things."

"Ready to put that knowledge to the test?"

Tamati sat up straight. "Are you serious? You're going to let me heal you?"

He nodded. "But there is one condition."

"What's that?"

"Don't tell your mother."

They both laughed, and the nurse walked back in. "Did I miss a good joke?" she asked.

And they laughed again.

. . .

"Excuse me, Mr. Tamati Smyth," an older voice came up from behind him.

Tamati turned to see the warden of the garden hobbling along on his wooden stick. The last time Tamati had seen him, he'd looked up to the old man. *If he hasn't shrunk, then I've grown a great deal these couple of years. I might be the tallest I've ever been.*

"What can I do for you, Mr. Zimile?" Tamati turned back to the plant and carefully pulled up a single root so that he didn't place unwanted stress on it.

"The doctor said I'm too old for my work." He shook his head. "But I feel fine. Well, my knees are sore and I'm tired a lot, but I can still work with the plants."

Tamati nodded, understanding. "Age is inevitable, sir."

He laughed. "I suppose it is."

"What is it that you want from me?"

He sighed. "I see you come in here collecting all sorts of things that others think are rubbish. But seeing your father recover like that, it's a…" he paused, looking for the right word. "A miracle!"

"Not a miracle, sir," Tamati corrected him. "Just a lot of hard work."

"I can see that. Would you help me feel better?"

"I can't click my fingers to make you feel twenty years younger." He laughed. "That's not going to happen."

"No, no. I'm no idiot. I mean… not younger, just not in as much pain."

Tamati nodded. "Can I have a think about it? I'm not sure what herbs or things I need. It'll take me a few days."

"Sounds speedy to me." He turned away and Tamati watched him disappear down the winding path. Exotic trees and plants littered the scenery, the glass dome full to the brim.

In all my lives, I've never gotten to grow old.

He breathed in the fresh air, filling his lungs. *I love this place.* He looked around, soaking in the sights. Trees towered up into the dome while bushes surrounded the edges. Flowers of all different colors were scattered across the ground and there wasn't any grass in sight.

The artificial light above illuminated the entire place without casting a shadow. The colors were so bright that Tamati often struggled with the strain it caused his eyes.

It's like I'm struggling to fit into the world more and more. He breathed in again, letting the natural fragrances calm him.

He gathered his pieces and stepped out into the cold, foreign place. The walls were always grey, and that annoyed him. *Why can't they paint them?* Even though it was a constant temperature, the look of the place made it feel so much colder.

The buildings stretched up to reach the roof, and Tamati lived with his parents six blocks from the dome. He took the stairs up the eighteen flights, and never passed anyone. Others always took the elevator.

He pushed open the door and smelt the strong fragrance in the air. It hit him hard, giving him an instant pain between the eyes.

"You're in for it now," his father said, coming into the open room.

"Tamati?" his mother called from where she lay stretched out in front of the projector wall, copying the positions the people were in. With her legs out in each direction, she stretched her arm up and over her head.

"In for what?" Tamati stood by his father and ran the roots he had collected under fresh water.

"Don't ignore me," she said, lowering the volume on the projector.

Tamati retrieved creams from the fridge and sat down at the table beside his father. He rolled up the sleeve of his shirt and applied it in the crevice of his arm.

"You know Zella?" His mother went on anyway. "The lady who lives a couple of houses down?"

"Yeah," his father answered, rolling his eyes at Tamati.

"She wants to know if you have a cure for her hair."

"Her hair?" Tamati scrunched up his face. A year after Tamati had begun his secret treatments, his father had stopped going to the doctor. He hadn't been able to handle the prodding and poking, and then the heavy pain killers. It had been messing him up. Everyone had thought his recovery was a miracle, even his mother, until they'd bumped into the doctor in the food court.

"I thought you were dead!" the doctor had exclaimed, and then checked him over, fascinated by his transformation.

His mother had marched them both back to the apartment and not let them leave until they'd explained themselves.

"You let him conduct experiments on you?" she'd yelled.

"Look at me," his father had said. "The boy has a gift!"

"For stupidity!"

Tamati had stood up. They'd both looked to him, and he'd explained how he understood plants, and what he needed to take from them to insert into the human body. After that, she'd never been able to close her mouth about it, telling nearly everyone in their quarter.

"Remember how she had so much hair? But then she lost all its color."

Tamati nodded, but concentrated on his father in front of him.

"Well, she was using lots of dyes and colorings, but then her hair started to strip. Now it's nothing but bald patches. Poor thing. Can you do something for her, Tamati?"

"For hair? Really?"

She flopped out of her position and stared. "Tamati! She's having a hard time."

Tamati and his father sighed at the same time. "Okay," Tamati said, sounding deflated. "I know! I have a treatment plan just in mind."

"You do?" She sat up straight, tucking her legs beneath her.

"What she needs to do is shave it all off and buy a wig."

His dad burst out into laughter.

His mum got up and threw the closest ornament across the room, missing him by miles, then turned and stormed off to her bedroom.

"Oh, you're going to pay for that one over and over again."

"I know." He continued applying the cream on his father's other arm. "But she has to stop telling people I'll heal them. I've got too much schoolwork to do."

"You're doing heaps better than I did, kid."

Tamati looked up from his arm and saw the sadness in his eyes. "Why did you choose to get supplies?" Avoiding the conversation for years, Tamati had never pushed his father about what had happened—not since the first day at the hospital. Even though he desperately wanted to know, he saw the pain in his eyes when people mentioned anything. A friend, a time, even a name of a particular tool caused him to glaze over and avoid speaking. It was like he turned off.

"Are you worried about finishing school?"

"I'm not worried." He heard the defense in his own voice.

"I thought you'd go into medicine."

He shook his head. "It's not what I want."

His father placed a hand over his own. "What do you want?"

I haven't a clue.

"It's okay not to know."

"But my birthday is in three days, and I'll receive my first mark. There are kids in my school that already have six."

Stupid things. Why does everyone need a mark to advertise what they've accomplished? What if I don't want to live to their standards? I want to do what's right!

"The first mark is your adulthood. It'll give you access to places that you haven't been before."

"Like the surface?" Tamati asked.

He nodded, but it was reluctant. "Sure, but for the love of all things you know that're good for you. Don't tell your mother."

He laughed.

"I was hoping you were going to say Market Mall," his father added.

"Isn't that place, er..." He couldn't find the right words.

"Don't say sleezy." His father shook his head. "Think of it as more of an eye opener."

Tamati took a deep breath in and held it. Then he answered, "they recruit people for the war there."

"They do that, too."

"I'll think about it," Tamati said, "but you have to tell me something. Why are people at war?"

"The surface is different, Tamati. People are fighting over the limited space, the air is either polluted or toxic, and there're no animals or plants."

"There have to be. How do people survive?"

His father shrugged. "I didn't see any of that from my cage, and when we left, all I saw was mud fields and death."

It's sounds like World War II all over again.

"We're safe down here. Things are different. The community doesn't have sides or politics, and we all have a role to play."

"It is peaceful here, but doesn't it bother you that there are so many suffering up there?"

His father nodded, and then asked, "are you thinking of going to the surface?"

Tamati took a deep breath in and held it before answering. "I just don't know."

Tamati woke on his birthday four hours before his parents.

He lay awake looking at the ceiling, wondering what to do. Finally, he got up, dressed, and slipped out the door, having collected an apple as he'd passed through.

I don't want another birthday. I've had more than my fair share.

He quietly closed the front door, hearing the locking mechanism click. He turned and faced out, pressing his head against the side of the hall and noticing that all the lights were dim along the corridors, lighting up only if someone was walking along.

Even in the dark, there was light. The city had had people here for generations who had never seen a real dark time.

I miss the moon and the sun and everything about fresh air, even though these lungs have never tasted it.

He walked along the hall and descended the eighteen flights, then walking out into the open. Small carts passed on wheels and trolleys stocked full rode past. Men and women working to get the city up and moving for the day ahead.

Even at night, it still keeps going. He wondered if the neighboring quadrant did the same.

He rushed across the busy walkways and between the buildings, past the dome and further. He knew exactly where he was going, to the center tower.

Don't ever go up there, Tamati, his mother's voice rang through his mind, a memory that he had never let go of. *It's not safe and that's why they banned children.*

But he wasn't stupid. He'd wanted to go up there ever since he'd heard about it.

If I go up there, I'll find my answers, won't I? He hurried his pace, feeling the burn in his muscles.

Not wanting to spend another day in school, he had to make a decision before leaving. It was their rule. They had people come in and offer all sorts of roles, telling kids of the wonderful payments they'd receive. One by one, the classrooms dwindled down to holding just a few students.

"Choosing before your birthday is best, Tamati," his teacher had said.

"What happens if I don't choose at all?"

"You are free to continue with school—"

"So, I'm not forced to continue?"

George beside him had leaned in. "You're not planning on being a bum, are you?"

The other kids had laughed.

Tamati had ignored him and turned back to the teacher. "The choices I've been given aren't suitable."

"Even medicine?"

He'd shaken his head.

A voice behind him had spoken up. "Doctors do what you do, except they're experts, and you're, well, not."

It was an argument he had heard all too often.

"Sure," he'd retorted back at them. "But there's not a cure for everything. And why walk down the same path that others have already tracked? None of you will find anything new."

The teacher had glared at him. "We all have a place in society. It helps build places like this; it keeps the water out and the people safe. Our place is what gives us our lives."

Tamati had nodded. *I understand that. But when you've lived as many lives as I have and fought against the same curse, the same outcome and nothing changes, it's so hard to then sit here and tell me my place.*

He'd stood up and aimed for the door.

"He's too good for us," the voices had teased.

"He'll end up scraping sewage out of pits." The kids laughed.

Tamati shook the horrid memory from his mind. *I just don't fit in anymore. They're right. There's no place for me and there never will be.*

The underwater city was too different from the rest of the world. He reached the bottom of the center tower.

He looked up. The tall black column was much thinner at the top and thicker at the bottom, with a spiral of stairs on the outside.

The door at the bottom was open, with the lift waiting. *I hate those things, but I wonder if it's worth climbing?*

Arching his neck, he considered just how tall the tower was. It was the only building that attached to the roof of the dome, and other sections had buildings forty stories high.

He stepped into the lift and pressed the button. Closing his eyes, he latched onto the side bar for support.

The lift flew up the column and stopped. The doors stood wide open before Tamati had caught his breath and gathered his bearings.

How anyone can use these things all the time is beyond me.

He stepped out before the doors closed on him.

"Are you old enough to be here?" A man appeared on his left, holding a hot drink.

"Am today."

"Happy birthday," he said monotonously.

"Er... thanks."

"Sorry, kid. You're not the first to come here on their birthday."

"How does it work?" Tamati asked.

The man breathed in and put down his coffee, pointing out the window. "We have views to five other towers." He pointed them out, across the top of the buildings.

Tamati saw the first four fine, but the fifth was hard to see.

"We all have signals to give one another at certain times. Each signal is a sign posted in certain colors; that way, we know if there is something going on in the other quarter, and we can either go in and rescue them, or shut it down so that our quarter remains safe."

"Shut it down?"

"Yeah, like massive walls to split the quarters. If their roof breaks, instead of killing us all, we close it off and only lose that section."

Tamati froze. "Are you serious?"

The man sat back in his seat and swiveled around. "You know there's an entire ocean above our heads?"

He nodded.

"So, how did you think this place worked?"

"Has it ever happened before?"

"Yep," he said, reaching for his coffee. "Back in the old days when the quarters were first being built. Didn't lose that many people, though—more workers than families."

"How did they fix it? Which quarter was that?"

He shook his head. "Once the quarter has been penetrated, it becomes a tomb."

So brutal. Tamati shivered and looked back to the man. "So, if our section shuts off, how do we get out?"

"Shuts off?" He laughed. "You'd be dead before you knew it."

"Er..." Tamati shook his head. "No, how do we get out of the underwater part?"

"You mean to go to the surface?"

"Yeah."

He laughed. "Each quarter is linked to a main tower." He pointed up to the roof. There was a hatch and a round lock. The man stood and turned it until it released and opened.

Tamati looked through the hole and saw a ladder extending all the way up.

"The surface is up there?"

"Yep." He returned to his seat. "Go on, kid. Knock yourself out."

Tamati nearly jumped out of his skin. He'd imagined this day since he'd first been told about the city. Not waiting any longer, he jumped up and hooked both hands on the bottom of the ladder.

It extended down to the ground and he stuck his foot onto the first step, quickly climbing upward.

The small space was just big enough for him to fit in it, and he climbed faster and faster, with small lights lighting up as he got higher.

Halfway up, he breathed in and, for the first time in this body, smelled fresh air. Pushing open the lid when he reached the top, he felt a strong wind rushing into his face, up his nostrils and chilling his skin.

Climbing out, he reached out, instantly latching onto the side railing nearby.

The lid behind him banged closed and he laughed.

Looking out before him, he saw endless water. The sky was dark, but the sun wasn't far from rising. The stars were starting to fade.

The water below lashed around him and big waves rose and fell. The air was brisk, and made all his hairs stand up on end.

"Excuse me?"

He turned and saw two young women sitting side by side in the middle of the platform.

Tamati nearly fell over the edge. In that exact moment, he took in both their faces, and everything hit him at once.

"Who are you?" the beautiful and young, brown-eyed girl asked. The other, blond and blue-eyed, smiled.

"Tamati," he said.

"I'm Ivy, and this is Rozelda."

Holding onto the railing as tight as he could, he felt the color draining from his face.

"I've never seen you in the quarter before." He shook.

"Oh, we must not come from your quarter. I come from Quarter B and Roze comes from EJ Quarter," Ivy said.

"We're not allowed to go to the surface in our quarters, so we come here."

"Oh." Tamati had held in his breath. He looked to the manhole that he'd just came up from, and felt it was best to go straight back down.

"Wait," Roze said, getting to her feet. "You're leaving already?"

He nodded.

"But the sun is just about to come up." She stood beside him and he felt a tingle between them.

Tamati paused and looked out to the nearby sea. It thrashed around and he couldn't help feel somewhat connected to it. Like it was mimicking his own feelings.

"Come," Ivy said as she waved him over. "Sit with us."

Reluctantly, Tamati sat down, and Roze sat even closer.

He looked down, trying to avoid eye contact, but he couldn't deny the way each of them made him feel.

"We've never seen you here before," Ivy said.

"I only turned eighteen today."

"Well, happy birthday." She clapped and smiled at him. Her gaze went right through to his heart, hammering at his body.

He looked up and smiled at Roze. The wind blew her hair and all the fragrance of her whiffed into his face. In that instant, he could have reached out to touch her, to hug her... to love her.

Rashmi, he thought. *And my Isaac.* He closed his eyes and their faces flashed in his mind. Then he opened them again and her face contained whispers from those lives.

I hurt you in that life. His throat swelled, his body struggling to look away. *If only you knew now, would you be so willing to sit by my side? Would you forgive me?*

The girls giggled. He looked back and forth between them and felt more uncomfortable as the time went on.

"Are you going to talk?" Ivy asked.

"Oh." He laughed with them. This life was much different than the last. He had the freedom to speak his mind, and every opportunity he desired was laid out before him to try, but something from last time, from each time before that, had carried over with him. Reserved, guarded, and emotionally tormented, he knew his choices would lead down the same path.

He looked to Ivy and locked eyes with her.

Every time, I fail to save you.

"What is your place?" Ivy asked.

"What I do?" he tried to correct her, never having gotten used to the term 'place' in the way they used it here. "I help my father heal," he said. "I'm a healer."

"Like a doctor?" Roze asked.

"Sort of. I don't use medicines, but rather create my own with natural products."

"Interesting," Ivy said. "Some might call you a witch."

They both laughed. Tamati shivered. *That word has never sat right with me.*

"No, Ivy," Roze said. "Men can't be witches; they're warlocks. Isn't that right, Tamati?"

"Um, no, I don't think so," he said. "Titles aren't necessarily gender specific."

Ivy poked her tongue out. "Know-it-all's got it wrong," she teased.

"Shut up!" Roze retorted back.

"There's an old man who wants me to make him feel younger," he said, and he laughed at the idea. In all his years, he'd never gotten to have the privilege of growing old. It seemed likely he himself would spend a millennium as a child, adjusting to a new time and culture and somehow never finding a place.

He froze.

"Are you alright?" Roze reached for his hand.

He accidentally brushed it away and got to his feet. "Um, yeah. I just thought of something I forgot to do." He reached for the manhole lid and opened it.

"Will you come back?" Ivy asked.

He paused halfway into the ladder. "Sure," he said, and then held himself back from promising anything. *I no longer want to* manipulate destiny. *I have no plans on determining how this curse is going to unfold.*

That's right, isn't it? I've got some sort of beef with destiny?

He kept climbing down, one foot after another going further below until the ladder dropped and he hit the floor.

"Girls too much, huh?" the man swiveled on his chair, his coffee mug no longer steaming.

Tamati pushed open the side door and began running down the spiral staircase.

I know what I've got to do. His legs burned, but he ignored the pain. *How haven't I see it before?*

Destiny?

Curse?

Ivy said she was caught on a loop! How didn't I know it then?

The memories never faded, they were clear in his mind, but after seeing the girls sitting in front of one another, as friends, each on one side of him, he now understood the piece that had been missing all along.

Tamati reached the bottom of the stairs and bent over to catch his breath. Sweat covered his body, and he yearned for fresh water.

Running all the way to the dome, he reached it more quickly than he'd thought imaginable, but he was lost in his thoughts.

I need to write this down. He had to see it on paper somehow, to understand what the puzzle actually was.

The dome was empty and he quickly ran towards the middle, reaching for the hose. After filling his stomach full of water, he then went to the other side, where he had once hidden a box of chalk. Retrieving it, he shoved it beneath his shirt and tucked it into his waist.

Slipping out of the dome, he wondered where the best place to write everything down would be.

No one can know about this. He paced, faster and faster. *If they see the girls' names, the girls might be ratted out to their families, and that's not right. I won't let that happen..* He shook his head. *I won't use words, I'll use symbols.*

He looked around. Only buildings and walkways and walls that held signs. Clean, grey, monotone. Everything was the same.

A sign in the corner of his eye made him turned.

No entry, it said. He walked calmly over to it and pushed the door open.

A short corridor with a large staircase running downward looked dull, but had enough light to see by. *This wall will do.*

He ran down the steps and went along further enough that no one entering the door would see him.

Taking out the first piece of chalk from the box, he began drawing on the walls.

Small circles and boxes, triangles and rectangles. Then he moved on to lines and arrows, squiggles and dashes. He filled the entire wall in minutes. Annoyed that he was running out of room, he continued down the corridor, sometimes spreading across the floor and even the roof.

"What the hell are you doing, son?" a voice came up from the other way.

Tamati paused. With the chalk firmly pressed into the wall, he turned and saw a round-stomached man.

"I'm not your son," Tamati said.

"Yes, I know that," he huffed. Rolling his eyes, he wheezed out his breathing. "Jeez, kids these days. I meant, what are you doing to these walls? You're not one of those crazies, are you?"

"On the contrary," Tamati said, standing up straight. "Are you having trouble breathing?"

The man leaned out and pressed his hand to the wall. "What's it to you? Come on, you can't be down here."

Tamati put the chalk down. "Answer me. Is your chest feeling tight?" He saw all the signs. The breathing was rapid but hollow, and the man struggled to stand while his lips weren't even a neutral flesh color.

He took a step towards the man and reached for his neck.

The man leaned back and held up his hands. "What the hell! Don't touch me!"

"I'm going to check your pulse," Tamati said, and he pressed two fingers to the vein in his neck. "Are you feeling alright?"

He wheezed again. "I'm just feeling a bit off today. But I don't need a crazy like you coming near me. Go on, it's time to leave."

"Can you sit down for me?" Tamati pointed to the floor. "I know what I'm doing; I'm a healer." Tamati held both his hands up, like he meant to surrender. "Please let me help you."

"A healer..." The guy pulled something from his pocket and clicked it on. It was a small flashlight, lighting all of the area. "Oh, I know you—you're... you're Drogg's son."

"Drogg?" Tamati stared at him.

"Yeah, Drogg. You ate him."

"Ate?" Tamati shook his head, then realized what was happening. "Sit down right now, I think you're having a heart attack or a stroke and I need to examine you."

"Healer? You sound like a doctor." He kept talking, but did as he was told.

"I hear that more than I would like," Tamati said as he held the man's wrist tight, counting the pumps under his fingers. "Call for help."

"Use yours," the man snapped, gesturing to Tamati's arm.

"I only turned eighteen today and my appointment to get it installed is later this afternoon. Now, stop arguing and do as you're told."

"You sound like my mother."

"I assure you, I'm not. Now, please, call for help."

The man unclipped the patch on the top of his arm. He

pressed the round tattoo on the top of his arm and spoke. "I need help. I got a kid here saying I'm having a stroke."

He nodded, then told Tamati, "She says they're using my locator tracker now." He wheezed more heavily. "Get out of here now, before they find you down here."

"I'm not leaving." Tamati sat down beside the man, looking up at the wall. "I'm not finished here."

"You aren't planning on flooding the place, are you?"

He laughed.

The man glared.

"No, of course not. I just needed a quiet place to think."

"Turning eighteen is half the battle..." he said, but his words had slowed, and he leaned towards the side.

Bang! Tamati jumped.

"They're..." The man slumped over and Tamati held out both his hands, catching his head before it hit the wall.

"You there!" voices yelled. "Stay where you are!"

Tamati didn't move as they rushed to each side of him, looking at the man. They replaced Tamati's hands with their own and pushed him out of the way. One pulled a syringe out of his medical bag and pressed a serum into his neck. The fat man jiggled and then rolled to the side. His muscles relaxed.

Tamati got to his feet and stood against the wall. A hover bed had followed the two men in and stayed back beside Tamati.

One of the men clicked his fingers, and the hover bed went up and leaned against the wall, floating down and underneath the patient as they rolled him onto it.

The men got to the feet. One took the hover bed while the other stood beside Tamati.

"What's all this?" He pointed to the wall.

"Thinking."

"Are you planning something?"

Tamati shook his head. "I'm eighteen today. I'm only trying to figure out what to do."

"We've all been there, kid." He hit him in the arm. "But this…" He gestured back to the wall. "This, not so much."

The man passed by and caught up to the patient. He leaned into the top of his arm and spoke. His words carried down the corridor as he did, making it easy for Tamati to hear. "Better get down here and check this out." He disappeared through the door.

Tamati sighed.

No matter what, I'll never have a place. But how did I not know that was the point?

He ran his chalky hands through his hair.

Tamati picked up the chalk and continued his work. He left the wall he'd been at and turned to the other, starting fresh. To anyone else, it would have looked like a bunch of symbols, shapes, and a whole lot of chaos. But it didn't matter. This wasn't for anyone else. This was for him.

He needed to map it out. Each event was an occurrence, something that happened in his life. The square was him, the circle Ivy, the triangle Roze.

Roze!

She's come to me since India… but why?

He thought it through. *Why India? What happened then?*

America was clearer in his mind. *Obviously, she wanted me to not choose Ivy, and she even tried to get her out of the picture, but why?*

And in India she threw a stone. She pleaded with me not to choose Ivy.

Tamati couldn't believe that she'd gotten in the way like that. Rashmi, of all people. *But what about before that?*

Pacing up and down the corridor, he had to think, and had to figure out what he was missing.

I've been so focused on Ivy and how to save her that I didn't notice Rashmi and Isaac, and her being able to save me.

The carriage to London. There was a girl, what was her name…

He continued his pacing up and down, going faster.

Nothing was coming to him because his wall of squiggles and lines and symbols didn't include that information.

Why didn't I think this was important?

He wiped the sweat from his top lip.

The girl coming to London with me... but she was late, and then I saw Ivy and got out. Was that Rashmi? Has she been trying to contact me in every life?

He stopped pacing and all his nerves tingled.

England.

How didn't I make the connection? All this time and I never saw it.

All the thinking hurt his brain. The information was just too much.

He studied the chalk symbols again. It was like they played a dance right in front of him. How hadn't he recognized the symmetrical layout before? How hadn't he seen they'd been playing into Ivy's original curse all along?

He fell to the floor then and looked up, tears in his eyes.

The original curse!

It was like it hit him over the head again.

Rose!

The Rose who I was supposed to marry before Ivy turned up and met me.

Was I destined to marry Rose?

Is destiny punishing me?

I have to break the curse!

More than seven hundred years ago, so young and petite, Rose had been in his life.

He had planned on marrying her.

But I didn't. The air went from his body. *I didn't marry her and everything changed.*

He got to his feet, trying to breathe, but he was bent over, pressing his hands against the wall and dry heaving.

Rose got Ivy killed.

How could she have done that?

Even after all this time, Tamati still couldn't understand.

Did she accuse Ivy because of me?

Was I the cause of the curse all along?

"You there!" a voice down the corridor yelled out.

Struggling to breathe, Tamati turned as his stomach still heaved. He was thankful that the apple he'd had that morning was well and truly digested.

Two men flashed lights as they ran towards Tamati.

"What is this madness?" the one on the left asked as he looked to the wall. The right one flashed the lights straight into Tamati's eyes.

"I'm not taking any chances," he said to his sidekick. "You're under arrest. Put out your hands."

"Yeah, we can't be too careful," the other man said under his breath.

Tamati did as he was told. There was no need to think anymore. He had worked out his puzzle, and now understood what he'd come down here to puzzle out.

He let the two men drag him by the arms up to the door. His head wobbled from side to side, the weight of his mind too heavy to hold it up. He needed sleep, and needed a fresh start.

I wanted something new in this life and I think I've got it.

It is true, ignorance is bliss. He thought of ways to break the curse, but his mind could no longer cope with any more thinking. *I can't... I won't...* He started to cry.

"Come on, we'll take you to the station and process you there." He stopped at the door, holding Tamati in place. "Don't forget to take photos of it, and order a clean-up crew, just in case," the man told his partner.

"In case of what?"

"I don't know what that is," he said, and turned to Tamati. "Care to elaborate?"

"It's nothing. It won't mean anything now."

"Whatever," he said to Tamati, and then he turned to the man down the corridor. "Get rid of it, just in case it's instructions. We don't want anyone else reading it."

The guy pulled a small water bottle from his little bag and sprayed it over the walls. The chalk ran in patches, but it didn't matter. Tamati saw the pattern, and he had it firmly in his mind now.

I understand everything I need to.

Dropping his head to his chest, Tamati moved forward as the man pushed him through the door and out into the walkways. The station was two blocks away on the ground level of one of the smaller buildings.

"Sit here." He shoved him down between other criminals sitting on yellow plastic chairs.

Tamati looked them over. They smelled bad and wore rags. He wondered what they had done. Everyone had a place—that had been drilled into his head more times than he would have liked. But homelessness was a thing.

"You—" the officer came back and pointed a finger at him. "How old are you?"

"I turned eighteen today."

"Show me your marking."

"I haven't received it yet. It's booked for this afternoon."

The officer leaned back on his heels and laughed. "Wow, you're real lucky, kid. Without that marking, I can't book you for a crime."

"What crime?" Tamati asked. "I haven't done anything wrong."

"We'll determine that."

Now I understand what these guys are here for. Tamati rolled his eyes. *They're pulling whoever looks suspect without evidence to back their case.*

"Let's call your parents. As soon as they're here, you'll be free to go."

Tamati gave them the number, and they showed up sooner than he would have liked.

"Stay calm, Miko," his mother said as she walked through the double doors holding his father's arm. She'd locked eyes with him instantly, and a small smile spread across her lips.

His father didn't even look his way. He crossed the room, shook the officer's hand, and walked straight back out again.

The officer unclipped the cuffs and Tamati was out the door, running to catch up with his parents.

"There was no crime?" Tamati asked, but his father continued to walk in silence.

"Would you stop?" he asked, reaching out and grabbing hold of his arm to twist him around.

"You are so lucky you didn't get your marking until this afternoon," he said, pointing a finger in his face. "Or whatever this was would have been something much different."

His mother caught up. "Calm down, Miko."

"It's okay, Mom. I can explain. I needed a quiet place to think and I had a packet of chalk. So, I went through a door that had a no-entry sign and drew on the wall."

"Drawing?" His father shook his head. "There isn't pen and paper about anymore?"

Tamati sighed. "It was what I had on me." It wasn't true, and he hated lying. Paper was limited by its edges and had a habit of getting into the hands of someone else. The space the wall provided, was what he needed. Most of all, he was desperate to step back and look at the entire picture to help him understand.

"No, what you had was two parents who woke up to celebrate your birthday and, instead, we found an empty apartment block and a phone call from officers. Happy birthday, Tamati!" He turned and walked off.

Standing beside his mother, he watched him go.

"Give him time and he'll calm down," she said.

He breathed in and out again. "I thought you would be the mad one."

"Oh, you're in all kinds of trouble and you know it. But the first time you muck up with your father, the police were involved." She shook her head.

Tamati came out of his room ready for the ceremony.

"You look handsome," his mother said.

"Ready?" his father asked, but his tone was stiff and distant.

Tamati nodded.

They walked together down the stairs and straight into the school building. "Shouldn't this be done somewhere better?"

His mother shrugged. "That's what I thought, but they haven't changed it in generations—why start now?"

"Does it hurt?"

"Yep," his father said, and he received a slap across the arm.

"Miko!" she snapped. "Cut it out."

"What's it like?" Tamati asked.

"What? The insert or the tattoo?"

"Both."

"The insert is more weird than anything, because you have to get used to it being in your arm."

"And you won't notice the tattoo," his father said. "Because they spend that time trying to adjust your ear piece."

"Sounds great."

"Wow, the sarcasm!" His mother laughed.

"Can you blame the kid?" Father laughed, too. "No one comes back for this stuff twice."

They arrived at the office and found the door unlocked. Tamati pushed it open to see the principal waiting for him.

"Congratulations, Tamati, you've been one of my best students." He handed him a certificate and they posed for photos.

"Unspecified?" his father asked, taking it from him. "Didn't you choose?"

He shook his head.

The insert was huge in his arm and jiggled against the skin. The tattoo felt more like a slice across the skin, but they never said anything about the insert in the back of his ear.

Pain was easy to compare to his death.

When it was all over, he was out of there like a flash.

"I have a special dinner at home," his mother said.

"I'll meet you there," Tamati said, kissing her on the cheek. "I need to stop off at the dome."

He took a slow stroll until he reached the dome, taking in all the sights.

Mr. Zimile came up from behind and poked him in the back. "What's going on with you?" he asked, and sat down in the nearest chair.

Tamati sighed and shook his head.

"Come on then, out with it."

Turning around to face the old man, Tamati slumped up against the wall.

"Let me guess, it's a girl." He laughed. "I've seen that look before."

"There's a look for it?"

Mr. Zimile nodded.

"Great." Tamati heard the sarcasm in his voice again. "Well, what's the look for two girls then?"

"Two? Getting a bit greedy now."

Tamati laughed. It was a small laugh at first, and then it turned into a big belly laugh. He slid downward, letting the floor catch his bum and the wall hold him up.

"You're losing your mind, kid."

"I think I lost it long ago."

"Ha!" He sat back in his chair. "Age is nothing to young ones like you."

"True," he said. *If only you knew, old man. If only...*

"I just want to do the right thing, and I know it's going to hurt everyone I know."

"What's that?"

"Walk away."

"From two girls?"

"From it all."

"That doesn't sound like you're hurting anyone. Might hurt yourself, though."

Tamati nodded.

"You're trapped under all this, aren't you?"

"Why do you say that?"

"Because I see the sunburn on your milky skin."

I didn't even see the sun! It's windburn.

"That tower gives anyone who goes up there a whole new perspective on life. Why do you think they put an age limit on who can access it? Imagine if all the little children got up there... they'd never come back down."

Tamati hit the back of his head on the wall. "I've made you cream and a heap of little capsules. There's plenty there; should last you more than a year, and then after that, you won't need it."

"I'll be dead then?"

Tamati laughed. "What? No! Because you'll eat right and only drink water." He poked a finger at the old man.

Tamati got to his feet and shook the old man's hand.

"Good luck out there."

He nodded and walked away.

Before he got to the edge of the dome, Tamati pulled out a little notebook from his top pocket. Scribbling something down, he then folded the message and crossed the main quarters, looking in the directory for a name.

Finding it, he ran all the way to the location and slipped the note underneath the door. Then he ran all the way back to his quarters, back home to his parents.

He showed them his marking and they celebrated his birthday, just like they were supposed to have done early that morning.

That night, Tamati left his room just before midnight. He hadn't bothered sleeping because he'd needed enough time to write out a letter to his parents.

It was the first time he'd told the truth.

I've lived over seven hundred years, he repeated the words in his mind. *And I still don't know what to do. I was once told it was a loop, forever repeating itself over and over.*

Perhaps it was all karma.

He'd told them about Wales and India, and Germany and Scotland, but he held back on England.

I'm sorry I didn't know how to fit in, and I know this was hard sometimes, but I have to go and live my life. It might be the only way I break the loop.

He'd finished his letter with: *I hope we cross paths again.*

He left the apartment behind and didn't think of it again. He walked through the quarters and climbed the main tower.

Up on the platform, he found that the boat was already waiting.

And also sitting there waiting, with her hair blowing in the wind, was the most beautiful woman he'd ever seen.

"I got your note," she said.

He smiled and sat next to her.

"Are you sure you wanted me?"

He nodded. "I have a story to tell you, Roze."

She laughed. "I bet you do."

The boat pulled away from the platform and headed towards

shore. The wind lashed their faces and he held a hand up to protect her face.

He looked into her eyes and fell into them like they were oceans. *She's been here with me all along and I didn't see it.*

I was never meant to break the curse for Ivy. I was meant to save Roze and myself. To break away from Ivy.

The boat pulled into shore and he stood holding out a hand.

"I can't promise you the world," he said. "And if you go back now, I won't hold it against you."

Roze stood and looked back towards the ocean, and then she scanned her eyes along the horizon until they rested on Tamati.

"But if you come with me, I will never leave your side," he said. "I will do my very best. And I hope I'll make you proud."

Tears formed in her eyes, and she stepped off the boat and into Tamati's arms.

She closed her eyes shut and breathed in. "I've never done anything so reckless, but for some unknown reason, this feels so right."

He smiled.

Turning their backs to the ocean and the underwater city, they travelled across the land and well into the farming region.

Tamati spent three years building a cottage by hand before their first child was born. Then he farmed the land until he grew old, watching all of his children grow and gain families of their own.

Before he knew it, his hair lost its color, and then he lost all his hair. And his face had more wrinkles than his hands.

One night, after Tamati helped Roze to her rocking chair on the veranda, he sat beside her and they watched the sunset.

"The grandchildren are coming to visit tomorrow, dear."

"Good," he said. Nothing excited him more than to see their vibrant young faces, even though he mixed up their names.

After a long moment of silence, Roze cleared her throat. "You're thinking again."

"I think I broke the curse," he said.

"After all these years," she said. "You never forgot."

"Too many memories... too much has happened. It's nice to grow old, for once."

"And you did it so well." She smiled.

"It's broken now," he said.

"Will we find each other next time?"

"Wouldn't that be nice?"

He rocked in his chair and watched the stars begin to sparkle in the sky.

Leaning back, he closed his eyes and drifted towards the stars.

It was the most peaceful of deaths.

EPILOGUE

2200

$\mathcal{B}$right white light was right in front of her. She felt the air fill her lungs and something in her mouth. She coughed, she screamed, she burped, and then she slept.

The white returned, and no matter how much she looked, she couldn't see.

Then there was something else in front of her.

A woman.

She recognized the woman's voice. She had heard it many times before. But before... when?

The woman came in close, and she sensed that this was where she had come from.

My mother.

She breathed in and out again. More sleep.

She woke. There was noise about her. She tossed and turned and moved her body. It felt light, easy, young. But there wasn't enough energy; she felt so, so tired. Her eyes closed again.

Time passed. Days? Years? She couldn't tell. She experienced food, love, cuddles, sleep, and a rotation of the same.

She woke to her mother's laugh.

Her eyes weren't as cloudy now. She could see she was in a

bed. Her mother so close, it was like her voice was all around her, like one big loveable cuddle.

A voice entered her head. *Wake up, Ivy.*

She looked, but couldn't see anything with her eyes.

You are blind.

Blind? She thought back. *But I can see.*

A light above her, round and bright, leaned in and kissed her forehead.

Open your eye.

Both her eyes flickered, and a third opened. There, hovering above her bed, was a bright light made up of many people.

The curse, she thought. *Is it broken?*

Far from it, the answering words entered her mind.

Oh my! She sucked in air and it caught in her throat. The woman picked her up and held her, tapping her on the back. *What have I done?*

Do you understand now? the voices asked in unison.

Understand what? That the curse will continue? That I've plagued the world for a thousand years? And every generation from that point on? What do you want me to understand?

The promise, child. You promised.

The body reacted to thoughts. Mumbles exited her lips.

She closed her eyes. Tired. So very tired. She opened them again.

I need to break the curse!

How?

Thoughts sped through her mind. *How? I don't know how! Tell me.*

Ivy... you are the one who created it. You are the one that must break it.

"So," a mother's voice spoke, jolting Ivy out of thought. The spirits disappeared around her and her third eye sealed shut. "What have you named him?"

"Thomas!" another woman's nearby voice said. "I've always

loved that name. If I were to have another boy, I wouldn't have a clue what to call him. I couldn't have two boys called Thomas." She laughed.

Ivy squirmed. *Thomas? I know that name.*

"Well, I've been struggling with names," she said. "But I think I've found the one."

"Tell me!"

"Ivy."

She froze.

"Isn't that just divine?"

Ivy screamed her lungs out until she made herself sick.

THE END

TRANSLATIONS

Wales
Mam - Mother
Tad - Father
Bach - Boy
Merch - Girl
Na - No
Ydw - Yes
Cachi - Shit

Scotland
Sasanech - English
Sgaoileadh - Blasted
Nighean - Girl
Balach - Boy
Màthair - Mother
Athair - Father
Tha - Yes
Chan eil - No

India

Massi - Mother's sister
Mama - Mother's brother
Bhau - Father's sister
Chacha - Father's brother
Diya - Candle
Ladki - Girl
Ladka - Boy
Maa - Mother
Pitahji - Father
Haan - Yes
Nahi - No

German
Mutta - Mother
Mama - Mom
Vater - Father
Papa - Dad
Opa - Grandpa
Mädchen - Girl
Junge - Boy
Ja - Yes
Nein - No
Arzt - Doctor
Krankheit - Sickness
Tod - Death
Heilung - Healing
Medizin - Medicine

ACKNOWLEDGMENTS

I would love to say a huge big thank you to everyone that helped me along my Heavy Dirty Soul journey.

Matthew for always pulling me back out of the rabbit hole when I've dived too deep. For making sure we all have full stomachs and to remind me what day of the week it is.

To Brittany for helping me make the impossible possible, and to remind me that yes, I can achieve my dreams.

Ashton, you have become the angel that sits on my shoulder and guides me in the right direction even though I have a tendency to take the much harder route.

To Dr. Gareth James and Sunny Jhawar for your cultural expertise.

ABOUT THE AUTHOR

A.A. Warne writes elaborate, strange, dark, and twisted stories. In other words, speculative fiction.

Located at the bottom of the Blue Mountains in Sydney, Australia, Amanda was born and artist and grew up a painter before deciding to study pottery.

But it wasn't until she found the art of the written word that her universe expanded.

A graduate of Western Sydney University in Arts, Amanda now spends her time wrestling three kids and writing full time.

www.aawarne.com

facebook.com/AAWarne

twitter.com/AAWarne

instagram.com/aawarne

ALSO BY A.A. WARNE

Beginnings: An Australian Speculative Fiction Anthology
Hidden Truths Trilogy: Concealed Power